Tracking Bryon

Book One of a two book series

Joy Bischoff

ISBN-13: 978-0692377420
ISBN-10: 0692377425

Published and distributed by Raqia Publishing

For more information regarding this and other books, please visit www.raqiapublishing.com

Cover design by Rebecca J. Greenwood

Dedication

To my son Bryon who was a babe in my arms when I first had
the idea for this book. Thank you for encouraging me so much
as I have struggled to become a writer.

Tracking Bryon

Prologue

A sweeping panorama spread out before the bewildered child cuddled in her father's arms. Being of tender years, she did not understand what her father was telling her, yet she sensed the intensity in his voice and responded by squirming nervously. Normally she was soothed by his overly articulated, flowery speech but there was an intensity to his words that was new.

Hungrily, Anthony gazed over the valley and unconsciously gripped his young daughter too tightly. "Upon your mother's grave, I promise you shall be mistress of all this one day. I failed to win it for her but I shan't fail you, princess."

The little girl squealed unhappily and tried to wriggle loose from the imprisoning arms that bound her. The child was too young to know that his passions were threatening his reason; nevertheless she sensed something was very different about her father.

The distracted parent finally grew aware of his daughter's struggles and eased his grip, patting her to calm her down then trying again to direct her attention back down toward the mansion. He waxed eloquent as he tried to help her appreciate its elegant lines and pristine, white exterior. He was vaguely aware that his colleagues thought him pompous but he never allowed his inferiors to affect his actions. Soon they would be forced to acknowledge his superiority.

He glanced down at the child again and discovered that she was more interested in the flight of a red-tailed hawk than the enormous colonnaded mansion that glistened in the valley below. "Someday you'll swim in that lake, my darling, and pick me bouquets of flowers from the gardens. And Papa will take you on walks in the woods." He breathed deeply, picturing them wandering in the lush forest that framed the grounds and created such a beautiful setting for one of the premiere residences in all of England; Ivy Downs Estate. Queen Victoria herself had lauded the estate as fit for royalty and was often a visitor there.

Before climbing back into the surrey, Anthony gave one last promise, "Don't worry, my sweet, I shall see you ensconced within those walls. Papa will take care of everything."

Chapter One

Swallowing hard, Adrian rubbed his chin and stared vacantly at the golden hills that surrounded the small town. He resented being forced into such a devastating decision. He thought back on his life. Certainly he had committed some petty crimes when he was a child in England, and maybe as an adult he had crossed the legal line for his boss back home in London and in Philadelphia, but he had been sincere about reforming since he came to Oregon. He truly thought that was all behind him. It wasn't his fault everything had gone so wrong. He was desperate but was he so far gone that he could do what Richard was asking? Adrian turned and frowned at his companion. "What am I supposed to tell my wife?"

Richard Stewart impatiently threw up his hands and glared at his cousin-in-law in disgust. "You really have no imagination, Adrian. You tell the woman we want the boy to spend some time with us here in town so he can get to know his cousin, Belinda. Living out there on that pathetic ranch of yours gives the kid no chance to makes friends."

"I don't know, Richard. Bryon's only four and he's been unwell lately. My wife may not want him that far away from her."

"See, this has been your problem from the beginning. You threw away a fortune for a woman and you're still letting

2

her call the shots. Be a man, tell her your son is visiting us. Don't make the mistake of asking her!"

"If you're implying I'm not the head of my home," Adrian bristled, "you don't know me very well. It's just that I don't want her to grow suspicious of me when Bryon never returns."

"What does it matter? Even if she does wonder, it won't be long until she's out of the picture anyway."

Adrian Hancock looked away from the big man's hard glare. Instead he watched some laborers building the new livery stable down the street. Baker, Oregon was growing fast, but he wouldn't be around to see the livery finished.

He tried to keep his features passive so Richard wouldn't see the conflict inside him. He was willing to give up the boy, after all Bryon was flawed, but he didn't know if he could sell out his wife as well. Cecilia was a beautiful woman, and Adrian worshipped beauty.

#

The boy's eyelids slid down in ecstasy and he took a slow, deep breath. The afternoon sun had warmed the pines so their scent poured over him like a tangy magic potion. Turning, Bryon looked back across the farmyard at the small cabin that was home. Through the kitchen window he could see his momma washing the dishes. He hadn't realized how stuffy it had been in there all those days he had to stay in bed with a nasty cold. Finally he was free and it felt so good to run through the grass that covered the hill overlooking the cabin.

When he reached the top, he threw himself to the ground and rolled down the far incline, picking up speed until he tumbled into a crooked heap at the bottom. His face was buried in a patch of clover and before sitting up he took another deep breath and realized he had made yet another exciting discovery. Clover was sweet. But nothing prepared him for the miracle that met his eyes as he sat up.

The boy froze in astonishment and his lips formed a soundless 'O'. His four-year-old brain raced to find an

3

explanation for what lay before him.

The dry spell the previous spring had inhibited the flower pollination so as a three-year-old, Bryon hadn't learned about bachelor buttons. This year however, rains that had given the boy such a bad cold had spawned a riot of spring color. Spreading over the meadow were hundreds of bachelor buttons in various shades of purple, blue and pink. Bryon sat in stunned disbelief for what was a very long time for a small boy.

This child had a gift; a gift so rare, and so powerful that it affected people whether they knew it or not. He had the ability to put himself into the moment with all his soul.

Throwing himself to his stomach, he rested his chin on his folded hands and focused on a purple bachelor button. He became immersed in the essence of it the same as a sunbeam would penetrate the translucent petals. The delicate veins in those petals became his own as he merged with its color and scent. The joy of that small flower exploded through him, leaving the child breathless.

A sudden thickening in the air was so dramatic that the boy wheeled around. He was shocked to find no one behind him but he felt no fear. The child felt as if someone was standing near him. He was certain the light was brighter than it had been a moment before. Being so young, he didn't have a problem believing in an invisible world but he wanted to know what it was that was near him. His mind raced with confusion and until finally, it dawned on him. The fairies had come to Oregon.

Scanning the pines that surrounded the big meadow, he could detect no sign of the wily visitors, but he knew they were there. Momma had told him stories she had heard at her father's knee about the little people from Ireland. Elves, fairies, and all sorts of wondrous creatures inhabited the earth alongside the mortals but were rarely seen. Grandpa Peter's mother had come from Ireland and she had seen them. They were her friends.

He had to let Momma know. *She'll understand*, he thought as he crawled from one luscious bunch of flowers to another, gathering the treasure as fast as he could. Green stains streaked the knees of his faded over-alls but he didn't notice.

4

Once his arms were full he raced back over the hill. The excitement built as he crossed the farmyard. Unable to contain his enthusiasm, he crow-hopped from one foot to another, making the dust puff up in little clouds. The soft dirt felt silky and warm as his toes sunk with each step and the sunny smell of good soil mixed with the scent of the flowers in a heady perfume. Everything felt better, smelled better and he was sure the world would remain much brighter now that the fairies were here.

When he reached the house he went to the kitchen window and began jumping up and down trying to get his mother's attention.

Cecilia looked up from the pan she was scouring and grinned at the sight of her four-year-old's golden hair bobbing up and down above the window seal. Wiping her hands on her apron she hurried to the door and swung it open to reveal her little boy with that look of wonder on his face that she knew meant he had made another incredible discovery. This time though, he seemed more thrilled than usual.

Taking in the armful of flowers with a smile of thanks, she looked into those deep chocolate brown eyes that seemed to have their own light source. She felt a moment of panic realizing that something profound was in her child's mind. It wasn't often anymore that he became frustrated when she couldn't discern his thoughts.

Bryon was mute. He had never been able to speak but their souls had become so attuned that she rarely needed to search long to know what was in the heart of her beautiful, silent child. Then like a whisper on the breeze, understanding came. Kneeling, she wrapped her arms around her son, the bouquet between them sweetening the air. Nodding to the boy, she said, "The elves have been blowing their kisses on the meadow haven't they, lad?"

She knows, she really knows, Bryon sighed as relief swept through him. He knew that he would never forget this day. With the arrival of the fairy people, he would never feel lonely again. He had friends.

Perhaps the happiest day in his young life helped

balance the coming night, which would be the beginning; a foreshadowing of the darkness to come.

#

Cold chills swept over the child as the sun was blotted out by a shadow covering the ground around him. A small part of his mind knew he was still in bed in the loft but the dream was so intense that it was hard to believe this wasn't real. It felt very real. Trembling, he slowly raised his eyes to learn what had made the ominous shape that practically enveloped him, but the evil was so overpowering he became frozen, unable to move and hardly able to breathe. The shadow loomed larger and he could feel fetid breath wash over him like poison, making his belly ache.

"Help me, Elves, help me," he cried out in his thoughts. Almost immediately a light appeared, rapidly growing brighter and spreading its warmth over him as a protection against the putrid breath and overpowering blackness of the shadow. He peered into the light trying to discern the origin but all he saw was an indistinct shape.

"Run . . . now," a voice in his head urged.

With that warning, he bolted awake and leapt from his bed, rushing down the ladder of the loft. He didn't notice the fading light drawing to a pinpoint, then disappearing behind him. Rushing through the sitting room he plowed through his parent's bedroom door and threw himself onto his sleeping mother.

"Bryon . . . Bryon what is it?" Cecilia asked her son panting in her arms. "Baby, are you hurt?"

He shook his head but his trembling didn't subside.

"A nightmare?" she asked brushing his thick honey colored hair back from his eyes.

Bryon shrugged, never having had a nightmare. It seemed so real.

"Get back to your own bed, boy and stop acting like a sissy," his groggy father grumbled. Adrian had no patience with his handicapped son. He felt that treating him gently would only ruin what chance he had to make his way in life. Not that he would have much of a life. As far as Adrian was concerned,

Bryon was retarded, an embarrassment to be hidden away as much as possible, and the heartbreaking reality was, most of society in 1856 would agree with him.

Cecilia tensed at her husband's coldness but trying to make her voice as soothing as possible, she pleaded, "Dear, I've never seen him like this. He must have had a terrible nightmare. Just this once let him sleep with us."

"If it happens once it will never stop, you know that. No, take him up to bed."

The tenderhearted mother gently lifted the boy off of her, rose and slipped into her threadbare, bottle-green robe. Scooping him into her arms, she moved into the sitting room and placed him on the rocker. After stirring up the dying coals in the fireplace, she dropped a log on the reawakened flames. The hungry red tongues hissed and spit as she settled in her big rocker. Cuddling her child close, she sang softly in his ear. The child began to relax as his face pressed into her neck until finally, he slept.

There was a fundamental difference in how Cecilia saw her son and how her husband saw him. She believed his life had value. She thought he was of equal worth to a child that was whole. She hoped with all her heart that she would be able to pass that conviction on to Bryon.

As Cecilia ran her fingers through her son's silky hair, she was mesmerized by the cozy fire. She saw the past in the leaping flames and her mind went back to the fear she felt the day he was born. Doc was so supportive through it all. He had told her there might be a problem with the baby. Doc had even feared the pregnancy would not come to term. But no preparation stopped the eerie feeling she had when Bryon was first laid in her arms. He was making all the motions as if crying but no sound was coming from his mouth.

After an examination, Doc said he had no vocal chords. "Just didn't develop 'cause a your sickness, ma'am. Just be glad he lived at all and if I do say so, I have never seen a prettier baby in all my days." Looking at her thoughtfully as if to take her measure he added, "The good Lord will make it up to him in other ways, you watch if he don't."

7

It was true. Bryon was so intelligent, why couldn't Adrian see that? For him to think his son was retarded was willful blindness. Cecilia didn't believe there could be a child with a sunnier disposition anywhere?

Adrian was always irritable whenever Bryon slipped into one of his 'moments' as they called them. This was when the child discovered something so splendid that he would light up like a candle. The object of beauty might be an animal, a delicious treat, or a new thought that would appear as if by magic. To his father, this was proof of his retardation. "No one gets all giddy like that if they aren't crazy, Cecilia," he was always telling her.

Her husband was also angry when he saw his son's crude attempts to draw. Being a painter had been Adrian's dream and he felt it was a mockery for this inferior child to scribble his babyish drawings on his slate board. Of course, as a four-year-old, he couldn't recreate reality but there was surprising detail and imagination for so young a child but Adrian never noticed.

The boy's strangest gift was only known by his mother. Bryon so often knew what she was feeling as if he was experiencing the same thing. This was like his 'moments' only deeper. Sometimes, especially when Adrian was angry with her, Bryon would come and lay his chubby hand on her leg and the look in his eye showed such empathy it took her breath away.

She was very glad he had lived. For that matter, she was glad she had made it through that illness that almost took both their lives before she was even aware she was carrying him. At the time it occurred to her that it might be better to just give up and join her parents in heaven. Life with Adrian certainly hadn't turned out as she had hoped.

A heavy sigh drew her attention from the fire and the past, down to her son cradled in her arms. Bryon had awakened and was looking at her as if feeling her sadness. Slowly he reached up and touched her cheek as if comforting her. Turning her thoughts from darker times, she smiled down at him and searched for a happy thought. Maybe tomorrow would be fun. She would do her best to make a delicious lunch to please her husband's relatives. Perhaps she could try harder to make friends with them and Bryon could have more people to love him.

Bryon's eyelids drooped as she studied his perfect features until finally he slept again. Cecilia thought back to the day she and her husband had gone into Baker to visit her cousin and his family. She had been so excited to get to know Richard, Opal and their daughter Belinda. They had just moved clear from England to live near Cecilia, Richard's only living relative. She had only learned of his existence after her mother had died. Feeling alone in the world back when she was eighteen years of age, she had a terrible need to learn if she had any relatives back in England where her father, Peter Stewart, had come from. After searching through her father's papers, she found the address of a solicitor's firm in London and had written asking if they knew of her father and if he had any relatives.

After months of waiting, a letter arrived from the firm. To her astonishment she learned of a small inheritance they were holding in trust for her. Apparently her grandfather, Hiram Stewart, had known of her existence. The letter from Mr. Peterson, the senior solicitor, informed her of a nice little property on the moors in Devonshire that was worth about two thousand pounds. The missive further stated that one of their law clerks, a Mr. Hancock had some business for the firm in New York and he would be glad to come to Baltimore and finalize the details of the trust.

Cecilia struggled with guilt over her regret that Adrian Hancock had ever shown up on her doorstep. If it had not been such a humble doorstep, her future could have been different. She tried to love Adrian but he was so different after they married.

The ranch they had purchased in Oregon was beautiful but she wondered if it was too lonely for a boy who grew up in London. Maybe if they spent more time with people Adrian would come out of his shell again and act like the man she first knew. Tomorrow they would finally have company but Cecilia couldn't help but wish it was someone other than her cousin

9

Richard. They hadn't seen much of Richard since before Bryon was born. Neither he nor Adrian seemed inclined to friendliness and to tell the truth, Richard's wife Opal was a bit too cold for Cecilia's taste. That thought brought a wave of guilt. She had to try harder, make a greater effort.

Looking into the dying fire Cecilia drew Bryon closer to her. She hoped she was doing the right thing in letting her son go spend some time with Richard's daughter Belinda. They were coming by tomorrow to fetch him back to Baker.

Should I let him go? she wondered. Do I want to turn down the overture of friendship the Stewarts are offering? After all, they came out here for family. Bryon has no friends so maybe it is best to give it a try. Belinda is three years older but that shouldn't matter. Would she be patient with Bryon's impediment? Cecilia didn't know. Tomorrow would be here very soon she realized, so wrapping a quilt around her boy, she slipped back to bed.

#

Smells were such interesting things. Bryon had been discovering a whole new world of smells since yesterday. He grinned as he thought of what Momma would say if she saw him sniffing the big brown back of the plow horse he was lying on. He loved riding old Honey. She was the only horse he was allowed on alone and she was easy to mount. When she was grazing, he would sit behind her ears and then she would lift her head and Bryon would slide down to her back. When he was sleepy, like now, he would turn around on her broad back and rest his head on her silky rump. She was placidly chomping clover behind the barn while Bryon waited for his cousin to come and get him.

The droning of a fly lulled the boy and he dozed. Suddenly, he became aware of voices near him. They must have been coming from inside the barn. Had his cousin arrived?

"You have no proof and even if you did, with what I know about you, I could have you hung. If you would be a man and just go through with it, I would share everything."

"I don't trust you, Richard. I've heard enough about

10

your father to realize that the apple didn't fall far from the tree."

"You know that I was supposed to kill you too, so why do you think I haven't done that?"

"You haven't done any of it because Doc is watching you too closely since you poisoned my wife!"

"That's why you're going to take her away from here. I'm being watched like a hawk and I'm tired of waiting. What you're going to do is announce to the folks around here that Cecilia can't stand thinking of her poor lost child, so you're taking her back to Baltimore where she grew up. Instead you'll take her to St. Louis. I'll meet you there and we'll finish this business once and for all. It's a good thing you've come to your senses after all this time. I hope you can see none of this has been worth it for a woman, and certainly not for an imbecile like your kid."

"All right, all right. You've made your point so let's just move on." Adrian was trying hard not to lose his temper. He glanced nervously at Stewart then looked down at his shiny boots. *I shouldn't have told him I don't trust him,* he realized.

He didn't want Stewart to detect the full extent of the rebellion simmering in his blood. He had no intentions of taking Cecilia to St. Louis. He was not yet sure where they would go but it wouldn't be any place obvious. He felt bad about sacrificing the boy but they would have more children in spite of what Doc said. He felt shame over the weakness he had for his wife. She had no idea what a sacrifice he had made and was still making to keep her alive, but he loved her. In spite of himself he loved her.

Honey switched her tail at a fly and the course hairs brushed Bryon's hand, startling him as he was trying to understand the meaning behind the words he had overheard through the thin, back wall of the barn. The vague conversation was too much for a four-year-old to grasp. Only one message got through his young brain. *Papa and Momma are going away . . . without me.*

Momma told me this morning I was going into Baker but she didn't say I would never come home again!

11

Fear clutched at the child as he scooted to the back of the plow horse and slid down her long tail. He had to get away.

The boy began to run as fast as his short legs could churn, across the dirt yard toward the woods to the northeast. *I have to go find the fairies,* he decided. *Momma will find me there when these bad people go.*

The two men were leaving the barn when Richard noticed the child disappearing into the trees. "Where's the boy going?"

"I don't know," Adrian replied. He called out to his son. "Bryon, come back here. Bryon!"

Richard watched him increase his speed. "Is he deaf too?"

"No. He's a wild one though, does what he wants. I'll go get him." Adrian began running after the boy.

It didn't take long for him to catch up to the child. "Bryon, stop right now!"

The terrified boy stumbled and rolled into a ball in the dirt. He screwed his eyes shut and covered them with his hands and held his breath. Since he couldn't see with his eyes covered, he was convinced he was now invisible. *He can't see me now. If I hold still, he'll never find me,* he decided.

Adrian felt the boy begin to shake as he picked him up. Richard met him as he was walking back through the trees. "Why did he run away, Hancock? Do you think he heard us?"

"Doesn't matter if he did, he can't talk." Adrian looked down at the boy who was watching him out of those bright eyes. He studied his son's features, so perfect, but clearly projecting fear. His conscience smote him as he contemplated what would soon happen to Bryon. "Don't do it, Richard. He's my son, I can't let you do it."

"Don't be a fool. It's too late. Besides, if you don't give him to me, I'll tell Cecilia everything."

"And implicate yourself?"

"I'm not the one with the criminal record in England, am I?"

"But I can tell . . ."

"With what proof? My wife saw you put something in

Cecilia's tea that night . . . "

"You're a liar! You almost killed my wife, and the doc said that sickness is why my boy is like this!"

Bryon looked over at the man his mother said was their cousin. He pressed himself against his Papa and felt surprise and hope at his father's defense of him.

"Adrian, calm down. You have no choice and you know it. I'll give you some money to help you get to St. Louis."

"How much?"

"Five hundred. That'll get you there and set you up just fine. And don't forget what you'll receive when it's all over with."

Angry and discouraged but resigned, Adrian refused to look at his son again. "Okay, let's just get this over with."

The noon dinner in the cabin was a quiet affair. Everyone seems listless and preoccupied except Bryon. He clung to his mother so fiercely that she could hardly eat. He ate nothing at all no matter how much she pleaded. Cecilia's feeble attempts to reach out had fallen on barren ground and she found it all too easy to give up. Now her only concern was for her son. "Adrian, he is awfully upset. Maybe he's too young to go off for a visit."

"Coddling the boy again; I won't have it Cecilia, so don't start with me."

Opal Stewart cleared her throat. "Come now, my dear, he needs to be around other children, you know that. Don't worry, honey. I'll take good care of your chick. He and Belinda will have a marvelous time together and you'll find he won't even want to come home. And I didn't tell you, he'll be making loads of friends. Belinda is quite popular with the other young children in town and she will make sure he makes friends, oh, and she'll protect the poor little fellow from . . . you know. I've noticed all the little ones do just what Belinda tells them to do. She's quite the little leader."

Cecilia tried not to give in to the feelings of revulsion she felt for her cousin-in-law. Opal's condescending manner grated on her nerves to the point that she could hardly speak to

13

her. "Yes, but I think next year he'll be much more ready to go."

Everyone jumped as Adrian's fist slammed down on the table. "Woman, what did I say to you? He's going and I won't hear another word on the subject."

His wife lowered her head, fighting to hold back her tears and mumbled, "Whatever you say, Adrian."

"Well, why don't we get a move on so it won't be dark before we get home." Richard was suddenly feeling great. "Sorry Opal can't stay to help clean up, Cecilia, but we'd best leave now."

"Certainly, Richard. I'll get Bryon's things." She went to the corner by the fireplace and picked up the drawstring bag that held the child's favorite blanket, and his best over-alls. Bryon followed her as she put the bag in the back of the wagon. Picking him up, she embraced him. She didn't want to make things worse for him by showing her distress so she did not see the look in his eyes that would have made her keep him home at the peril of her life.

Richard pulled him roughly from her arms and lifted him up to Opal in the front of the buckboard. You hold onto the kid for a while so he isn't scared, Opal."

"Of course, Richard." The cold woman pasted on an empty smile for Cecilia. "Don't you worry, we'll have a lovely time together."

After watching the buckboard disappear into the trees, Cecilia gave a shuddering sigh and pressed the heels of her hands against her closed eyelids to force back the tears that pricked the back of her eyes. She tried to control her fear for her beautiful boy and her anger towards her husband. Two very different men seemed to war inside of Adrian and she never knew which one would show up. Almost from the beginning she had had a burning desire to understand more of his past so she could pin down the reason for his strangeness. He would never talk about his past. He had worked for that solicitor, Mr. Peterson, only for a few years and she could never get a straight

14

answer as to what he did before that. Occasionally she would hear a note of bitterness when he would mention how much he had wanted to be an artist. Sometimes he drew sketches of her that to her untrained eye seemed marvelous. She knew he loved her but he seemed to resent her for some reason and he took a perverse pleasure in taking that anger out on Bryon. It wasn't just that the boy was a mute, there was much more to his rejection. And sometimes she caught him looking at her with the same bitterness she saw on his face when he stared at Bryon. If she didn't know better, she would say he felt he had been betrayed.

She didn't believe her small inheritance was sufficient inducement for Adrian to have married her for greed. No, he loved her. She remembered the day she had opened the door and found him standing there with a look of surprise on his dark, handsome face. "You . . . you are Cecilia Stewart?"

Even in her faded gingham dress and half-starved condition, Adrian had been astonished at her striking beauty. He had always loved beautiful things and was cursed with a fierce desire to possess them. Cecilia had inherited her mother's large, dark green eyes and her father's thick, golden hair. Tall and lithe, she exuded intelligence and a liveliness that Adrian's artistic eye found fascinating. She had to admit that she had also been attracted by his looks, though from the beginning there had seemed to be something missing in his character. But it was so hard to be alone with no prospects of taking care of herself. Her father had died when she was twelve. She and her mother had taken in sewing that offered only a bare subsistence and they were forced to move to the humblest of lodgings.

Once she had matured, there had been offers of marriage but she resisted these. Cecilia feared that she must have a snobbish heart. The would-be beaus all seemed so uncouth. At least Adrian had a polish that, if a little overdone, was at least more comfortable to a girl raised by a refined mother.

It was apparent that something had been dogging Adrian. They had been married only a few months when the money from the sale of her property came. Immediately, Adrian made arrangements for them to go west immediately. While she was packing for the move she came across a strange note tucked away with Adrian's personal effects. He was so private that she felt nervous about going through his things, but curiosity prevailed. The note, dated two months before was curt and ominous.

Adrian,

Why did you do it? Other arrangements have had to be made. You will have to live with the consequences of your actions. Don't believe for a moment that I won't be watching you closely.

Just before the couple departed for their journey, Cecilia received a letter from her cousin Richard. He wrote of his excitement in learning he had a living relative. The solicitors had tracked him down after long efforts and informed him of his American cousin. Richard wrote that he was glad she had made inquiries since the trust had almost elapsed. He assured her he didn't need the money and was thrilled it had come in handy.

After reading the letter, panic seemed to grip Adrian until they had reached Eastern Oregon. He bought a ranch he named Grand View, in the beautiful Blue Mountains fifteen miles west of Baker. He had seemed happy for a while. He was not a good rancher although he enjoyed playing the role. Certainly no one would argue that he was the best-dressed rancher around. But he changed.

It was around the time her cousin Richard moved to Baker with his family. Cecilia was stunned to learn that Richard was yearning so much for relatives, he would move this far to be near her. Maybe that was what was wrong with Adrian. Could it be he was jealous of her having ties to any man but himself?

She remembered the first night they had supper at the Stewart's home in Baker. The house was a pleasant two-story clapboard on the main street of town. Adrian was silent all through the meal. Richard tried hard to be pleasant but it was

16

awkward. That was the night Cecilia became so dreadfully ill.

Doc didn't think she would live through that night and he seemed so watchful and concerned after that. Food poisoning, he thought at first until he learned that no one else had taken ill. That was also when he informed her that she was with child.

Chapter Two

The relief Bryon felt upon their arrival was intense. The large, hateful woman had smothered him the first half of the trip and almost shook his teeth out the rest of the way. To begin with she pretended to be kind but he knew she was simply trying to keep him from getting away. At length she grew tired of the hypocrisy. Keeping a firm grip on his over-alls, she shook him whenever he squirmed.

Taking the boy from his wife, Richard helped him out of the wagon, but instead of putting him down right away, he lifted him up in the air as if playing with him. He held him high gripping him tightly and stared into his eyes.

Perhaps the boy did not know the word 'calculation' but he recognized the sentiment he was seeing. The moment somehow felt powerful but not in a good way. He knew he would never forget the icy feeling of being helplessly pinned by hand and eye. Bryon believed the man was a threat to him and he knew Richard wanted him to be afraid.

When he was finally on the ground again, he scurried after Belinda into the yellow clapboard home. In spite of his fear, he looked around curiously. This was a real house, not a cabin. What would it be like to stay in such a big place and right in the middle of a town?

Walking into the parlor, he looked around at the fancy furniture. There were bright colors and fancy doodads everywhere. In the corner he saw a full-length oval mirror trimmed in a glossy, dark wood. He walked up to it in great anticipation. The only mirror he had seen was the small one that

Papa used for shaving and Momma for her hair. He could barely see his face in that one but now he would be able to see his whole body. As he was staring at himself in wonder, his cousin walked up behind him. He studied her as she came. She was chubby like her mother, and her nose was long like her father's. Her ears stuck out of her mousy brown hair, reminding him of the rats he saw in the barn back home.

"You never seen a real mirror before have you, Bryon?" He shook his head. "At least now you can see why everyone feels so sorry for you." Through the mirror she watched the question in his eyes. "Oh, you know. You've heard how ugly everyone thinks you are, haven't you?" Again he shook his head, slower this time. "Of course. Everybody knows your eyes are too big and too dark. And your lips are fat, just like an old cow's. Look how stubby your nose is, and your eyelashes are way too long for a boy. They make you look like a sissy."

Leaving her poison to work its way in, she turned and skipped toward the kitchen. "I have to go help Mother with dinner. You can't help 'cause you're just a baby." She left the boy still staring in the mirror, tears coursing down his pink cheeks, his heart crying out the magic word, "*Momma*!"

Bryon gazed unseeing at his bowl of soup as Opal watched with disapproval. "Eat your supper, child. I'll put up with none of your spoiled ways."

The boy's mind raced with questions. *Am I going to live here forever? Do they hate me 'cause I'm so ugly? Will I ever see my momma again?* Tears brimmed over his eyes again and plopped into his soup.

"That's just about enough, boy. Don't go ruining my good soup with your bawling. If you want to starve, then I'll help you out." Turning to her daughter she said, "Belinda, take him to your room and put him to bed."

"But, Mother, I want to eat my supper!"

"Of course you do, dear. Come back when he's in bed and you can finish eating. I don't want him ruining my meal."

The little girl reluctantly took her cousin's hand and led him up the stairs to her room filled with colorful toys lining white shelves set against lemon colored walls. Bay windows let in the last light of a dying day. Belinda plopped down on a beautifully carved window-seat and ordered, "Take your overalls off and get in bed. Told you you're a baby."

Bryon complied as quickly as his trembling fingers allowed and was soon under the big quilt in Belinda's big bed. "Bryon, if you wiggle I'll make you sleep on the floor so watch out." He watched her leave, jerking when she slammed the door behind her.

Darkness fell like a shroud, smothering the cheerful bedroom. Before last night it would not have been such a trial to be left alone in the dark in a strange place but memories of the nightmare haunted him. His body shook from his silent sobbing. Soon, exhausted from the emotional upheaval, the boy was swept into a deep sleep.

He did not wake when Belinda came to bed nor when Richard came in to look at him. "Belinda, I want you to go to sleep right away."

"All right, Father. Why are you staring at him that way?"

He looked at his daughter with concern. I'll have to be careful with her, he decided. She's such a blabbermouth, she'll tell all her little friends that I took him if she wakes and sees me. He decided to wait longer than he had planned just to be on the safe side. To his daughter he said, "I'm just concerned for the boy since he missed two meals. Do you think he'll be okay?"

"If he was hungry he would have eaten his soup instead of crying in it. He's just a big baby, Father." Belinda was by nature cold and cruel but she had heard her parents speak so disparagingly about her little cousin that she felt she had permission to unleash her darkest side. It seemed to actually please her parents and that egged her on even more.

"I guess you're right. See you in the morning, sweetie."

#

The dream came again, but this time it was with a force that paralyzed Bryon with its intensity. "Run, Bryon, it's time.

19

Go now!"

But he couldn't move. The shadow was lowering over him until he thought he would suffocate. He was close to complete despair when the light grew stronger and drew close. Bryon could feel the battle between the light and the shadow as each struggled for dominance. Finally, the light burst over the shadow, driving it behind. "Now Bryon . . . run, hide!"

The child threw himself forward and woke sitting up in the big bed next to his cousin. Belinda mumbled and turned away from him. He was confused, without any idea of what he should do. Momma had told him this was just a dream and not real.

If I get up I'll get in trouble, he worried. *Should I go to sleep again? No!* His shattered nerves screamed out against staying in this bed and taking the chance of falling asleep. Carefully, he crawled out from under the patchwork quilt and went to the window seat where he had left his clothes. As he finished fastening them, he heard footsteps coming down the hall.

The voice from his dream came again, but this time he was not asleep. "Go, Bryon, hide now!" Hope came as he realized that even in this huge, scary house, his friends were still with him. The fairies would help.

Unable to think of anything better, the boy lifted up the lid on the window-seat and crawled in with the toys, then carefully eased the lid back down. It took effort to curl into a tight enough ball to fit in the small space but the child was determined. The footsteps stopped before the bedroom door and he heard nothing for what seemed like an age to a four-year-old. Eventually he heard the door creak open and footsteps move toward the bed. A gasp sounded then low curses followed. Bryon could not identify the thud that sounded which was Richard dropping to his knees and looking beneath the bed. If Opal had been searching she would have gone straight to the window seat, but Richard forgot it was more than a place to sit. Belinda's favorite toys lined the shelves and the ones in Bryon's hiding place were old and unwanted. Richard went to the closet and rummaged angrily, shoving aside his daughter's dresses and shoes.

"Father, what are you doing in my closet?" Belinda asked angrily.

Maybe this was better. Belinda would be a witness that the kid was gone and he did not have him. "I got up to make sure our guest was all right. He's gone, Belinda. Do you know where he went?"

"No. I've been asleep," she answered crossly, still upset at the rude fuss her father was making over that boy.

"Well, I'll go look for him. Maybe he sleep walks. Go on back to sleep, sweetheart."

Richard hurried out the room and down the stairs, his mind racing. I'll find him. He's too small to have gotten far. He's probably on the road to home.

Bryon had no idea what to do. His only conscious thought was to try and keep his breathing quiet and not shiver so hard that he moved a toy.

"Bryon, run. Go now!"

He wasn't afraid of the voice. It had saved him from the shadow and now from the man. Carefully, he lifted the lid and crawled out. A glance at the bed showed him that his cousin was asleep again. He tiptoed out the open door and softly descended the stairs, then he began to run. He raced out the front door and down the main street with the intent of following it straight out the way they had come in, but as he ran he saw the darkness ahead and felt the same kind of oppression that the shadow had brought. Coming to a stop, he hesitated, not knowing what to do.

A tiny light appeared to his right and without questioning, he followed as it moved onto a side street and led to the church. The voice came again. "Hide, Bryon. Don't be afraid now."

Reaching up, he pulled the latch on the door and entered the chapel. An inexplicable peace stole over him as he walked down the aisle. It felt like Momma's arms encircling him. He walked up to the pulpit, went around to the back and crawled into the space underneath. In moments he was asleep.

An hour later, Richard returned home and woke his wife. She helped him thoroughly search the house, *including* the window seat. After that, they began searching the town. Opal was the one who came into the church. She looked under all the benches. Unaware that the pulpit wasn't solid, she left without detecting the sleeping child.

When it was light, Richard saddled his horse and rode for miles in the direction of Bryon's home. Hours passed before he gave up and went home. He started to hope that perhaps the boy had done his work for him. Either the wild life or starvation should take care of the problem.

#

A loud growl woke Bryon. His stomach was cramped with hunger. As another rumble escaped his little body, he wrapped his arms around his belly and squeezed tightly to ease the discomfort.

Waking in a strange place would have been frightening enough, but to be in such danger overwhelmed his senses. It was too quiet in that church and worst of all, his mother wasn't there. A heavy loneliness began to crush the child. Although he was often alone, he rarely noticed because his world was filled with so much love from his mother and such wonder in a landscape teeming with life. This was a different kind of being alone and it made Bryon's heart almost physically ache.

Light was coming in the window as the boy crawled out from the pulpit and walked down the aisle of the church. His desperate desire to see a friendly face and the need for food overcame his fear and drove him into the street.

The sun was almost straight up in the sky by this time. Bryon looked toward Main Street then turned his head in the other direction. The buildings thinned to a scattering of small houses on the outskirts of town. He focused on a cabin set on a hill above a thick stand of cottonwoods and willows. A small creek meandered nearby. The cabin looked a lot like his home and drew the boy like a magnet.

Belinda was playing with a group of her friends by the willows when she saw her small cousin approach the cabin

22

where her best friend Georgettc lived. The girl loved Georgette for two reasons. First, her friend always did what she asked, and second, Belinda loved the feelings of superiority she felt over the poorer girl. Belinda felt quite proud of herself to be able to inform her best friend and the other kids of a great adventure her family was experiencing with the disappearance of her idiot cousin. Her sudden shriek of angry surprise focused everyone's attention on Bryon who turned and ran as soon as he recognized his cousin. The children began shouting and chasing the boy as he ran away from the willows and into the cottonwoods beyond. Soon the children caught and surrounded him.

"Where have you been, you naughty little boy?" Belinda sneered at him. "My parents were worried sick about you. How could you pull such a dirty trick on us?" She rushed forward and pushed him hard. Bryon flew back into a tall, blond girl. Belinda stuck her fists on her hips, thrust out her chubby chin and addressed her friends. "Maybe I'm as dumb as he is. Why am I asking him questions when I know the idiot can't even talk?" Loud laughter met this observation, which encouraged the girl. With a chuckle in her voice she said, "Maybe he just hasn't tried hard enough to talk. Maybe we should make him want to. What do ya think?"

Glaring at Bryon who was being firmly held by the blond girl she said, "Okay kid, all you have to do is say 'stop' and then you can be our friend. No dummies can be our friend so you'd better do it, dummy."

Turning to her friends, she said, "So, do you guys want to help me make him talk?"

A gleeful chorus of consent echoed in the glen. Bryon looked away from his cousin. He couldn't bear the feelings he sensed coming from her. The boy did not understand why everyone was angry with him and his confusion only grew along with his terror as the sun slowly moved across the sky.

A cool breeze caressed Bryon's wet cheek, drying the tears and making his skin itch. He tried to use his shoulder to scratch but with his hands tied tightly behind him, he couldn't

23

quite reach. Turning onto his stomach, he rubbed his cheek against the warm earth which helped some but the movement brought back the nausea. Hoarse dry heaves erupted from the child, hurting his empty stomach worse than the vicious kicks Belinda had given him.

A few of the children had protested the kicking but Belinda's fierce stare backed them down. They all knew from experience how miserable life could be if they got on her bad side.

At first it had been darkly fun to torment the little boy with slaps and poking him with sticks. Tying him up had seemed little more than a game until Belinda began kicking him. Now the fun was gone but they still vied with one another for Belinda's approval and would quickly glance to see her reaction when they would toss out an insult or pelt him with rocks. One small boy, not much bigger than Bryon strutted forward and kicked dirt in his victim's face. "Dummy!" he yelled. The small boy puffed out his chest when he saw the look of satisfaction on their leader's face.

Bryon's body, affected from his recent illness and the lack of food, felt strangely weak. Waves of blackness washed over him as words of hatred slammed into him from the mouths of children. Again dry heaves racked his body.

"I guess you really can't talk, cousin. You know, a dog is worth more than you. They don't talk neither but they can do lots a stuff you can't."

These words settled with more clarity in Bryon's impressionable mind than anything else that was said that day. He never forgot them nor the feelings of self-loathing they engendered. He had no worth.

"Lookee there, he can't even throw-up right. Ain't a thing comin' outta him," a boy noticed.

"I don't think nothing can come out of his stupid ole mouth. Not words an' no puke neither."

"The little fella's too dumb to know how to puke. Maybe he needs some help," Georgette taunted.

"That's right," Belinda agreed with her friend Georgette. "Let's help him throw-up. I know just the thing to teach him."

Leaping to her feet she hurried to the creek that ran below. Shouting over her shoulder she said, "You guys just wait there. I'll bring him his dinner."

She returned with a large slug, which she held up in triumph for her friends to admire. "Doesn't it look yummy?"

"Now he's gotta swallow it," the boy explained. "My ma does this to my sister when she don't take her medicine."

Until this, Bryon hadn't been desperate enough to fight hard but now he twisted and squealed with such violence that some of the children became nervous. Seeing such terror in his beautiful eyes some of the children suddenly began to realize that the mutt boy was a real person. It was almost as if a blinding fog of excitement was sliding away, leaving only ugliness and shame in its wake. "Let 'im go, Belinda," one suddenly pale little boy called out. "This ain't right."

"Yeah," a skinny girl with brown braids added, "ya'all don't wanna kill the baby do ya?"

Belinda narrowed her eyes and glanced around aggressively but when she saw more than a few looks of concern, she tossed the slug aside and sat back. "Okay, I think he learned his lesson."

Bryon had been hyperventilating so much that a feeling of unreality washed over him making sights and sounds seem at a distance.

Not fully content with the punishment and the glory it brought her and realizing she was losing her grip on the other kids, Belinda began thinking of what fun it would be to see what her father would do to her naughty little cousin. "I have to go get my father so he can punish him too." Looking very dignified she gave her orders. "Keep him here while I get my father."

Without Belinda's leadership to enthrall the influence them, the children began to experience sharper twinges of guilt and pity for the bruised and bloodied child. Having no experience with mob-mentality most of them felt bewildered by their own actions. They all backed away from the boy and not one of them had the courage to look anyone else in the eye. The little boy who had held Bryon's nose began to cry, his angelic face screwing up with stress and confusion.

Within minutes, Richard Stewart came striding up the hill. The big man stood surveying the scene in silence for a long moment. "Children, before I take my little cousin back, I think we had better have a talk. Come with me please."

Leaving Bryon as he was, Richard led the children out of the gully that had secluded them from prying eyes and beyond a thicket of cottonwoods. Their apprehension grew as he stopped and looked them over. Quietly, he spoke. "I understand there are times when we are so aggravated by a situation that maybe we lose our heads and let things get out of hand. I can easily understand why you were so upset with Bryon. He ran away and purposely caused my family great distress. He is a willful, rebellious child and he needs a strong hand and you recognize that. However, we should be quiet about what happened here today. A lot of people . . . people including your parents, wouldn't understand at all. They would probably punish you for what you did."

The children exchanged cunning looks of relief as they listened to the grown-up. "You all need to promise me that none of this will go any further." He looked sternly at each child. "Give me your word and we'll never speak of it again."

One by one the children promised. "You kids go on home now. Your parents will wonder where you are. Belinda you go on back to the house to your mother."

"No, Father! I want to stay and help you with that boy!"

"Absolutely not. You go on now." He watched the children move through the trees toward the path to town before he returned to the gully.

Hovering between consciousness and darkness, Bryon concentrated on taking slow breaths through his raw throat. He had rolled onto his stomach to ease his aching shoulders and with that accomplished, he reached for the soothing nothingness he sensed was near.

Just as he was slipping away, he felt a coldness cover him as if a snowman had swallowed the sun. Cowering, he tried to draw himself into a ball but the pain was too intense to move. Opening his eyes to just slits, he noticed a dark shadow on the

26

ground around him. The horror of the nightmare rushed over him and he began to shiver uncontrollably, his teeth chattering loudly. Fear held two faces. Which was worse? To look and see the winged monster, or to only imagine its horrors? This question demanded a decision. Carefully, the small head turned and looked up at the hovering peril. Pale blue eyes glowed from a hatchet-shaped face above him. An ink black beard covered the bottom half of the menace looming above him, making Bryon wish he hadn't looked. He did not recognize Sheriff Barnes until he heard his deep voice. "Well, if it isn't Bryon Hancock."

A noise caught their attention. Richard came walking into view. When he saw the sheriff he stopped. Bryon looked back and forth between the two men as they stared at each other. Something significant was going on in that look but he was unable to interpret the meaning, but he knew there was some kind of understanding being communicated between the men. Then they both turned and looked at him. Confusion grew as the child was flooded with feelings coming from the men, intense, filled with . . . hatred.

The shrill cry of a hawk hunting overhead drew a silent moan from the waiting boy and reminded him again of his nightmare. The darkness swooped down in concert with the bird as Bryon at last fell unconscious.

#

The round face appeared so good-natured and the bright smile was so genuinely kind that Bryon immediately relaxed. The room took on a rosy hue to his sleepy eyes. Recognition dawned as he studied the freckled face above him and a small answering smile rewarded his six-year-old nurse.

"That's right, you know me now don't ya, little Bryon." Betsy Carter patted his hand. My papa is your friend. Your's and your mother too. He thinks she's sweet and sad and you are . . ."

"And you are a handsome little boy." Doc Carter said as he walked into the room and gave his chatty daughter a warning look. "Let your patient rest, darling."

27

Flipping back her cinnamon colored hair, she lifted her pert, freckled nose high and gave her professional report while patting the boy's head. She believed firmly in the healing power of patting. "He smiled a little, Papa. I think he's going to be okay."

"I'm sure he is, Betsy, but he is going to need lots of rest." The Doctor took Bryon's wrist in his hand and began timing his pulse. "Well young man, you looked a little better last month when I treated your cold." While palpating the boy's stomach, he looked into Bryon's eyes to gage his reaction. The pain he saw there made his face flame with fury but he tried to keep his features calm so the boy would not be alarmed. Bryon folded his arms over his stomach and grimaced.

"Betsy, go and get me the bayberry mix and a spoon. Hurry now." Smoothing back the boy's hair he tried to reassure him. "I know it hurts, son, but we'll have you fixed up in a few days and get you back to your ma. Try not to worry."

After administering the herbal remedy, Doc Carter tucked the covers around Bryon and patted his hand just as his daughter had earlier. Let me go heat up some chicken soup and we'll get that down you before you sleep again. He smiled as the child's eyes lit up in anticipation of food.

Betsy drew up a stool and sat next to the bed. "I'll bet that nasty ole Belinda Stewart was 'sponsible for hurting you, huh!" She nodded at his look of confirmation. "She's always making fun of me 'cause I help my papa instead of playing with her and that bunch. Do you wanna know what Papa says about her? He says . . . "

A loud voice came from the other room. "Betsy, quit talking that boy's ear off. Come in here and help me, child."

#

The days flew by at Doc's house. He kept apologizing to Bryon about not taking him home, explaining that he was expecting a difficult delivery at any moment at Mrs. O'Malley's. Bryon wondered how he could be a doc and a postman at the same time but was unable to decipher the puzzle. His time was spent mostly with Betsy and an old Indian named

28

Storm-That-Kills. Doc called him Carver since he was the best carpenter anywhere.

The second day of Bryon's recovery, the Indian brought Doc a beautiful dresser carved from maple with designs from nature engraved in the middle of each drawer. When Bryon was able to get up, he often rubbed his hands over the glossy wood and traced the carvings. Storm-That-Kills talked to him about the blessing of working with wood and was gratified with the boy's rapt attention.

Betsy loved having the silent boy in her home. He was such a good audience and she did love to talk and fuss. He even cheerfully ate the results of her attempts to cook. The warmth and peace of Doc's home did more to heal the traumatized boy than the good herbs and soups. After five days, Doc gave up waiting on Mrs. O'Malley's imminent arrival and asked Storm-That-Kills to take Bryon home. The obvious rapport between the old Indian and the small boy gave Doc confidence that Bryon would be comfortable on the trip.

All went well until the Indian showed up on the doorstep of the Hancock cabin with Bryon in his arms. When Adrian opened the door, he blanched white at the sight of his son.

Storm That Kill's eyes narrowed at the father who could not hide his revulsion toward his own boy. Adrian turned his frustration on the Indian. "What are you doing with my son?" When no answer was forthcoming, he tried again. "A bloody murderer like you has no business touching a child." Reaching forward, he wrenched Bryon from the Indian and set him down behind him.

"How did you come by my boy? Where is Richard?"

The proud Indian turned on his heel and walked slowly away.

Chapter Three

The clouds performed a swirling dance for the enjoyment of the five-year-old boy leaning against the gnarled old oak. A warm breeze ruffled his thick golden hair and carried the sweet, tangy scent of the currant berries.

Bryon glanced at his straw hat nestled in a thick tuft of grass at his feet. The bright berries were heaped so full they almost spilled over the sides. The boy felt pleased that he was old enough to do such hard work. His mother was proud of him and she trusted him. At five, he no longer had to stay constantly in her sight, as had been the case since he returned from Doc Carter's when he was just a baby the year before. Maybe he had been a freak back then like the children had told him, but he had grown a lot bigger and he could tell by the things his mother told him and by how she treated him that he wasn't a freak any more. He was content with his quiet life.

The child heard her softly humming on the far edge of the clearing but he could not see her behind the bushes where she continued to pick the ripe berries. A soft rustling noise attracted his attention and to his great delight, only yards away was a small, gangly grizzly cub frolicking in the grass, grabbing his furry feet and rolling this way and that. He had only seen one at a distance so this was a great event. He had been warned about the bears but he had the hardest time believing that they were dangerous when they looked so cuddly, just like his kitten; only much bigger.

Bryon concentrated all his gentle nature upon the little cub, letting peaceful good-will fill his heart and spill out his eyes in an offer of friendship. The little animal sensed the lack of danger and scooted a few feet toward the boy. Bryon slowly bent over and grabbed a handful of berries from his straw hat and eased closer to the cub. Placing the berries on a flat stone, he drew back a few feet and waited patiently.

The cub studied him for a long moment, learning to trust his quiet nature, then slowly moved to the stone, never taking his eyes from the child until the berries were in reach. Quickly he gobbled the treat then rose up on his little hind legs to challenge the strange creature. Again the trust came as they looked into each other's eyes. The gift that was uniquely Bryon's washed over him in a rush of empathy for the creature. It was as though a part of him was drawn out and joined with the cub. Almost immediately the little animal dropped to all fours and rambled over to the boy, crawling into his lap and bawling out some story he thought would interest his new friend.

Smiling in the pleasure of the moment, Bryon stroked the furry baby, oblivious to the giant form that watched with deep curiosity from the shadow of the woods. Time seemed to stop as the two young creatures enjoyed each other and the spell was only broken when the humming of Cecilia grew louder as she made her way back to her son. She rounded a thick bramble of bushes barely in time to see the cub scamper off Bryon's lap to obey the call of the mother grizzly who did not feel the same trust in the large human as she did in the child.

Glancing nervously around and seeing no further sign of bears, Cecilia wiped the anxiety from her face. "I see you made a friend, son." Bryon grinned happily and jumped up to take her hand. "Bryon, I've never heard of anyone having such a gift of soothing animals as you have. I've seen it work with people too. Thank God for blessing you with that power, son. I know it's the greatest gift in my life."

She squeezed her child's hand and asked, "How would you like to cuddle up with me and have our story-time here today? I may not be furry like your bear cub but I'll have to do. I don't feel ready to go back to that stuffy cabin. What do you think?"

Bryon enthusiastically nodded his head. His father had joined with other ranchers to drive cattle to Nampa, Idaho so mother and son had enjoyed spending long days in the autumn sun playing and watching green leaves bleed to riotous colors. Together they curled up under Bryon's tree. Cecilia laid her head on her shawl and held her son close to her breast. She softly sang Bryon's favorite song and stroked his hair and appreciated the dancing clouds almost as much as the child had.

After the song she told Bryon an Irish tale her father had

often recited before putting her to bed. She knew how her son loved to hear about the elves. When she finished, thoughts of her father overwhelmed her. Suddenly she could smell pipe smoke and felt as if a blanket of safety and comfort poured over her. She hadn't felt like this since she was a child, before her father had died. The pipe smoke smelled the same as his had.

"Bryon, I want to tell you about your grandfather Peter. I never knew a better man. He wouldn't talk much about his childhood but I know he grew up very wealthy. Something terrible must have happened because he left England suddenly and as far as I know, he never spoke to or about his relatives again. I think he must have felt very badly about something he did and he spent the rest of his life trying to make up for it. Your grandfather became a very religious man, truly religious, not the fake kind. He showed kindness to everyone he met.

Your gift with animals must have come from him. He told me once that he didn't think there would be animosity between people and animals if people changed their attitudes towards them. They must have sensed this from him because he had the magic touch. Not quite like you but to a remarkable degree. To tell you the truth, son, I don't think there is anyone as wonderful as you on the face of the earth. And some day others will know what you're made of. Life won't be easy for you, Bryon, but I have no doubt that you'll be able to stand up to any challenge that crosses your path."

He looked up at her with question and a touch of self-doubt in his eyes. Her words reminded him too much of Belinda and her father, and especially of the horrible fear he had suffered since awaking beneath the pulpit. He hated being alone.

Brushing back his hair, she smiled and spoke in a soothing voice. "Don't worry, baby. I'll always be there to help you. I know you don't like being alone. The thing is, son, you're not really alone at all. See, there is something very unusual about you but you need to be a few years older for me to tell you what happened to me when you were born and what I was told. In the meantime, remember, you're not alone."

As the breeze lulled them to sleep, Bryon drew in the

smell of wild herbs in his mother's beautiful yellow hair. The moment that he shared with the bear hadn't fully left him and so when this new awareness hit, the impact of its sweetness brought tears of joy to his eyes. He fell asleep with his favorite word resting in his mind; *Momma.*

The storm hit with surprising speed and force, the wind bringing Cecilia awake with a jolt. She shook Bryon and had to shout for him to hear her. "Leave the berries, we have to get home quickly, the rains are coming!"

Bryon had a terrible time understanding reality as they stumbled through the buffeting winds. The nightmare had come again, the dark shadow that brought terror and danger. Only, now that he was awake, it should be gone, but it wasn't. The dream stalked him like a specter. He shivered violently and his mother wrapped her shawl around him thinking he was cold from the wind. In an instant, the skies opened up and the torrents swept down.

Bryon did not hear the crack of the rifle above the storm and only realized the crisis when he felt his mother's knees buckle and saw her slump to the ground. Frantically he knelt down and turned her over. He stared in disbelief at the red stain spreading on her breast. He looked into her eyes for answers. They always held the answers, but this time they were closed.

It took great effort for Cecilia to open her eyes. She didn't know why Richard hated her and her son but she knew he did. Ever since Bryon returned from his fateful visit she understood this. He was supposed to have moved back east with his family but now she knew he was not gone. He was right here. She wasn't sure why she was so certain of that but she felt the truth of it to her core. She looked up at her beloved child and knew he was in mortal danger. Just as she opened her mouth to warn him, the faint discharge of a rifle was heard above the storm. The bullet tore into the turf next to Bryon, paralyzing her with fear. She needed to tell him to run but she was frozen. Bryon was holding her arm and rocking back and forth in silent terror.

Unable to accept the gravity of what was happening, not

33

willing to face leaving her child to a world without her, Cecilia's mind focused on one thing only. Regret was as bitter on her tongue as the coppery blood in the back of her throat. Why hadn't she told him? He was old enough to understand and more than that, he had such a power of discernment that he already felt how thin the veil was that separated this life from the unseen world. Bryon thought the presence he felt was the fairies. She should have told him the truth, she should have told him what happened to her right after he was born. He needed to know about himself, about why he had to live. Would he still be able to accomplish what he was sent here for? The letter! She had almost forgotten; she had written it all down. Would Adrian ever think to give it to Bryon when he was old enough to read?

As her sight began to fade and sounds became distant, she noticed a bright light growing behind and above Bryon's head. A peace that defied logic stole over her and she no longer felt frozen. Cecilia tried to squeeze her hands into fists, thinking somehow this would keep her spirit in her body. She didn't want to feel peace, she wanted to fight. Bryon needed her. No, I won't go, she thought.

The light grew brighter and she saw him more clearly. No, please, who will protect him, make sure he survives everything they'll throw at him? she cried out from her anguish, but no words passed her lips.

Bryon watched his mother staring at the light, a fierce look of defiance on her face but he was unable to sense her thoughts as normal and he could not see what she did within the light. He watched her shake her head as if communicating with someone.

But if I go with you, Cecilia communicated to the man, you have to promise me to watch over him. Be his guardian angel. He can't talk, he won't tell anyone so you can do more for him. Surely God will allow you to do more for my baby.

The little boy saw tears in his mother's eyes and he buried his face in her shoulder, unable to bear the sight.

Pressing her cheek against his silky hair, Cecilia gave in. Okay, Papa, then you will keep your promise. Okay, Papa.

Pressing her lips to Bryon's ear, with no more strength

but to whisper, Cecilia said, "Run, Bryon, run fast and hide in the line shack on the mountain."

The boy shook his head in horror. Leaving his mother was impossible. He could not do it.

"You have to do this, son. It's the only way." Another shot rang out, the sound much closer. "I have to go with Grandpa now, but you have to stay here. Obey me if you love me. Run, now!"

Bryon rose and leaned over his mother and gently kissed her on her mouth. He felt the pressure of her hands on him, urging him to go. Trying not to think, wanting only to show her he loved her by doing as she asked, he turned and ran into the darkness. He did not see the dirt kick up behind him from another bullet as he entered the trees and sped over the uneven ground, nimbly dodging the entangling brush. Thankfully, he did not hear the final shot that sent his mother into her father's waiting arms, or see the light disappear.

He ran until his sides felt like they were tearing. He had no idea where he was or how to get to the line cabin. He told himself that he would see his mother again as soon as he found his way home. Nothing else was acceptable.

"Bryon!" That voice had haunted him for two years. "Bryon, wait. I can help you. Your mother wants me to bring you to her."

The child was not fooled. The same feeling from the nightmare followed him and was embodied in that voice. A voice that was pure evil!

As he ran, his mother's recent words echoed in his head. "I have no doubt that you'll be able to stand up to any challenge that crosses your path."

I have to go back, he told himself. No, no, no, his mind screamed. I can't do it, Momma! I'm not brave. I'm scared, Momma. He tried momentarily to tell his body to turn back and face the danger but his feet keep running until he feared he would collapse. She needed him, she needed help and he was running away.

A muffled explosion broke through the roar of the storm and the boy felt a sharp tug of wind next to his cheek. He saw the splat from the bullet as it plowed into the muddy hill in front of him. Bryon found hidden strength and ran as fast as his five-year-old legs could carry him. Whenever he could hear the voice above the storm, it sounded closer than before. His labored breathing grew painful, a feeling of dread clutching his chest. He pushed himself to keep going, gasping loudly with every step. The ground had become steep and at times he would come to an incline and he scooted down on his seat through the mud. Cresting a sharp ridge, he began descending into a ravine, mostly sliding down a slick deer path.

Bryon could no longer hear the voice over a roaring that was growing in front of him. The sound was frightening but nothing like the horror that followed him. The child did not see the shadow that loomed up behind him or the hand that reached out for him. How close behind him, he would never know. The hand closed on air as the prey suddenly disappeared.

The shock was so great that Bryon had no time to fear as his feet flew out from under him as the embankment gave out and he was hurled into a raging river that had been a large, quiet stream a mere hour ago. He didn't know about flash floods and he had no frame of reference for what was happening to him as he was swept rapidly downstream. Instinctively he dog paddled to keep his head above water but the turbulence drove him beneath the water again and again. At one point, he thought he heard the crack of the rifle again but this time he hardly cared.

The exhaustion from his flight suddenly washed over him and his movements turned to slow motion. The sense of unreality that had been with him since he awoke in his mother's arms became all encompassing. He was not even aware when a swirling current drove him close to shore and he reached out to grab the bush that hung out over the water. He clung to the thin branches that stung his hands as the current tried to tear him away.

Hand over hand, he inched his way up the whipcord branches until the top half of his body was out of the water.

A huff of air exploded from him as his ribs were struck by a heavy weight. The object wrapped around his hips by the force of the water. His hands slipped and he had to use all his strength not to be dislodged. He wriggled desperately, trying to throw off the dark shape that seemed to stick to him. His eyes grew wide and he opened his mouth in a silent scream as he recognized his friend, the small grizzly cub. He focused on the small red hole in the middle of the cub's back. Slowly, the limp body slid away, swept downstream by the current.

Closing his eyes against the raw emotional and physical pain, his grip tightened on the bush until the blood began to drip from his hands. He had no memory of how long he stayed like that or how he crawled from the water. He had no memory of how he struggled up the bank and took shelter under a thick blue spruce. One thought alone had taken root in his untutored mind. He had left his mother to die. Bryon no longer remembered his mother's command to him to run. Pain dulled the edges of the scene of her death until all he remembered was that his courage had failed and he had fled. He had failed her. And because he had failed her, he was alone. He would always be alone.

He was deep in sleep when Richard walked past him in the pitch dark of the storm. The man found the cub two hundred yards downstream, caught on a log.

Mistaking the cub for his prey a second time, Richard used a stout stick to drag the body to shore. He picked up the cub and studied it for a moment. "If only you were that obnoxious child." With a grunt of disgust, he threw the bear cub back into the water. As it floated away he continued his search.

Having no luck, he retraced his steps to look for any sign of the boy leaving the river.

The rain had slowed to a soft drizzle when Richard found the bush and saw the smooth gouges the boy had left in the mud as he dragged himself ashore. He knew the kid could not have gotten far. He began a systematic search, moving back and forth in a semi-circle. He was elated when he came upon a dark shadow the shape of a child, lying beneath a large blue spruce.

Softly, he crept forward and swung his rifle up to take careful aim. He didn't see the mother grizzly behind him. Enraged at smelling her cub on the man, she roared with fury.

37

Richard spun around in time to catch the mighty swing. The long claws of the grizzly raked skin and muscle from the cheek and jaw of the terrified man. The force of the blow carried him ten feet through the air where he rolled down the bank and into the cold floodwaters. This act likely saved his life by carrying him away from certain death and allowing the chilly waters to slow the bleeding. He failed to appreciate the blessing.

The events of this night would leave scars on both boy and man, changing forever the way they perceived themselves and the world.

#

The loud scolding of a jaybird woke Bryon in the soft pink morning light. His mind took pity on him and refused to function. A sense of sorrow lay heavy upon him but he would not let his thoughts move beyond looking for the bird. Instead, he found the stern face of Sheriff Timothy Barnes watching him. For a moment he thought he was again four-years-old and Belinda and her friends had been tormenting him. He scooted back against the trunk of the tree, shaking with apprehension.

"It's all right boy, I won't hurt you. Come on out of there now."

Bryon shook his head determinedly and the sheriff sighed. "Okay, I'll come in there and get you then." Slowly, the hatchet faced man moved toward the child until he heard shouts from the ridge above them. He froze for a moment then looked above them at the men who came into view.

"Sheriff, did you find him?"

"Yeah, he's down here. Doesn't trust me though."

As three men came stumbling down the incline, the boy and the man looked at each other again, each wondering what the other was thinking. Both would have been surprised had they known.

Chapter Four

Bryon stared through the window into Sheriff Barnes eyes as the train slowly pulled away from the station. The sheriff watched him through the glass, still and silent in his usual way.

The boy remembered another time, six years ago when they had looked at each other with the same questioning stare. He could hardly believe that much time had passed since his mother's death. Much of his life since then was a vague memory; days and nights had little meaning to him.

As the train picked up speed, the eleven-year-old child thought back over the years. He wondered again, as he often had if it had been his imagination that made him believe that a giant grizzly bear had warmed his ice-cold body through that awful night. *No, that couldn't be right.* Shrugging his shoulders, he figured he'd never be certain.

Doc Carter patted the seat beside him. "Come, sit beside me, Bryon." He sighed as the boy folded his arms protectively across his chest and looked at the floor. "Son, I know you're scared but it might not be so bad. At any rate, it was your pa's decision and there's nothing I can do about it except go with you to make sure you get to Portland safe and sound. Maybe you'll like it better than the life you've been living. Adrian worked you way to hard these last years. I wish he'd left you with us after your ma died."

Bryon thought back to the months following his mother's death. Since his father had been away on a cattle drive, Doc had taken him in and cared for him. He knew his father had returned because occasionally he saw him; usually going into or out of the saloon. Any day he had expected to be taken back home but it was almost a year before Adrian had showed up at the Carter home and in a resentful and surly voice, demanded his son back.

Bryon's memory of living with the Carters was hazy, but at least it was a cozy, safe hazy. Betsy kept the emptiness at bay with her constant happy chatter and Doc was kind, always patting his head in his distracted way. He remembered always feeling an underlying tension though. Doc and Betsy were the only people who believed in him and that made him feel a vague sense of shame. His mother had also believed in him and he had betrayed her, leaving her to die. He probably could have saved her if he would have had the courage to remain by her side. He was sure that if Doc knew how he had left her to die, he would no longer treat Bryon with respect.

The next years were a blur of a different kind. Thinking back on it, color seemed to be missing, a gray pall hung over those memories like cobwebs.

I don't know what was worse, Bryon thought. *The year Father ignored me and let me run wild, never speaking to me, just drinking himself sick, or the years of hard work after that.* He understood that his desperate father had put him to work because he didn't have any more cattle to sell. The money from his lumber bought his alcohol.

Bryon closed his eyes, leaned his head back against the cushion and pictured the first day he started working with his father. With no other income, Adrian began logging the forest on his property to scrape by. At seven, Bryon was taught to use a hatchet to chop the smaller branches off the felled trees. By eight, he could take off all the branches and at nine he was chopping down smaller trees by himself. As a result, his shoulders, arms and chest were thickly muscled for an eleven-year old. He looked down at his hands. *I wonder if I'll lose these ugly calluses now? Maybe I'll have to chop down trees where I'm going? Could be that's why Father is sending me away, to hire me out to a logger in the Willamette Valley.*

The click, click of the wheels on the track and the gentle sway of the train car lulled the boy to sleep. Doc Carter gazed with tenderness at Bryon's beautiful features, softened in sleep. A chill ran down his spine as he pondered what laid in store for the boy.

#

"Wake up, son."

Bryon tried to retreat from the gentle pressure on his shoulder but it became more insistent.

40

"Come on, Bryon. We're in Portland; it's morning. There's a great little restaurant right across the street. Hurry or we'll miss all the chow."

Together they made their way across the wide dirt road to the quaint little café unoriginally called *Grandma's Place*. They found a small table in the corner and Bryon sat facing the wall. He hadn't felt comfortable around crowds of people in six years.

"Let me order for you, pal." At Bryon's nod the friendly doctor turned to the waitress. Rubbing his beefy hands together, he grinned. "Make sure we have the best of everything. I'm hungry this morning. We'll take a stack of buttermilk pancakes, half dozen eggs, fried potatoes, sausage, bacon, biscuits, and a pot of hot chocolate to drink." He grinned at Bryon then shrugged innocently at the waiter's raised eyebrows.

"I hope you can help me," Doc said to Bryon. "My eyes might be a lot bigger than my head." He was rewarded with a real smile of anticipation from his dining partner. He knew the boy usually had to fend for himself if he wanted food. Hancock's priority had leaned toward liquid sustenance. He shuddered to think how Bryon was going to be fed after this. He had heard far too many stories.

The doctor watched the hungry boy gobble his food and hoped Bryon didn't notice how little he was eating.

A feeling of well-being spread through Bryon and for a moment he had hope that maybe things would not turn out so bad after all. As he was reaching for the pot of cocoa again, Doc noticed his hand.

"You know, I feel a little guilty about those rough hands of yours. I benefited from their work, you know. "Did Storm-That-Kills tell you that I've gotten a lot of great comments on the carvings you sold me?" The boy nodded and Doc went on. "He told me he brought you food and candy when he sold me your two best carvings. Did you enjoy that?"

Bryon was relaxing and remembering how he had once trusted the doctor and Betsy. He rubbed his tummy in response and smiled.

"Good, you deserved a reward. As much as I love the

41

mother grizzly, it's the carving of the boy with the cub in his lap that I prize the most. I can't imagine where you came up with your idea and how a mere child could put so much feeling into something. Never forget how gifted you are, Bryon."

Finally, the child was really listening to him without fear or reserve. "There's something else I want you to remember. I'm your friend, son. I really do care about you. I hope someday you'll come back and look me up. I'll be wondering how you are."

With a serious look Bryon nodded once, slowly, confirming the agreement. As they both quietly sipped their chocolate, a slight smile tipped the left side of Bryon's mouth. As he watched the traffic out the window, his memory slipped back to the one bright spot that had given his life purpose the last two years. Storm-That-Kills had given him two treasures. He had trained his hands and provided practically the only human voice he heard.

Since his cabin wasn't far from the Hancock ranch, the Indian kept abreast of the events that took place down the mountain. Recognizing isolation similar to his own, he reached out to the lonely boy two years ago. Storm-That-Kills often helped Bryon meet his daily quota of felled trees, careful to disappear if Hancock ever came to check on his son. That freed up enough time so he could teach Bryon to carve.

The older man had a talent that was widely recognized and appreciated even if the maker wasn't. He was feared because as a young man he had often become violent after the traders passed around the whiskey. He seldom remembered his actions afterward but they were shocking enough to earn him an ugly reputation, and his name. Even after years of sobriety, he was still an outcast among his people and most of the whites. This boy was an outcast too and that created a bond between them.

Storm-That-Kills had recognized Bryon's feel for and appreciation of wood when he first met him and he guided that feeling to bring out the boy's artistic nature. His hands, strengthened from hard work, showed surprising dexterity. The Indian soon recognized that the child had the potential to surpass his own talent and he worked patiently to bring that about. In the two years that Bryon learned from him, the quality of the carvings increased astonishingly for one so young. Storm-That-Kills had heard that the boy's father once fancied himself an artist and the old Indian delighted that this talent was so generously manifested in the child.

Bryon remembered how honored he felt by the bestowal of his Indian name, Bear's Brother. *How did he know about that day with the cub?* Bryon wondered for the hundredth time.

His friend had shown him how to carve a simple grizzly print on the bottom of all his carvings as his signature.

A frown replaced the smile at the memory of his final day with Storm-That-Kills. His friend was encouraging him to carve a likeness of his mother as the boy remembered her. Something long dormant was unfurling inside Bryon as he worked to re-create the beloved features. With determination, he had tried to force away the feelings of guilt that assaulted him when he thought of Cecilia.

Adrian was more drunk than usual as he quietly stole into the clearing where the pair were carving. In the exaggerated movements of a drunk, he had snuck up to surprise his son with a sharp slap to the side of his head. Grabbing the carving, he threw it as far as he could. Storm-That-Kills rose to his feet, his own carving falling unnoticed to the ground.

Adrian ignored the Indian and with a face mottled dark with rage he shouted, "I'd heard rumors," he shook his son hard, "that you were cavorting with re . . . with red," his angry speech was interrupted by a loud belch. "You've been seen with red men but I didn't really believe it 'til now!" Grabbing the boy by the collar he began dragging him toward home. Pulling up short, he spun around, almost falling over with the effort. The hated Indian had been following a few paces behind.

"I told you once to stay away from my kid, Injun. I've been having a hard ti . . . time, making a decision about his future. You just did the job for me."

With a soft but lethal voice, Storm-That-Kills spoke. "If you harm Bryon in any way, I'll slit your throat and feed you to the coyotes."

43

Adrian tossed his head. "I'm not going to hurt my own son. In fact, I'm sending him somewhere safe where he won't be around bad influences like you, red man."

Bryon remembered the look on his face the last time he saw his friend. The Indian knew they would both now be alone.

As soon as they returned to the cabin, Adrian had pulled a worn letter out of his desk. Bryon had seen him first open the letter and read it a few weeks before. His father had been distracted ever since and had occasionally pulled the letter out to ponder the contents. *Whatever was on that paper is the reason I'm going away. I just wish someone would tell me where that is.*

#

The heavy wooden door swung open on the thick, steel hinges. Doc touched Bryon's back to encourage him forward although he felt anything but encouraged himself. "If he didn't have the law on his side," Doc muttered under his breath.

Bryon did not understand what he meant but he knew Doc didn't like the look of the huge, gray stone mansion any better than he did. The building couldn't be that old since Portland was a new city, but it sure did look old, set out here all alone in the woods. Old and haunted.

"Please come in out of the cold." The sour looking woman at the door tried to hide her impatience but Bryon sensed it. He grabbed Doc's hand and clung to him desperately. He tugged to get the man's attention and violently shook his head. *I can't stay here; you can't do this to me, please!*

Doc's heart broke as he read the plea in the child's face. Bending down to Bryon's eye level he whispered, "Son, there's nothing I can do about it. Your father signed the commitment papers. If I tried to interfere, I'd be put in jail. Believe me, I know. I was already threatened with it." He watched all the ground he'd made with the boy on the trip fade away. Bryon drew into himself, his eyes dulled as he pulled his hand free.

He did not see Doc's tears flow as he watched the boy walk into the dim interior of the lunatic asylum.

Chapter Five

"Hey, what's ye name?"

Bryon was curled into a ball in a dark corner of a small, filthy cell that was bare except for two slate colored blankets and a bucket overflowing with human waste. He sat on his blanket to avoid the cold flagstone and breathed from his mouth to ease the stench.

He felt the soft poke on his back again. "Hey, whatsa matter with you? I wanna know yer name!"

Bryon peaked over his shoulder at a redheaded boy who looked to be about eight-years-old. The ravaged look on Bryon's face silenced his roommate who gave up with a sigh and began slowly pacing around the tiny cell. After a few turns the boy stopped abruptly and demanded loudly, "I wanna know yer name right now! Please, please tell it to me and then you don't gotta tell me nothin' more." He stood with wide spread legs, the palms of his hands turned outward, fingers spread in determined supplication. Hazel eyes too big for his thin face gave him a mournful but comical appearance.

Desperate to be left alone, Bryon turned to him, pointed to his own throat and shook his head. Shrugging in dismissal, Bryon buried his head in his arms and resumed his effort to think of nothing.

"Do you got a frog in your throat, huh?" The redhead nodded with satisfaction. "Maybe that's why you don't wanna to talk to me. Maybe you don't hate me after all, right? Maybe?" He did not seem to need an answer. "Gee, maybe you don't even got no name. I knew this real little girl that was here once and she didn't have no name neither. She died. Whatdya think they put on her headstone? Oh yeah, my name is George. You know, like Washington." He looked confused for a moment. "He's the capitol."

He shifted his feet, a far away look coming into his eye. "Ma said once she wished she'da saved my name for my little brother Herbert, 'cause George Washington was a real brave man, not a idiot like me." Looking back at his new roommate he defended himself, defiance in his voice. "She was wrong, I am *so* brave! Really I am. Once, I saved Herbert from drowning when he fell into the creek but he was only little and couldn't tell Ma what really happened. She thought I was trying to hurt Herbert so she sent me here. I weren't trying to hurt 'im," he whined, "I wouldn't do that. I took real good care of him."

George went over and sat beside Bryon. "I heard my ma tell my little brother once that he had a frog in his throat. I was so, so glad it weren't me what had some slimy ole frog down my throat." The boy leaned over his new roommate whispering conspiratorially. "Maybe if you stuck yer finger way down there, you can grab that frog by the leg and yank 'im out? We could give it to cook to fry up for our supper. It'd be better than that nasty soup they give us, whatdya think?"

When an answer wasn't forth coming, the mentally retarded boy sighed dramatically, rose and resumed pacing his habitual circle until the door opened revealing the burly head orderly. George backed hastily against the far wall and held his breath until he saw that the dark-haired man was moving toward his roommate.

The orderly grabbed Bryon's arm and pulled him to his feet, motioning for him to follow. "Miz Simondson be ready to see ya now."

Bryon trailed out the door behind the man who stopped to turn the key in the lock before leading the way down the long hall. Bryon hadn't noticed his surroundings when he was brought to his cell the day before but now he looked with morbid curiosity at his new home. The rough-cut gray, stone walls reached up to high, roughly plastered ceilings. Since being led beyond the marginally pleasant, family reception room yesterday, the only color he had seen was on his body. His brown homespun slacks and pale yellow cotton shirt were, oddly, a comfort to him. They let him know that the world wasn't slowly fading away the way paint used to when his tears fell on one of his drawings.

The asylum administrator was waiting behind her desk in a large office situated just past the family reception room. There was certainly color in this room. Green plants dominated the back wall where two large windows let in the pale, autumn light. Shelves lined the right hand wall, packed with mementos; ceramic bowls, clever trinkets, even beautiful wooden carvings that made Bryon's pulse speed up at the thought of Storm-That-Kills. Miss Simondson's cherry wood desk and lovely, Elizabethan style chair dominated the left side of the room.

Agatha Simondson was a thin, nervous woman in her forties whose confident, authoritative demeanor was belied by her constant habit of primping her coiffure. Her dark hair was liberally sprinkled with gray and her twitching fingers smoothed and tapped constantly at the stern hairdo.

"So, you are Bryon Hancock!" She tapped and twitched as she waited for his response but a painting hung between the two windows caught his attention. He stared wistfully at the depiction of two bear cubs cavorting in a berry patch. This brought such an intense yearning that the boy paid no attention to the administrator. He was so lost in the power of the art, he did not hear her clear her throat expectantly.

She shared an annoyed glance with her head orderly and looked back down at the form on her desk. Addressing her orderly she said, "The father only filled in that he was mute. He must have meant deaf/mute. Get him his clothes and when he's dressed, take him back. Tomorrow morning you can start showing him his chores. He's to clean my office, the surgery and the waiting room. Is that clear?"

"Sure, no problem." The orderly turned to Bryon, took his arm roughly and pulled him out the door. Assuming it was useless to speak, he did not waste the effort. He led the boy to a laundry room and motioned for him to remove his clothing.

"Do it now!"

Bryon bent down and slowly removed his boots. When he stood back up he just stared at the frightening man. His black hair was slicked back with too much greasy stuff and his big nose was oddly shaped from too many fights. Small, dark eyes glared fiercely."

"I said take them clothes off, kid."

I'll be lost if he takes my clothes, Bryon thought as he clutched the front of his shirt and pressed it to his chest. He did not understand his own reaction but he instinctively sensed that a loss of identity was to follow.

The orderly spit out a few choice words as he tore the boy's hands away and pulled his shirt apart, sending buttons flying through the air. Spinning the child around, he stripped it off his arms, then efficiently removed the pants from the squirming inmate. When he reached to unbutton the faded red long johns, Bryon shook his head, and backed up, a wild look in his eye.

"Either you take them off or I will and I ain't gonna tell ya again."

Quickly, the shaking boy turned his back and removed his underwear.

The man shoved a bundle of faded gray canvas clothes into Bryon's hands. He felt like he had grown extra fingers as he struggled into the stiff pullover shirt and matching drawstring pants. He watched his own clothes being stuffed into a gunnysack. Looking back down at what he was wearing, he felt as though the world and all its color had just been washed away. Hope of rescue was gone; they owned him now.

#

Several weeks passed and Bryon was now proficient in his chores. As horrible as life was here, there was one bright spot. He alone, of all the inmates had color in his world after all. His chores consisted of cleaning Miss Simondson's office, the family reception center, the surgery and the pretend room. At least that is what he called the pretty little room that was shown to families as an example of the living quarters. Three of the rooms had paintings, plants and colorful dust-runners. Only the surgery made him wish to be elsewhere. Too often, he had to clean up blood and throw away the contents of stainless steel bowls filled with things he had no wish to identify.

While he was engaged in his favorite chore, polishing the ornaments lining her shelves, Miss Simondson was chatting with the orderly as she glanced through her mail. "So, Dr. Williams is taking care of Andrew, right?"

"That's right."

"Good. They get to be such a problem at that age

otherwise." Her eyes narrowed at a letter in her hands. "Oh bother, not that awful do-gooder again?"

The orderly put on his most attentive expression, which looked ghastly on his dull features. "Bad news?"

"It could be. I've told you about Dorothea Dix? She is trying to push through some more legislation to reform the asylums. She's back in New England though, so hopefully she'll leave us alone. She wants to change asylums from places of control, to treatment. I'd like to see her try it. Since 1848 when the first institution was opened in Yarra Bend, it has been understood that we exist in order to control what the families are unable to control. If they could handle things then they wouldn't bring them here. If treatment were possible, it would be far better done in a loving family so when they are forced to inter them, any idiot should see that as an admission that there is nothing more to be done. And I'd just like to see what that woman would come up with to treat what everyone knows is the primary reason for insanity; demonic possession. If she gets her nasty law passed then she'd better be prepared to march right in here and cast out all the devils herself or I'll give her what-for!"

Agatha knew her head orderly was too stupid to understand much of this but she loved impressing him with her knowledge. Plagued by acute insecurities, she appreciated a lackey who basked in her glory like a hound at her feet.

"Well now, you are doin' jus' fine then 'cause that there new preacher is comin' in here ever Sunday and doin' somethin' 'bout that. Don't ya just feel proud?"

"You're right. I am giving treatment, I have nothing to worry about at all do I?" She looked thoughtful for a moment. "Come to think of it, just in case that theory is wrong and the other one, you know, lunar influence is the main cause, we help that too by not letting our inmates outside when there's a full moon. Or any other kind of moon at that."

"Never did git that one."

"Lunar stands for the moon, dummy. Some people believe the moon affects people like it affects the ocean and that interferes with their brain waves or some such malarchy. That's where the word lunatic comes from." She scrunched up her sharp face. "If it is true, I wonder if it affects people even if they stay indoors?"

"If that ain't the stupidest thing I ever heard. The ocean is made o' water. We ain't got no water in us now do we? Not unless we jis' drunk some or haven't peed!" Feeling very proud of his logic, he beamed at his boss waiting for approval.

She cleared her throat and looked away from the big man chewing on his thick bottom lip. "Um . . . well, anyway those are the theories." At times she felt like an idiot herself for even attempting to have discussions with this man. Loneliness could do funny things to a person. The doctor was the only person she ever saw who came close to her intellect so she was forced to communicate with morons. "Why don't you go check and see if the laundress has come yet. She has a big load this week so get some extra flour from cook for her."

Her attention switched to the boy lovingly rubbing a wooden carving of an eagle. "Take the boy out before he wears that wood away. Have him clean the reception room next to give Dr. Williams a chance to finish."

As the orderly was getting the boy's attention, Agatha looked at Bryon intently and wondered if he learned his job so quickly because he could read lips?"

The orderly tapped Bryon on the shoulder and pointed toward the door. Bryon had failed to hear the woman's instructions for him to clean the reception room. He knew they thought he was deaf and he felt safe letting them think that. Somehow that made him feel cocooned in his own little world.

After ushering him out of the room, the orderly promptly left, forgetting to direct him to the reception room. He headed for the surgery according to his regular pattern. Lugging the big bucket of water and rags, he opened the door into the most hated room in the asylum.

Concentrating on bringing the bucket through the door, he walked a few steps into the room before he looked up. The sound of the door closing alerted Dr. Williams to his presence. "How did you get in here, you little creep?"

Bryon barely heard his words as he stood, paralyzed by the embarrassingly horrible sight before him. A deaf boy a few years older than him named Andrew lay strapped to the table with his pants off. Blood was running thickly from his genitals. Gratefully, the boy had passed out on the table.

Bryon was stung back to reality when the doctor slapped him. "That door was locked. How did you get in?"

Bryon shook his head and pointed to the lock. The doctor grabbed him with one of his bloody hands, pulled the door open and hurled him into the hall. Bryon fell in a heap on the hall floor and covered his head protectively as the bucket of water was thrown out on him. He heard the door slam and the click of the lock.

The brown water running into his lap reminded Bryon of what he had just witnessed. Nausea slammed into him like a fist. He threw up just as the head orderly came back down the hall, having finally remembered his instructions concerning Bryon.

With a foul curse, he kicked the boy in the ribs and told him to clean up the mess. As soon as the room stopped spinning, the bruised boy clambered slowly to his feet and with thoughts racing he began to clean.

A week later, while dusting the reception room, Bryon heard the clang of the heavy doorknocker. Knowing the door was locked he waited expectantly as Agatha Simondson passed through the room into the entrance hall and unlocked the door. The boy heard the murmur of male voices and watched as two men entered with a woman held firmly between them.

Bryon's heart ached at the look of fear and despair on the pretty blond woman's face. He was fascinated with her delicate, refined appearance. Her sprigged muslin gown was an aching reminder of his mother's Sunday dress. At a scowl from the administrator, he turned back again to his work but listened attentively.

The men sat on either side of the woman on a brown, horsehair sofa, the older one speaking. "You understand we hate to do this, Miss Simondson, but we feel we have no choice."

"Of course I understand. Families are the real victims in this situation. The mentally ill are safe in their little world of make-believe while you suffer for the consequences of their actions. I see it all the time."

The older gray haired man sighed with relief. "That's right. It *has* been an embarrassment to us but we'd put up with it if it weren't for the sake of the children. My son here has a little boy and girl that have to be considered."

"How dare you!" the woman shrieked. "You tear me away from my children and imply I wasn't a good mother! What did I ever do to make you think that?"

"Now, Patricia," the younger man interceded, "you know that children learn by example. Having a mother who is a nymphomaniac could . . ."

"Oh, Alan, how could you? You're the one . . . "

She cowered back in fear as her husband squeezed her arm and roared at her. "That's enough, Patricia. No more of your dirty lies."

Alan's father sent an apologetic smile to Agatha Simondson. "We find this a little embarrassing but Patricia has been falsely accusing Alan of having an affair. Which he isn't," the man quickly added. "It's just that, he won't, well, he doesn't, um . . ."

Alan rescued his father. "She places unreasonable, lewd demands on me that are unnatural for a woman. I'm afraid the children may have noticed. For their sake, I think this is best."

Patricia glared at her husband then spoke to the administrator. "Could I speak about this with you in private?"

Cold eyes met the young woman's pleading look. "Certainly, but not yet. There are a few details to see to, then we can have a nice chat."

Opening a folder, she handed the necessary paperwork to Alan Strouse to sign. After he had read through and signed it he glanced nervously at his wife. "I guess that's about all, Patricia. I hope they can help you here. I'm sorry things had to turn out this way."

"I'm beginning to think you aren't sorry at all. In fact, I'm beginning to wonder if you didn't plan it this way from the beginning. Please, Alan, you can't really be this cruel can you?"

The man's face twitched and what might have been guilt

made him blink and look away.

His father felt no guilt, however. "Don't you put this on my boy. I've seen how you sidle up to him and give him those sultry looks. Touching him and trying to hold his hand." His eyes glinted with malice. "Why, I'm ashamed to have to tell this good woman, you've even given me some come hither looks when you thought my son wasn't looking."

"That's a disgusting lie! I've always loathed you. And I won't deny holding my husband's hand. I was trying to improve our relationship. Trying to get back what we had that first year. I didn't do anything improper and you . . ."

Standing up, her father-in-law over-rode her. "Nobody wants to hear any more of this, Patricia. It won't help and this just goes to show how argumentative you always were. Your kids will certainly be better off without you."

His son flushed a bit at this last statement and looked a little sorry. "Miss Simondson, I want to know what things are like here? Where will she be kept?"

"Why, I'm glad you asked. Let me show you one of the rooms. Your father can stay with your wife while you follow me." She led Alan Strouse out of the reception area and down the hall. Across from her office was the room kept ready to show inquiring family members.

Opening the door, she ushered him in. "It is best not to bring family into the interior of the building. Sometimes, seeing strangers can upset our guests, but this room is just like the others so you can feel comfortable about leaving your dear wife in our hands."

The man felt relieved as he looked around the cozy bedroom. The bed was neatly made with a cheerful counterpane. A maple dresser, a cane rocker with an embroidered pillow, and a soft prayer rug completed the furnishings. A watercolor of Jesus holding a lamb hung above the bed. "This is fine, just fine. Thank you for putting my mind at ease, ma'am."

"My pleasure." She patted her hair and simpered at the handsome man.

Shortly after the men had left, Bryon finished the

reception room and moved on to clean the pretend bedroom. As he was dusting the dresser, he heard the pretty woman's raised voice pleading with the administrator.

"You need to listen to me! You haven't heard my side of things yet."

"I've heard all I need to, Patricia."

"But you only listened to what *they* had to say. Don't I have any rights? Don't I have the right to be heard, the same as them?"

"Actually, since your husband signed the papers; no. You don't have any rights at all!"

"I won't stay. I won't stay in this place, I tell you," the woman screamed hysterically. "Get your hands off me!"

Bryon heard a resounding slap and after that, only sullen murmuring. Shortly, the office door opened. The head orderly led the softly weeping new inmate down the hall into the bowels of misery.

Chapter Six

The smell of stale cabbage and vinegar fought for supremacy over the stench of sour sweat and urine in the large common room that Patricia reluctantly entered. She had initially felt relief when an orderly had led her out of her horrible little room but her apprehension grew as she wondered about her fellow inmates. Her cellmate, an old man who truly was out of his mind, shuffled after her, mumbling incoherently, spittle sliding down the corners of his mouth.

Patricia felt self-conscious in the stiff, sack shaped gray dress even though she knew all the women would be wearing the same. Even worse, the orderly had taken her hairpins, citing a rule about dangerous instruments, so her thick, long hair hung indecently down her back.

As they were the last to arrive, the orderly shoved them before him into the room and locked the door behind him.

"Grub's on the table. Git to it afore someone else does."

Two long tables dominated the room, rough-hewn benches on either side. The windows were high, small and dirty, letting in little light. Patricia walked to the table and noticed the boy she had seen upon her arrival. He was beautiful. His coloring reminded her somewhat of her Frank, just five years old. A gasp of pain clutched her heart at the thought of her children and she slapped her hand over her mouth to stifle a sob. Hurriedly, she grabbed a small wooden bowl and one of the heavy, sturdy spoons and sat by the boy. She smiled down at him, trying to forget her own sorrows. "Hello. I hope it is all right if I sit by you?"

Bryon looked back adoringly and nodded.

"Thank you. My name is Patricia. What's yours?"

The boy pointed to his throat and shook his head. A small redheaded boy poked his head around the blond child and spoke accusingly, "He won't tell me his name neither, but mine be George."

"Pleased to meet you, George."

"He stays with me in my room and it's been 'bout a hundred years since he come and he still won't tell me. If he ever tells you, will you give it to me? I need that name!"

"Certainly I will."

The man sitting across the table from her interjected, "Kid's name is Bryon. That's what the orderly calls him."

"Bryon!" George lit up with excitement at finally knowing his roommate's name. "Whatdya know?"

Bryon slumped with relief, beamed at George, turned and shyly grinned at the lovely lady. He nodded his head and patted his chest.

She reached out and took his hand and shook it warmly. "Well, I am most happy to meet you, Bryon." She watched him flush as he turned back to his food. She picked up her spoon, dipped in into the watery soup and froze. The smell had reached her and she knew that it would take more hunger than she currently possessed to induce her to partake of her prison fare.

The grizzled man sitting across from her stared hopefully at her bowl. "Are you going to eat your supper, ma'am?"

She was startled at the polite words and the genteel accent that came from the haggard inmate. "Why, no. You're welcome to it if you like." She scooted the bowl toward him and he gratefully accepted the gift.

"I know it must seem like poison to you but it is truly amazing what the body can adapt to when forced." Between spoonfuls, he spoke. "My name is Barker Frohme. Do you mind my asking yours?"

"Not at all, Mr. Frohme. I'm Patricia Strouse. I'm pleased to meet you."

"Where are you from originally? You sound northeastern."

"Very perceptive, sir. Yes, I was raised in Hartford, Connecticut."

"Lovely place. My family is from Boston."

"I've heard of a Frohme family in Boston. I don't suppose . . ."

"Suppose away. My prominent family is duly horrified to have a sheep as black as I." He shrugged dismissively. "Do you still have family back east?"

"No. My mother passed away last year. She was all I had left." Patricia tried to hide her surprise that this man with the long, scraggly beard and wild hair could be a Frohme.

"I'm sorry."

"My husband wasn't. I inherited her estate. He was thrilled."

"So now your husband has your money?"

She jerked back as if he had slapped her face, eyes widening in suspicion. "I, uh . . . I guess I hadn't quite thought of that."

"I'm sorry. It's none of my business. You sound like a highly education woman. It's a shame this had to happen to you."

"I have to say, Mr. Frohme, you definitely do not seem to belong here either." Although her first impression had convinced her that this man was a typical worn-down bum, his demeanor and the intelligent light in his eyes reminded her of her mother's admonition not to judge by appearance. Patricia began to believe it would be possible to not lose her mind with these children to love and a compassionate friend like Mr. Frohme to converse with.

"You look surprised. You expected to be the only sane one in here, correct?"

Looking a little shamefaced, she nodded. "I'm afraid so." Looking around her, she continued, "and I have to say, it looks like we're not alone."

"Oh, we have our crazies, like that poor man you came in with. But by and large, most people here are sane enough."

"I don't understand? I thought this was an asylum for lunatics; crazy people?"

"It is. It's just that my definition is different than the commonly held belief of what constitutes crazy." Encouraged by her keen interest he went on. "I'd say that out of the hundred or so inmates here, only about twenty are really insane. You have to understand, they mix a variety of disorders together in these institutions. At least it is better than it used to be."

"You're kidding?"

"No, really. Not many years ago, all the people in here would be crammed together in jails. If they weren't so lucky, they would be put in filthy stalls that almost make this place look clean." A look of disbelief crossed her face as she looked around at the walls streaked with unspeakable grime and a floor covered with refuse. He went on. "I said almost. We don't have to lay down in inches of our own waste as was the case with many back east until very recently. Those considered violent, or likely to escape were chained in closets, cages, pens or cellars, usually naked. Those in colder climates suffered greatly since heat is, even now believed by most to be unnecessary for those of us judged no better than animals."

"So we won't have any heat? Even in winter?"

"I'm afraid not, ma'am."

"I don't understand? How could this be allowed? Why don't the families stop it?"

"They either don't know, or don't care, Mrs. Strouse."

"How do you know all this, sir?"

"I am, I'm afraid, an inebriate. I tend to have a hard time

controlling my drinking."

"But why are . . ."

Holding up his hand for patience, he continued. "As I said, all kinds are put in together. We have the insane, the mentally retarded, the deaf and dumb, who are generally considered retarded although I haven't personally found that to be the case." He smiled at Bryon who, curiously enough, appeared to be listening intently. "We have the inebriates like me, the criminally insane, and just plain prisoners when the jails are full. And to answer your question, I have had the dubious honor of being in two asylums before this one. Both were back east where my family is. With my own eyes, I have seen most of these conditions, and heard of others from those who suffered them. I knew one poor fellow who was chained in a tiny, windowless room for seventeen years. They sent me in every week to clean out his bucket."

He lowered his voice after glancing nervously at the head orderly who was leaning against a far wall. "I have seen men, women and children beaten or lashed bloody. It happens here but not as much as the first place where I was a guest."

"Oh no, Mr. Frohme, something has to be done."

"Things are slowly getting better thanks to a woman named Dorothea Dix. She has worked tirelessly for years to expose the inhumane treatment and is making some real changes through legislation.

People around them were rising and stacking their dishes on one end of the table. Patricia rose with Barker and did the same.

"We are allowed to stay in here and visit for an hour after supper in the evening. Except for the hour for chores, the rest of the time is spent in the cells so enjoy it if you can."

He was interrupted by a shrill laugh. Patricia saw a young woman slapping at the orderly in a coy manner.

"You keep your hands off me, you dirty old man. The only one who gets to touch me is Dr. Williams."

"Shut yer mouth, ya idiot. Do ya want the administrator havin' me put ya in another straitjacket?"

"I'll pull her hair out if she tries it. She's just a jealous old biddy is all."

"Knock it off or I'm a gonna have ta report ya. Unless ya wanna be nicer to me and change my mind," he leered.

"Who'd want that?"

"I thought nymphomaniacs were suppose ta want any ole man. What's wrong with me?"

"Look in a mirror."

The big orderly swung his fist and caught the woman on the side of the head sending her crashing against the wall. "Ya gone to far, Theresa. Yer gonna pay for that, I don't care what the doc says. Yer gonna pay!"

Patricia noticed how upset Bryon was and motioned him to a far corner. "Would it be all right if I told you about my children?" At his nod she began regaling him with anecdotes about her five-year-old son, Frank and three year old Lisa. Soon the boy relaxed and smiled at the stories. She felt a little of the ache lift from her heart as she talked to the child and in return, she made him feel like Frank and Lisa were part of his family. As she continued, she ran her fingers through his long, golden hair.

"Git yer hands off that there boy."

She did not hear the orderly at first, lost in her story about Lisa's pranks with her terrier puppy. "I said, don't touch him!" She was spun around and jerked away from the boy. Her face flamed red as he continued. "Yer another one of those nymphos. Miz Simondson told me. That there boy is too young fer ya. Don't let me catch ya touching him again or you'll get what she got."

Bryon lost his temper at the treatment of the beautiful lady and was ready to plow into the big orderly when Mr. Frohme grabbed him by the neck and whispered, "Don't be a fool. He'll eat you for lunch." He held on until the boy had himself under control.

The horrified woman backed up against the wall, her hands over her face and slowly slid to the floor. She didn't notice Mr. Frohme's hand resting on her shoulder. How am I going to bear it? She wondered. Maybe I really will lose my mind.   #

Meal times became the most pleasant part of the day for Bryon. Patricia never seemed to run out of stories to tell George and him. Sometimes they were about her children, other times she told of her own idyllic childhood and sometimes she told him wonderful fairy tales that transported him to colorful worlds of adventure and happiness. These were George's favorites. She was careful not to touch either boy, even casually on the hand. Barker enjoyed the stories and at times would tell one of his own although he was shy about it, saying Patricia was so gifted that he hated to ruin the mood.

The first Sunday brought a momentary ray of hope to Patricia Strouse. After the morning meal, the orderly ushered a minister into the common room. Theresa cupped her mouth and whispered to Patricia, "The last minister was real nice, but this here fella is plumb crazy. Stay away from him."

Patricia did not trust anything Theresa said and hoped fervently the woman was wrong. She clamped down on her impatience as she listened to his fire and brimstone preaching. When the sermon was over, he approached Patricia who had flattered him by her attention.

"Good morning, young woman. I am happy to see you are concerned about your eternal welfare."

"Good morning, Reverend." She extended her hand, which he held only for an instant. Beaming his cheeriest smile, he then generously offered to throw the devil out of her, assuring the woman that this would most likely solve all her problems.

She was a bit startled but still determined to get his help. "Reverend, can I talk with you a moment?"

"Why certainly, child." The man looked about her age. "What can I do for you?"

She took a deep breath and tried to sound calm and rational. "There has been a terrible mistake. I don't belong here, you have to help me get out." Unconsciously she began to pluck at his sleeve with growing desperation when she saw his doubt.

"Now, now, I'm sure there was good reason to bring you here for help. Give it some time and I'm certain things will come right."

"You don't understand. My husband and his family put me here. They say I'm a nymphomaniac but I'm not."

The minister removed her hand and moved back in revulsion. "I can't help you with that. Why don't you talk to the administrator?"

"I have. She doesn't believe me. Look, I can prove it. My husband has been having an illicit affair since my daughter was born. I can give you witnesses. He barely tried to hide it. He told me that his mistress wasn't afraid to please a man. She wasn't cold like me. I tried to change, to become affectionate like he wanted and as a reward he called me a nymphomaniac and said he did not want a woman like me raising his children. Now his mistress is living with him in sin and Alan said she is going to raise my children. Surely as a minister of the Lord, you can't let that go unnoticed?"

"Do you see how unladylike you are acting? Please find some dignity and accept your situation."

"Then at least could you get a message to my uncle in Connecticut? He'll pay you! Please!"

Panicked at being drawn into a difficult situation, the minister put his hands out in front of him as if to ward off danger and straightened to his full height. "Woman, you must repent!" he shouted with authority. "Liars are surely in danger of hellfire. Repent!" Whirling around, he started away. "Let me hear no more of this." Tossing those last words over his shoulder, he hurried from the room.

Chapter Seven

A dramatic grimace of defeat was fixed on Bryon's face as he watched his hand being pressed relentlessly toward the grimy floor. With a thud it hit and a cheer went up from his redheaded challenger. "I won, I won. Wow, Bryon, I can't believe I finally won you in arm wrestling. I'm getting real strong, huh? Whatdya think?"

"Bryon grinned and nodded. It pleased him that after all

these weeks George was finally gaining some strength. Daily, Bryon would arm wrestle him, changing hands so George would work both arms evenly. Of course, he insisted the young boy use both hands and all his body but even at that, Bryon had to ease back quite a bit to let him win.

He had been worried about how frail his cellmate was and had come up with a few different games and exercises to work different parts of George's thin body and the benefits were starting to show. George wasn't so pale and his lungs, which had suffered terribly during the winter from the unheated conditions, finally sounded clear.

In return, George aided Bryon by helping him escape the confines of their miserable cell. Although retarded, the red-headed boy had an amazing imagination. He remembered parts from the books his mother used to read the family. Embellishing upon those stories, he would pretend that he and Bryon would travel by magic carpet to exciting places all over the world. Bryon loved listening to the adventures they had in George's colorful, make-believe stories.

Reaching out with both hands, George grabbed Bryon's right hand. "Let's do it again," the younger boy enthused.

The sound of the lock in the door, as normal, had George scurrying back to the far wall. He watched in terror as the orderly came in.

"Chores," he barked out. "Hurry it up."

George scrambled to his feet but in his haste he tripped and sprawled against the orderly, knocking him back against the open door.

"Yeow!" The big man kicked him away and rubbed his shoulder where it had hit the edge of the door. "Ya did that on purpose didn't ya, twerp?"

George stumbled back out of his way.

The orderly turned to Bryon and stuck his face next to the boy's. He spoke with exaggerated emphasis, his putrid breath fanning Bryon's face. "I think you can read my lips, so listen. Ya git on down an do yer chores. You know the way. If I find ya been goofing off or ya gone somewheres ya weren't s'pose ta, I'll lick ya but good. Now git!"

As he hurried out the door, Bryon looked back at his cellmate's face that grew in terror with each slow step the orderly took toward him. Bryon stood in indecision until the man reached out and grabbed George by his shirtfront.

Running back into the room, Bryon threw himself against the orderly. He felt as though he had just hit a solid wall of stone as he bounced back and fell to the floor. The orderly whirled on him with a growl. "Ya little fool! Just what the devil are ya trying to pull?" He picked Bryon up by the back of his collar and the seat of his pants and tossed him out the door, slamming him into the far wall. He grunted with satisfaction when he saw the blood trickling down the unconscious boy's neck from a damaged ear. "That'll teach you, ya idiot." He turned back, closed and locked the door behind him.

Only a few minutes had passed when Bryon regained consciousness. He wiped the blood from his neck and gingerly stood up. His ear and head ached but he ignored it as he thought of George. He pressed his good ear against the locked door and heard sobbing within. Knowing there was nothing he could do and wanting to avoid further punishment, he hurried to do his chores.

There was comfort in polishing what he considered friends; the knickknacks in the office. He knew he was luckier than the other inmates. He had the most coveted chores in the place. He was the only one who regularly saw anything beautiful and he tried to constantly feel gratitude for that opportunity. Although Bryon wasn't aware of it, eight months had passed since he came to the lunatic asylum.

He hadn't been listening to the desultory conversation between Miss Simondson and Doctor Williams until he heard the woman swear.

"I'm telling you, Avery, this could be trouble."

"Don't worry. That law will never pass. Nobody who has a brain really wants what it implies."

"But you do realize that if it passes and it's no longer illegal for the deaf and dumb to have children, then you will have to stop sterilizing them."

"Won't happen. I remember you reading me some

statement by an asylum administrator back east. It pretty well stated the prevailing opinion."

The woman nodded her head. "I know it by heart. He said the deaf and dumb are in an animal state and do not even possess the dignity of man."

"Too many people feel that way for the laws to change."

"You can't be sure of that and if you have to stop sterilizing them, that means we won't be able to get rid of unwanted inmates that way."

"Agatha, you know we haven't only gotten rid of the deaf and dumb."

"Yes, but you've been able to come up with other ailments that needed a special operation, and since there have only been two of those, it hasn't been a problem. There isn't even a hint of suspicion and it must stay that way. There *will* be a problem however, if the sterilization stops. Too many deaths from a variety of operations will definitely raise suspicions. It's just so common for the knife to slip and an artery get nicked during a sterilization that no one has questioned it so far."

The doctor brushed the sides of his silky moustache with his finger and thumb while he was thinking. He was inordinately proud of his thick head of dark auburn hair and his moustache that covered his top lip. Bryon could see he was thinking extra hard today when the man stopped stroking his moustache and began chewing on it nervously like a mouse nibbling cheese. "I've been meaning to talk to you about that, Agatha. There have been a half dozen in the last two years and I'm thinking we should slow down before there are questions. You could turn down a contract or two without hurting us. We've both made a tidy sum already."

"But I thought you needed the money? You're always harping about it."

"I do but I can wait a few months. I can't get by for too long though, not with three children back east in private schools. And Marge has been begging for a new buggy."

"Avery, you promised not to talk about your wife."

"Come on, Agatha, you know I'm married. It's foolish

to pretend otherwise."

"I'm not pretending anything.   I just don't want it thrown in my face is all."

"Who's throwing it in your face?"

"You are. You just don't want to forget!" Agatha buried her face in her hands.

"Don't start. I mean it, don't do this or you'll be the one to regret it."

"There it is. Out in the open finally. I'm the only one who really ever cared, isn't that right, Avery? Or am I just getting too old?"

"You fly off the handle quicker than anyone I know. Why are you doing this? Is it that young woman? That dark haired girl you're so jealous of?"

"Shut up, just shut up!"

"You have nothing to be jealous of Agatha. I don't care that you're a few years older than me. Theresa doesn't mean anything."

"She's a nymphomaniac, Avery. How could you?"

"Most of the women in here are supposed to be nymphomaniacs, so that should make you feel right at home. Or is that why you hate them so much? They're your competition for me?"

Agatha made two fists, her voice rising hysterically. "Touch her again and I'll kill her myself. I'm not joking!"

"You're hysterical. You'd better calm down before you go too far."

"I'll calm down when you promise to stay away from the other women here. I know about you propositioning Patricia Strouse. Turned you down flat didn't she?"

"I'm telling you to knock it off. We've both got a good thing going here. Don't ruin it. You get what you want and I get the money I need. You will leave it at that, if you're smart." He took one look at her furious face and shook his head in disgust. "And I'll leave here right now if I'm smart." Turning for the door he added, "I'll see you later, Agatha."

A movement in the corner behind the door attracted his attention. "A kid!" Spinning around he confronted the administrator with a loud, long string of curses, fought for control and demanded, "What are you thinking?"

The woman stood up slowly and looked at him with amusement. "What's wrong, Avery? Are you afraid of the animals in the zoo?"

"Agatha, don't play games with me." He grabbed Bryon by the neck and pulled him forward. "Why didn't you tell me someone was in here?"

"Relax. He's just the cleaning boy. Deaf as a post, a total idiot. We don't have anything to be afraid of. To tell you the truth, I'm so use to him now I never even notice when he's in here. Let him go, he's almost done." She smirked at him. "I think he's afraid of the big, bad doctor. He just froze back there when you came in."

"I hope you're being careful, Agatha." He spun on his heel. "I've got to see to some patients."

After the doctor left, Agatha motioned for Bryon to get back to work. The administrator sat staring at the door, then with a sigh she began opening her mail. She noticed an expensive looking envelope and with curiosity, she drew out a cream colored piece of stationary. "Well, well, it looks like you won't be with us much longer. Our fine chap from England is coming to deal with you himself. Oh well, you would have only had four or five months left anyway. I wonder how long it will take our dear Anthony to travel clear from the British Isles?" She read further and exclaimed, "Oh, he isn't coming so far after all. He's in St. Louis visiting his sister so it won't take him as long." She stared at the ceiling, estimating traveling time. "Between trains and stage coaches, it shouldn't take long at all."

Bryon looked at the letter in her hand and something tugged at his memory. Thick, creamy stationary. With a jolt, he remembered. Slowly he edged behind the desk and peered over Miss Simondson's shoulder. There it was, right at the bottom where he knew people put their names. Even though he could not read, he had enough of the artist in him to recognize the same scrawl that had been at the bottom of his father's letter. His eyes followed the paper as she laid it down and he stood transfixed as if in a trance. He didn't see the woman turn to look at him.

"Boy, did you understand what I was saying to you?"

Bryon saw his peril in her eyes and bolted for the door. As he was swinging it open, she slapped her hand to the door above his head, slamming it shut. "Oh, no you don't." The twisted part of her personality had come to the forefront in her confrontation with Avery. Grinning like a demonic caricature, she lowered her face to his. The gloating in her voice grated on Bryon's frazzled nerves. "It looks as though Anthony won't get to meet you after all. That's too bad, but I don't anticipate any real problems. Certainly your father has no interest in you and I don't believe you have anyone else. I've learned from long experience that family and friends may call or write the first year, but after that, they seem to forget their embarrassing idiots in the asylum. It's no accident that this monstrosity of a building is so gloomy, you know." She laughed low in the back of her throat making chills raced up and down Bryon's back. "Not only does decorating cost money, the atmosphere discourages families from wanting to come here for their Sunday outings. They are quite content to leave their dear ones in our hands." She saw the question and confusion behind the boy's fear. "You see, sometimes a family member gives me a little something extra to get rid of their relative. We have to be very careful, especially with other family who know nothing of the arrangement.

"Anyway, we find it is very easy to dispose of unwanted animals after a year and that was my plan for you, but now things have changed. You are going to be sterilized, and I am very sorry to say the knife is going to slip. You've already made the doctor and me a nice bit of extra money. You know that painting of the cubs you like to stare at? That is what your future death paid for. I'm glad you've enjoyed it. It only seems fair after all. In a way, you could say that is your painting."

#

Bryon sat pressed into the corner of his cell, holding his bloodied and bruised cellmate in his arms. He had tucked the thin blanket around the younger child and cradled him close.

"You was real brave, Bryon," George whispered through battered lips. "We're just the same, you and me. I'm brave too. Did you know that?"

Bryon nodded sadly and tried to smile at the child.

"Ma should'a kept me 'cause I could'a protected Herbert for all his life." He sighed and continued. "I miss my little brother. Bryon, are you my friend?" When the older boy again nodded, George's eyes lit up. "Guess what?" He whispered conspiratorially, "I never had no friend before."

Both boys froze when the key grated in the lock. The orderly surveyed them and mocked, "Oh my, what a touchin' scene this be. Yer gonna make me bawl in a minute. Say goodbye to yer pal there, George. Bryon has ta go have himself a little operation."

"No, please," the child whispered hoarsely. "The last one; the woman, she didn't come back. Them said she died. Purty please don't take him!"

The orderly ignored the boy and dragged Bryon out from under George. Bryon fought hard and it took real effort for the orderly to subdue and drag him out the door.

The orderly helped Dr. Williams strip Bryon and strap the struggling boy onto the table then he quickly left, not having the stomach for what went on in that room. He enjoyed cruelty, but the operations were simply too much.

"So the little sneak can hear after all?" The doctor smiled coldly at him as he stroked his moustache. He didn't smile like Miss Simondson smiled, which reminded him of some of the crazy people here. His smile was pure evil. Bryon watched him pick up his scalpel and test it, his anticipation growing as he felt the boy's tension increase to the breaking point.

"Perhaps I'll skip cleansing the area with alcohol since there's no worry about you getting infection," he laughed. He stepped up to the table and put his left hand on Bryon's leg. The boy jumped and shook as if he had the palsy. The whites of his eyes showed bright around his dilated pupils, and his breathing was ragged and labored.

68

Satisfied that the proper moment had come, the doctor positioned himself over his patient.

A loud knock at the door startled him into dropping his scalpel. "What the . . ."

"Dr. Williams," a small voice hollered through the door. "Dr. Williams, come quick. A bad thing be happenin'."

The doctor swung the door open, his chin dropping in astonishment at the little redheaded boy, a very battered boy who stood before him. "What are you talking about? How did you get here?"

"Doc, Miss Simondson, she yelled fer me to get you in a hurry."

"What's wrong?"

"A big man, one of the crazy ones, he be hurtin' her."

Beginning to panic the doctor yelled, "Where is she?"

"The third floor, at the back."

The doctor started to run, checked himself and returned to the surgery. Grabbing his keys from the desk, he locked the door behind him then ran toward the stairs.

Hope had risen sharp and sweet in Bryon's breast when he first heard George's voice. As he listened to the boy's plan unfold he steadied his breathing and prepared to follow whatever instructions the brilliant mentally retarded boy gave him.

Hope died in a rush when he saw the doctor return and lock the door in George's face. Despair crushed him and he felt worse in some ways than the terror of minutes before. Tears gushed hot and fast from his eyes, and there was a roaring in his ears as dark emotions roiled over him. He didn't hear the key in the lock. His eyes were squeezed shut against the tears so he didn't see his friend until the little boy shook his shoulder.

"Bryon, we gotta hurry. He gonna be right back. Git up!"

Disbelief kept hope at bay as the mute boy stared at George. He pointed with his chin at the straps that the child hadn't noticed. Bryon was amazed at how fast those little fingers flew to unbuckle the straps. In seconds, he was pulling on his pants and following the younger boy out the door.

As they raced down the hall and through the reception area, George told his story. "When that orderly was fightin' you, I grabbed his keys. They was gonna kill you, Bryon. I couldn't let 'em. Not after you fought 'im for me today."

He glanced over for approval as they reached the massive front doors. Pulling a big set of keys out of his pants, he started trying each one in the keyhole. "The orderly forgot to lock our door or he would'a noticed his keys was gone. That be lucky, huh?" He fumbled with the keys and did not notice that he was repeatedly putting the same large key in the lock over and over.

Impatiently, Bryon grabbed the keys from George and found the right one on the second try. The two boys pulled the door open together and sprinted down the steps and into the yard beyond. As they were heading toward the forest, they heard the ominous barking of the guard dogs. The institute kept two attack dogs but the boys didn't see them, they only heard the fierce barking.

Reaching the safety of the trees, the boys plunged into the forest. Bryon heard a shout, then the sound of the dogs way too close. Glancing over his shoulder, Bryon saw the dark animals rushing across the yard toward them. *Too fast, they're coming way too fast*, he realized. *They're going to tear us up.*

He grabbed George's shoulder and swung him around to face him. Pointing up to a tree, he motioned frantically. George stood in confusion as Bryon leaped for a branch above his head. Quickly he secured his legs around the branch and swung his body down, reaching for the boy.

George backed away shaking his head. "No, I can't. I be scared of high things. You go up. Hurry, Bryon. It be you they wanna kill." He turned and hurried behind a tree, hoping the frightening animals would not find him.

The dogs were upon them. Bryon closed his eyes, unable to bear watching his heroic friend being torn up by the vicious animals. He tried to tell his fingers to let go. He wanted so badly to drop to the ground and try to fight off the dogs but he didn't move. *I'm a coward,* he told himself. *I'll let George die just like I let Momma die. I haven't changed at all!*

"Hold!" The command was shouted by the orderly who had just entered the woods. He could see the redheaded boy peaking from behind the tree. "Hold him, boys."

The dogs positioned themselves before the shivering child, growling threats.

Seeing he could do nothing to help, Bryon swung himself up and began climbing as fast as he could.

"Ya come on down from there, boy. If'n ya make me come up after ya, I promise yer gonna pay bad."

Bryon kept climbing higher. The tree was tall and the top branches were thin and precarious. Bryon knew he would rather die falling from that tree than go back into that surgery so he climbed almost to the top where he knew a full grown man would not come.

With a sigh of disgust, the orderly told him, "All right, kid. Jest as soon as my assistants git here, I'm gonna go git my gun and shoot ya plumb out o' that tree. Jest see if I don't."

Chapter Eight

As Bryon watched George being roughly dragged back to the asylum, he had a feeling he would never see him again. With a lump in his throat, he followed the progress of the bright red hair until it was out of sight.

He had never felt more alone in his life even though a pack of human bloodhounds stood baying at his tree. They were having a whispered conference about what to do with him. Every once in a while one of them would raise their voice to emphasize an opinion. The head orderly kept yelling about getting his gun, the doctor repeatedly used the word axe and Miss Simondson occasionally mentioned hunger. The other two orderlies seemed to agree with whoever was speaking at the time.

Finally, a decision was made. A man was sent for an axe. The men began taking turns at the tree, each trying to outdo the other. They made rapid progress and the jolts were beginning to nauseate their victim. Although he felt little hope for the final outcome, Bryon wasn't too concerned with what they were doing at the moment. He waited to ensure they wasted a lot of energy, then climbed further up the thin trunk until it slowly began to bend under his weight. He was deposited gently onto a sturdier limb of a neighboring tree. Climbing trees and playing dangerously had once been his favorite past time when he had not been with Storm-That-Kills and his work was far enough along for him to steal some playtime.

Despite the gravity of the situation, he couldn't help grinning just a little as he watched the men continue to swing away at the tree he had just left. Half an hour later, he heard with amusement the shout; 'timber'! The tree picked up momentum and slammed into the thicket opposite Bryon.

Shouting followed as everyone looked for the fallen boy. While they were diverted, Bryon carefully and silently made his way two trees over to the largest tree in the area. He secreted himself high among the densest foliage. The leaves were just beginning to dress in their Sunday best; orange, yellows and reds trimming the rich emerald green leaves, but they were still full and helped conceal the boy.

His tormenters were quite alarmed at his disappearance. Fearing he had somehow escaped, they loosed the dogs and signaled for them to track the boy. His scent was still in their nostrils from the earlier chase and they ran frantically back and forth searching the ground and the air for any trace of him. If it hadn't been for the dogs, he would probably have gotten away but something alerted them to his position and they took up their post at the base of the large tree where he sat hidden and set up a racket.

"There he is!"

"Where?"

"You can see a bit of gray through that clump of leaves up there."

Relieved that they had again found their prey, the group assembled once more to discuss the situation. The two assistants, tired from chopping took up the head orderly's part

72

and called for the gun.

"We can't afford an investigation. You know the authorities can be so ignorant about what we have to do to control our inmates," Agatha insisted. "We'll starve him out. I want one of you orderlies with one dog to camp at the base of this tree until he comes down. It won't take more than a day or two and then everything will be back to normal."

With the doctor agreeing with the administrator, the others had no choice but follow her orders. Soon all were gone but one disgruntled man and a sleeping dog.

The first night wasn't too bad except for hunger. Bryon had grown use to cold, it often being chillier in the building than outside. His nerves would not have let him sleep even if he dared, which he didn't. He knew the chances were that he would fall if he nodded off and he wondered how long he could keep this up and what other option he had? None! The bloody operation awaited and he would rather die from a fall than go through with that.

Several times he tried to sneak to another tree as he had before but each time the dog would growl and the man would shout, "It don't matter to me where you go. We'll be right below ya, kid."

Bryon finally decided that he had the best spot after all and he stayed put.

The second night was far harder. His muscles ached worse than his empty stomach and exhaustion was making him hallucinate. *Why don't the fairies come? They're late, they said they'd be here by now, he thought as his mind wandered further from reality. Maybe I need to open the door? They always came before when I needed them.*

Again and again he caught himself as he began to lie down, forgetting there was no floor beneath him. Jerking his head up repeatedly was making his head pound. The cold was affecting his depleted system severely.

If I close my eyes real tight and relax, I'll be able to lie down on the soft ground. It won't hurt for more than a second once I fall, and I'm too tired to care if it does.

A floating sensation came over him, waves of peaceful

unawareness. Gradually consciousness completely fled leaving him in a dream state. That is when the light appeared. As it grew brighter, the boy fell deeper into sleep.

"Bryon . . . Bryon, reach out and put your arms around your mother. She's right in front of you, son."

In his dreams, the boy saw his mother as she had been that last day in the meadow. Her basket of berries lay beside his hatful. Wrapping his arms around her, so desperate to feel her embrace that there was no fear of him letting go of the thick branch he was clutching. Peacefully he drifted into a long, dreamless sleep.

The birds woke him just before dawn. His head felt fuzzy with unsatisfied sleep but his headache was gone and he was more optimistic. He did not remember dreaming and was puzzled to find himself remembering his mother's stories about the fairies from the old country. He could hear her voice in his head and the details of the stories were amazingly clear.

The day did not move as slowly with vibrant fantasies to occupy his thoughts until his thirst grew unbearable during the long afternoon. By evening it was a raging obsession and the hallucinations set in again. He had felt hunger the first two days but now, by the third day only thirst remained.

His body had adjusted to its new demands and that night, he was able to sleep without the threat of falling. He woke often with strange thoughts in his head of rivers, lakes and rain. Near morning, the thoughts of rain were so overwhelming that he imagined feeling the cold drops running down the back of his neck. His eyes opened and he felt disoriented by rain cascading through the bright, fall leaves. Then his confusion turned to relief and he opened his mouth beneath a large maple leaf that formed a perfect funnel. The slow trickle was a tease until he had enough mouthfuls to satisfy the worst of the craving. The downpour lasted almost an hour and he took turns resting and drinking. He shivered with the chill but that didn't bother him too severely. The life-giving water didn't dampen his gratitude for this gift.

The fourth day began easier but by mid-afternoon his thirst was growing again. He actually feared it like a monster, knowing it would grow to frightening proportions. But one monster was traded for another.

Agatha Simondson arrived beneath the tree before evening. "Bryon Hancock! You can come down now. Your supper is waiting and you have a visit to get ready for."

Bryon peered around some leaves and squinted down at her, questions and mistrust clear on his countenance.

"I believe you were brought here by a Dr. Carter? I just received a letter from him. He is coming to visit in a few days. Isn't that wonderful? I'm sure you will enjoy that so climb on down and come back with me. I'll give you some bread with your soup tonight. We don't want the good doctor to think we're starving you, do we?"

Bryon's chapped lips curled in revulsion as he stared at her ghastly smile. *Could she be telling the truth? That would be a good way to trick me. I wonder if he is coming to take me home? Maybe I'll get to live with him again.*

The mere possibility was enough to make his decision. Muscles protesting, he slowly began to descend the tree.

When he reached the bottom the orderly had to grab him when his knees buckled. Miss Simondson patted him on the head and said, "I'm going to put you somewhere by yourself so no one will try and steal your bread from you. I can see we have to fatten you up, Bryon. I can't understand why you would do this to yourself."

With the man helping him and the dog growling in his wake, he returned to the hated prison.

#

Five days and he still isn't here. Was she lying? This question kept running through Bryon's mind. He had little else to occupy his thoughts shut away in complete isolation. Twice a day the orderly brought his food but didn't speak. Bryon was reminded of the years of silence with his father but at least then he had the world to move around in and not an eight-by-eight foot cell given to those in solitary confinement.

When he heard footsteps, he assumed it was breakfast

and could hardly believe it was real when the orderly told him the doc had arrived. He was taken to the reception room and when the door opened to reveal Doc Carter, the boy lunged toward him and threw himself into doctor's arms.

The doctor could feel sobs shaking the boy and had to brace himself to accept the fact that the horror stories must be true. Little Bryon was living in hell.

He held the child and patted him awkwardly, trying to comfort him. "There, there, it's all right. You're okay, son. Happy to see me, huh? I wasn't sure after I left you here. Thought you might not ever want to see me again. I just couldn't stay away any longer though. I've felt uneasy about you lately and just had to come. "

The doctor led Bryon to the sofa, keeping his arm comfortingly about him as he caught him up on life back in Baker. They both tried to ignore the nosy orderly sitting nearby but he was an intimidating man. When the doc ran out of conversation, he remembered the peppermint candies in his pocket and pulled them out. "Here, I almost forgot about these. I remembered you like this stuff. Do you still?"

Bryon enthusiastically nodded his head and grabbed for the candy.

"I'm afraid that's against the rules." The orderly came forward and held out his beefy hand. "Yer gonna have to give that there candy to me."

The doctor glared at him fearlessly. "I'll do no such thing. That candy is my property and I'll not give it to you. If you won't let the boy have it, I'll take it back myself."

"Suit yerself, mister. Jest don't give none to the boy there. It ain't good to spoil the inmates."

The doctor put the candy back in his pocket and wracked his brain for more stories to tell Bryon. Every time the orderly would glance away, the doctor would slip a piece of candy into the boy's mouth. Bryon kept his hand cupped on the side of his jaw that faced the orderly and thoroughly enjoyed the sweets. When he was done, Doc Carter stood and looked regretfully at his little friend. "I'm afraid I'll have to be going, son. But I've told Miss Simondson that I'll be back in three or four months to check in on you again. Her and I, we had a good talk and I think we understand each other, so don't you worry."

Relief washed over the child. Somehow Doc understood he was in danger and was helping. He didn't know how, but he knew his death was being postponed. At least until some Englishman got here.

#

His world was a tiny stone cell. Sometimes reality became clouded and he doubted anything existed outside this dark hole. He hadn't fully outgrown his fear of being alone so now, in these circumstances, he was haunted by his isolation.

Thinking had become a chore. Only the secrets he had overheard had the power to remain in his thoughts. The secrets of buying death, torture, bloody scalpels and a man named Anthony. He understood why she had to keep him here. She couldn't take the chance he would find a way to communicate with anyone.

Bryon tried to keep track of the days but he lost count and finally gave up. His guess was that he'd been alone for around eight weeks. The boy was good at counting. His mother had taught him a little and Betsy had played counting games with him when he lived with her. To a child, two months was an eternity. To anyone alone, it was purgatory.

Few would have recognized him. The flesh hung from his gaunt, frame and his skin was pale as death. The extra food had stopped after Doc's visit and although he now received the normal twice-daily ration, the food went right through him and refused to stick to his ribs. The sparkle in his eyes his mother had loved was gone and with it, the hope from his heart. He rarely rose from the hard, icy floor. Any effort was too much for him. Although he did not consciously know this, he had made the decision to die and was making rapid progress to that end.

The pale November sun struggled to penetrate the opening near the top of the wall, a foot below the twelve-foot ceiling. The boy often lay in a trance-like state staring at the opening. There were two bars in the window to brace the last

77

layer of stone above it. He thought he might fit through those two bars if he had a way to climb but the room was empty. Not even a blanket had been supplied. He had nothing but the clothes on his back.

That afternoon he didn't really see the window but it was a natural place for his eyes to rest. He didn't notice the small, dark object that descended slowly on a thin, white strand. It wasn't until the spider hung before his nose that his eyes focused and he saw his new cellmate. His first reaction was to recoil up into a sitting position. He had never been afraid of spiders but the revulsion most of the women here felt toward the homely creature was catching.

His second reaction was curiosity. The spider dropped onto his chest and crawled toward his arm, journeying to his hand that rested on his knee. When it reached its destination, it stopped and stared back at him.

Long forgotten instinct took over and he found himself connecting with the spider. That old sensation of joining returned in a rush. His natural empathy for all living things was such an innate part of what made him who he was that he hadn't recognized the danger its absence had been for him. Two months in the cell with nothing that represented life was killing him. Now he realized his will to live was still there. It was reaching out for anything to sustain it. That thing happened to be this spider.

His dormant mind began to function again. *Hello, little spider.* He sent the message hoping the small invader would feel his good intentions. *Do you need a friend as much as I do? If you stay with me, I'll share my food with you. Sometimes I even have flies in my soup so I'll save those for you. I like you, little black spider.*

Perhaps the spider felt the connection for it stayed on his hand for what must have been a very long time for such creatures. Later, it explored the floor, the wall, then disappeared above the doorframe.

The next morning an excited boy watched his new friend ride down its silken cord to the floor below. Quickly, his breath coming fast, Bryon brought his offering to the spider.

In the night he had decided that a spider probably would not eat human food so he had risen in the faint light of the moon and scraped with his fingernails at a loose chunk from a stone in the wall. The stones were thick but the edges of a few were loose and cracked. Often he had heard tiny scratching sounds indicating bugs, probably roaches. It never occurred to him to make friends with roaches but now he wanted one to feed his new cellmate. The crumbling mortar between the stones was easy to dig out once he had pulled loose a few small chunks. Patience was now necessary and it took over an hour of intense watching until he saw a roach. He struck it with a piece of stone and held the stunned pest in his hand while he lay back down to rest. Occasionally he felt its legs wiggle frantically and this pleased him as he thought spiders may prefer fresh food.

His diligence had paid off for now it was morning and the spider had come back. He put the bug down and hit it with the stone, killing the roach and laid his offering before his friend. He was overjoyed when it was accepted.

Over the next few days the spider would come and go, always disappearing above the doorframe. One day Bryon leaped up, grabbed the top of the frame and chinned himself high enough to see a large crack in the stone just behind the wood. A beautiful, intricate web had been woven across the crack. Satisfied he had found the spider's home, he sat back to wait for his next visit.

He was able to bear his prison now that he had something live with which to commune, spirit to spirit. His tension had eased and he began putting on a little weight and was sleeping more peacefully.

It was afternoon and his friend was perched on his hand staring at him. He was smiling and imagining adventures for the two of them the way George used to do when something wonderful happened. The sun was stronger that day, and although there was a soft breeze outside, it didn't feel as cold in the room. The light from the sun caught the last stubborn leaves of fall on a tree outside the high opening and their dancing shadows fell on his hand. The dappled sunlight on his hand and arm, in addition to the cheerful spider lifted him to emotional heights he hadn't known in ages. It must have been the sharp contrast from blackest despair to joining again with nature that brought back to him something he had believed he had only imagined. *The Moment!* That is what his parents would call it when he would become completely absorbed in a discovery or some piece of nature. He knew that his father thought he was crazy but his mother understood. She had a touch of her grandmother's gift the Irish called 'the sight'. She knew Bryon had the gift in full measure, although it was not the telling of the future, it was a joining. He connected with things and her own gift of empathy was augmented immeasurably when he would connect with her. They understood each other; they felt the other's heart.

This was his first intense 'moment' since the day his mother died. Bryon was transported beyond himself and together with the spider and the dappled leaves, he breathed in the very essence of life. With a tiny smile and tear-dampened cheeks, he absorbed the goodness of creation of which he was a part.

The closest he had come to this feeling in seven years was when Storm-That-Kills taught him to break through his emotional prison and carve what was inside him. He remembered his friend teaching him about the Great Spirit and how to get in touch with that spirit. Bryon concentrated, trying to recall the wise man's words.

"Bear's Brother, remember that the Great Spirit does not use the sound of a drum when he can get through with the song of a bird. Only the still, small sounds penetrate the heart and that is where life is lived. Remember this and you will have peace."

This is what Bryon now had. In spite of his conditions or surroundings or the hate of his enemies . . . he had peace.

The next morning, Bryon's eyes flew open as sleep fled in an instant. With the return of his natural optimism, he brain began functioning more clearly. The fully formed thought was there. *I can't stay here in this prison. I won't do it. I'm going to escape.*

Conviction that this was right had him jumping to his

80

feet. He began to pace and plan. It took all day to perfect his plan but finally he felt satisfied that it would work.

The next morning, with his gruel finished, he licked his spoon extra well and dried it on his shirt. Taking the spoon between his teeth, he grabbed the doorframe and chinned himself to the top. Jutting his chin forward, he deposited the spoon on the ledge then fell back to the floor. He had disturbed the spider web and felt bad for that but this was an emergency. After that it took him a few jumped to secure it neatly into the spider's wide crack behind the frame. Finally satisfied that it was well hidden, he waited.

The orderly came in for the dishes and stopped in confusion. "Where ya put yer spoon?"

Bryon shrugged and tried to look innocent.

"Show me where yer spoon is, dummy! Or do ya wanna git hit?"

The boy gave a dramatic Gaelic shrug and looked around diligently.

The orderly shamed the boy, searching his body for the spoon. Bryon hated that worse than when the big man slapped him against the wall.

When that had no effect, the man grunted and said, "Fine, suit yerself. You'll just have to slurp yer grub from now on."

After he was gone, Bryon leaped up to retrieve the spoon. The next few minutes were spent trying to bend the heavy metal. He balanced the spoon on the handle up against the wall and used his boot to try to bend it down. It took a long time to make much progress but finally he had it bent enough to apply good leverage and shape it like a horseshoe. This done, he waited and listened to a heavy downpour outside.

As soon as his supper bowl had been taken away, he went back to work. Stripping off his clothes, the boy used his strong teeth, and ripping with the grain of the cloth, he tore the clothes into multiple, thin strips. That done, he tied the strips together, folded it in half for extra strength, tied off the ends and firmly knotted his rope to the flat, broad end of the bent spoon.

Alive with anticipation, Bryon carefully tossed his

strange creation up to the opening. It took him four tries to get the spoon through the opening and then he began the painstaking operation of trying to hook the spoon onto a bar. His patience paid off as it settled with a soft metallic click.

Bryon stood staring at his means of escape for endless minutes. Then moving back toward the door, he stood for another minute, staring at the top of the frame. *Goodbye my little spider. I'll never forget you.* With a sigh he returned to his rope and after giving it an experimental tug, he began to climb, using his feet on the wall to help.

The opening was only an arm's length away when the rope slipped off the handle and Bryon fell in a heap on the stone floor. He stood, shook himself and glared angrily at the spoon stuck around the bar. The rope lay like his plan; in ruin at his feet. He grabbed his hair in both hands and pulled with a furious grimace. When that didn't help, he sat against the wall and tried to think. It was hard to concentrate with fear lying like a hot coal in his stomach at thoughts of what the orderly would do to him in the morning when he saw what he had done to his clothes.

Hours past as he stared at the spoon. At length he had an idea but it was a poor one. Feeling he had no choice, he decided to try it. Grabbing the crumbled pieces of stone by the wall, he positioned himself at an angle to best hit the broad end of the spoon and began tossing up the rocks. Only twice did he connect but each time the handle edged up more until it was precariously dangling with breathtaking hope.

Bryon used his long, ragged nails to tear more pieces from the cracked stone and began again to toss them at the spoon. He was shaking this time so his aim wasn't as good but finally a solid stone connected well and the spoon came flying down into his outstretched hands. With a thrill of delight he got to work.

Using the spoon as a pick, he began chipping away at a promisingly large piece of the rock. His frantic energy soon rewarded him with a nice sized chunk lying at his feet.

Next, he used the flat end of his trusty spoon to pry at the doorframe. This took a lot longer and his strength was beginning to fail when finally, with a pop, the frame came loose. After resting a few minutes, the determined boy used the rock to pound a sixteen-penny nail out of the frame. He was pleased with the size of the nail and took a moment to admire it.

Using the rock, he set the nail into the middle of the flat spoon handle and began to pound. Every few minutes he would wipe the sweat from his face and concentrate on breathing deeply. Time was his enemy now. He had to get away before the dogs awoke at dawn. After that it would be too late and he was sure he would be kept naked in future if found the next morning. Occasionally the nail would bend and he would pound it straight but his luck did not hold. First, the stone shattered and it took him precious minutes to break off another solid piece. Then the end of the nail snapped off and he had to begin the process of extracting another nail from the doorframe.

Panic drove him hour after hour until success was at last his. He was filled with elation when the second nail punched neatly through the tough spoon. He pounded the other side, driving the nail back out and admired the hole.

The sky was just beginning to lighten when he sucked on the end of his rope, twisted the cloth tightly and threaded it through the small hole. He tied it in a strong knot and sighed with relief. Wasting no time for a second goodbye to the spider, he tossed the spoon quickly through the opening. Luck was with him on the first attempt. He forced himself to slow as he maneuvered the spoon into place around the bar.

His exhaustion fell away from him like an unwanted embrace as he scurried up the rope. When he reached the top, he pulled the spoon from the bar and wrapped the contraption around his neck with one hand while holding the bar firmly with the other. The thin boy wiggled through the opening until his upper body was free. The branch that had given him the gift of the dappled fall leaves, now aided him in his escape. He grabbed it firmly and pulled himself free of his dark prison and into the dawning day.

Dropping lightly to his feet, Bryon glanced quickly around and began sprinting toward the woods. He had gone about fifty yards before he heard the dreaded baying of the dogs. The boy wondered if he was fated to repeat his first escape attempt.

The dogs were after him so fast that he had hoped their barks had not awakened anyone before the sounds faded with distance. Bryon had no hope of out-racing the dogs. As he ran through the trees, he knew he stood no real chance. His eyes blurred with tears as he listened to them getting closer.

The boy changed directions, angling toward the wide dirt road that led away from the asylum. They were almost on his heels when he broke through the dense growth and burst onto the road. He fought a desperate battle with his imagination regarding what kind of damage the fierce animals would inflict when they had him between their jaws. Shaking away the bloody image, still running full out, he unwrapped the spoon and rope from his neck and stopped dead.

The dogs were so surprised at this action that they hesitated. This gave him time to start swinging the rope with the spoon making a whirling sound through the air. The curious dogs watched this, giving Bryon the advantage. By the time they determined to attack, the spoon was spinning with such velocity that it looked as though the boy was completely encircled in a blur of rope and metal. The bravest dog struck first, and was smacked sharply on the snout for his trouble. He jumped back with a yelp.

Encouraged, Bryon began to back slowly up the road, his eyes never leaving the two animals. He kept swinging constantly as the dogs crouched and followed with whines and barks.

Now his thoughts were not on his danger from the dogs as much as upon his embarrassment. *If someone sees me like this, naked with only my old leather boots, I think I'd rather the dogs eat me.*

By the time the boy thought his arm would fall off, the dogs gave up and with a last threatening growl, they turned for home. Relieved that no one was on the road so early, he headed back into the woods.

Weariness returned with a vengeance as he plodded through the wet ferns and tangled undergrowth of the forest.

Trying to keep his mind from his exhaustion, he thought of his redheaded friend. *I wonder what happened to you, George. Did they hurt you for helping me? I wish you were with me now but I promise someday I'll come back and make sure you are all right. Someday, George, I'll help you like you helped me.*

He had come about a mile when he stumbled into a clearing with an old rundown cabin. What held his interest was a clothesline full of drying clothes behind the cabin.

Hearing the door open, he scurried back into the woods and watched. He saw a woman come out and bring in a load of firewood. He recognized her as the woman who did the laundry for the asylum. He knew she was given the clothing of the inmates to sell or use. As she had many children herself, the clothing was appreciated. Bryon debated whether it was all right to steal to clothe his nakedness since God would not want him to go about like this in public. Skirting the trees around to the back of the cabin, he stealthily walked up to the clothesline to examine the choices. He felt the shock clear to his toes when he saw his own yellow shirt and brown pants hanging in the middle of the line.

The symbolism of the moment didn't escape him as he scrambled into the beloved clothing, thankful to the woman for sewing buttons back onto the shirt. He didn't mind that the pants were too short for his twelve-year-old body. The world had color again. He was free.

Shoving his lucky rope into his pocket, he spotted the well. Knowing it was taking a terrible chance, but remembering the tortured thirst from his experience in the trees, he rushed to the well and let down the bucket for a much needed drink. The water was cold and sweet. Far better than any he had drank for a year. He was finishing his second dipper-full when he was startled by a light appearing suddenly in the woods.

His first thought was they had found him. But the light didn't move and then he noticed a vague shape in the light. He wasn't sure but the faint silhouette may have resembled a fairy. There was something familiar about all of this but he was under too much stress to remember what it was. He jumped when he heard a whispery sound next to his ear. He knew it had to be the

85

wind but suddenly it seemed the wind was inside his head. "Follow me. Hurry!"

Faint memories stirred of a night and a church, so with a trust and urgency he could hardly explain, he ran toward the light. It moved away as he approached so he kept his course and followed the orb.

He hadn't gone far when he heard the bark of the dogs and the booming voice of the orderly who must be speaking to the woman at the cabin. Doubling his pace he continued to follow the light that had moved farther ahead of him.

The dogs outstripped the orderly and were fast closing in on him. Everything he had gone through up to this point flashed through his mind. *This can't be all for nothing, I can't go through it again. Help me, oh please God . . . someone help me!*

Instead of help, betrayal is what he felt when the light suddenly disappeared ahead of him. He didn't know which direction to run and couldn't think of any reason it would help anyway, yet a strength from deep inside kept the winded boy upright on feet that were being sucked down by the muddy ground with each step. Every gasp was accompanied by a stab in his ribs and he had no idea how he could keep moving.

The thick mud, the stinging of bare branches and the sound of his own heaving breath as he ran on and on tugged at his strength until finally, Bryon's site began to blur. Against his will he found himself sinking to his knees, then toppling in a faint onto his side.

The dogs were baying in loud anticipation of reaching the prey that escaped them earlier. Bounding in great leaps, they saw the fallen boy. An instant later, they were confronted with a bright light. They skidded to a jarring halt and stood shaking under the glare of the awful apparition for perhaps five seconds before turning and running with their tails between their legs, whines pouring from their throats.

When his dogs returned, yelping as if they had been beat, the seriously superstitious orderly was greatly concerned. He yelled, and kicked his dogs, ordering them to the chase, but to no avail. His spine crawled when he stood still because he felt a presence in the woods that was foreign to him. The natural sounds of wildlife were silent as if confirming his feelings. If they would not resume the hunt, what could he do against powers so great as to terrify viciously trained dogs? He looked at his gun in disappointment and resigned himself to missing the chance to kill that ornery boy. With a curt command he headed back to the asylum in embarrassed defeat.

#

"Wake up, it is time."

A soft brush on the cheek woke Bryon. He looked for what had touched him but it was gone. In its place was a feeling of comfort. Gathering that feeling to him jealously, he rose and headed east. He didn't know what had happened to the dogs or the orderly and he didn't care to think about it.

He lost track of time as he slowly walked along and soaked up the sights and sounds of nature. He was almost sorry when he came upon a train track and knew it was time to enter the world of man again. He didn't have long to wait. A slow moving freight train came rumbling by and he was easily able to swing himself up the slats of a cattle car. Crouching against the far corner of the car, he closed his eyes and went to sleep.

Anthony was watching the landscape outside his train window that afternoon, anticipating his imminent arrival in Portland. The Englishman was looking forward to looking around the beautiful, new city before meeting with Sheriff Barnes that evening. He was trying to decide whether to stay at a hotel for the night after meeting up with Barnes or push on to the asylum immediately and end the years of tracking Bryon.

His view was interrupted by a freight train moving in the opposite direction. He blinked in surprise when he saw a boy in the cattle car.

Chapter Nine

"Get on down here, kid," Walter ordered. "We have to hurry and eat if we're gonna catch the six o'clock stage."

Backing away from the train car door, Bryon shook his head.

"You idiot. This is the end of the line. The train don't go no further. Do you want to live in this dung heap of a town?"

Looking around in consternation, Bryon's shoulders slumped in defeat and he followed Walter. The fifteen-year-old boy had taken him under his wing shortly after the younger boy had begun riding the rails. Now they had to change to the stage coach if they wanted to continue east and the only way they could do it was with the money Walter had stolen at a previous stop. He had tried to get Bryon to come into the houses with him while folks were at church but to no avail. Bryon hung stubbornly to his principles, but now he would help spend the money, like it or not.

Trying to make the boy feel better, Walter went on. "If you have any choice, I don't see it. I feel responsible for you, kid. I know you don't like that I took the money but I got no choice." He sneered at the skeptical look on the boy's face and continued to defend himself. "In this world, there's some of us get bad knocks. Life ain't fair and we gotta try an even up the score."

Bryon stopped in his tracks, folded his arms and looked sternly at his friend who promptly lost his temper.

"You come on with me or I'm gonna wallop you. I ain't leavin' ya here and that's final."

Fearing he really had no choice, and liking Walter in spite of himself, Bryon followed him to the ticket office.

. After a cheap meal of beans and corn bread at a boarding house, the boys continued their journey east.

Walter was an expert at begging for food and taught Bryon how to look pitiful and hopeful at the same time. Bryon hated every minute of begging but couldn't think of an alternative. He certainly ate better as a beggar than he had in the asylum.   #

Denver was the end of the line for Walter. "I'm gonna get me a stake right here and when I'm all set, I'm gonna get me a mining claim. Colorado is the new California and this is where I'm getting rich, kid. You should stay and help me. I'll take care of you."

Bryon's determination to move on irked the older boy but he had a feeling he couldn't bully him this time, so he did the next best thing; he found the boy another traveling companion.

Orville had lost part of a foot in a mining blast and was cursing his luck to whoever would listen. He had lost an arm in the war the year before and came here seeking his fortune after being discharged. Now he was heading back east and agreed to watch after the boy for Walter.

Concerned about how Walter would "work" to get his stake, Bryon hesitated to leave but he understood there was no way he could change his friend. He was determined that Orville would not draw him into a similar life of crime. He had, however, thought of an alternative to begging. He had gained back a lot of his strength with rest and hearty eating so he used that strength to chop wood for any kind woman who would spare them a meal. Orville didn't like it and tried to convince the boy it wasn't necessary but very early in the relationship, it was clear who held the reins.

The broken man needed a friend although he never would have admitted that. Day after day Orville poured his woes out to the boy who listened intently to every word he said. Sometimes he was unnerved by the strength he felt coming from the silent boy who would look him straight in the eye with confidence and compassion. At the same time, he found himself eased in his spirit by the calm power he sensed from the boy. Strangely enough, he almost felt as though the kid were with him in his head when he related his sad stories, stripping him bare to the soul. It should have been frightening but it was healing instead.

Unknown to either man or boy was the future importance of the day Orville first began to speak of Base-Ball. He had run out of woes and felt lighter of heart and this naturally brought him around to the exciting new sport sweeping the country.

"Bet ya didn't know I was an original member of the Knickerbockers?" He anticipated the boy's enthusiasm but was met with question. "You've surely heard of the Knickerbockers!"

Shaking his head, Bryon assumed his attitude of listening. Feeling encouraged, the man launched his story. "It was back in '45 in Brooklyn, New York. I was respectable back then. Good enough to be admitted to the first Base-Ball club in history. Before that folks played different versions of games with balls and sticks but they didn't resemble what we have now very much. The most popular version was called Town Ball. Its granddaddy was the game of Cricket from Britain. I played Town Ball as a kid. It sure could get crazy with sometimes dozens of players on the field at once. Usually there were between nine and fifteen players but no one had any set positions so we always ran into each other," the old man laughed. "Back then the infield was square and there were no foul lines. The Knickerbockers established the rules for the game we got now. Well, actually it was Alexander Cartwright that did most of the rule making but we all gave our two bits.

We played our first game at Elysian Fields in Hoboken, New Jersey. We lost to the New York Base Ball Club, 23-1. It was downright embarrassing since we started it.

He chuckled as he saw the boy's eyes glaze over. "You don't have a clue what I'm talking about do you, kid? Well, you sit right back and I'll tell you all about how it's played."

For days the lessons on the basics, then the finer points of the game were drilled into the silent listener who had actually become quite interested.

Orville was happier than he had been for years. There was something about this boy. Sometimes he watched him and wondered at his thoughts. He noticed a strange look in his eyes when the boy would watch things like trees, falling snow, birds. One day he noticed an arresting expression in the kid's eyes when he saw a spider crawling along the wall in the train car.

Bryon was amazed to learn the man was only forty. He

looked sixty. *Sometimes it's a good thing I can't talk,* Bryon thought. *I might slip and call the poor man Droopy. Everything about him is droopy. His shoulders, his eyes, ears, his mouth, even his eyebrows droop down the sides of his eyes. Come to think of it, his words are droopy too. Unless he talks about Base-Ball. Then he sits straighter and speaks almost like a gentleman, kind of like Mr. Frohme.*

On a cold day late in March, the pair were listlessly watching the heavy rainfall out the window of the train when Orville started again speaking of Base-Ball. "You know kid, playing the game was the one bright spot in my life. I learned for myself that the famous saying is true; Base-Ball has a way of 'Driving Away the Blues'. It surely does."

He noticed the calculating look that appeared on his young partner's face and that started him pondering. He thought for most of the day before speaking again.

"You know, kid, I was thinking . . . you really ought to make plans for where you're headed. Walter told me you were running from something back there but don't you figure you're safe by now? You need a place to lite. Now, I'd invite you to come along to Pennsylvania with me but I'm going to my sister's and she already has a brood so I don't have the right to bring you."

Bryon was a bit alarmed by this. He was attached to the older man and had no idea what to do without him. The idea of being alone again made his stomach cramp.

Seeing that alarm, Orville quickly told him his idea. "I have a notion you might like to see some Base-Ball. Am I right?" At the answering nod he went on. The season is just starting so I was thinking of taking you to Cincinnati, Ohio. It's on the way to Pennsylvania so it wouldn't be no trouble. In Denver I got a hold of a paper from Ohio and read about the new teams starting up this year. The paper says that an old friend of mine is going to be managing one of the smaller farm teams. Maybe he could use a ball boy. What do you think?"

Since Bryon had no idea what else to do, he readily agreed.

Knowing the kid was nervous, Orville kept up a steady stream of Base-Ball talk the rest of the day.

"We're really respectable now you see, because in 1857 they started the National Association of Base-Ball Players and they codified rules like; only nine players can be fielded at once, and no one can catch the ball in their cap anymore. Stuff like that."

"You know, ole Abe Lincoln and his son Ted use to watch games out behind the White House. If that doesn't make it a respectable game, what does?" He was pleased when the boy agreed. "And I don't know how I would have kept my sanity during the war if I couldn't look forward to an occasional game. Why, one day during the war, when I was down in Texas, our Union soldiers was needing to relieve some tension. So we started a little game between battle lines. I guess that wasn't too smart, looking back on it, but who would have thought a gentleman's game like that would be so rudely interrupted? The Rebs opened up on us. I was playing left field and I can tell you, I was scared spitless. That's how I lost this arm. Us three fielders got the brunt of the attack. They injured and captured our center field player and the other fellow and I barely managed to get back into our lines. We beat back the attack but the darn thing was, we lost a great center field player and worse, we lost the only base ball in Alexandria, Texas."

He saw the doubtful look on the boy's face. "I swear that truly happened, kid. You could probably look it up in the history books in a few years. Didn't you ever hear truth is stranger than fiction?"

#

The rains had gone by the time they reached Cincinnati. A soft breeze played with the wispy clouds and brought the scent of freshly growing grass to Bryon's nose. He felt a tingle of excitement that he would learn with time meant one significant thing. Base-Ball season was here!

The year was 1866 and it was the first time organized ball had come to Cincinnati. A number of smaller teams popped

92

up like the one they were going to see. There were two ball clubs, the Buckeyes, and the Cincinnati Base Ball Club, that were higher caliber teams, both in the same town. Everyone was expecting an exciting rivalry.

The club was out on the field, shouting insults to one another and laughing good-naturedly.

When the team's manager, Sam Jenkins, saw his old friend Orville, he did a poor job of hiding his shock. "Orville? That you, ole son?"

Orville saw the pity and recoiled. "Yeah, well you ain't getting any younger either, Jenkins. And where'd your hair go?"

Laughing, Sam turned around and rubbed his fingers through the fringe of graying hair on the back of his head. "Like it?"

"Charming. You look good for . . . what? Forty two, three."

"Twenty- nine, my friend. Twenty-nine forever. So what happened to your arm?"

"You wouldn't believe me if I told you so we'll leave it at this; the war happened."

"So where you been?"

"Colorado. Had some trouble back west so I'm going back to Pennsylvania." He knew he wasn't the man he'd been when they'd played ball together fourteen years before but he didn't need reminding, and he didn't want pity. The kid was the only person he'd ever allowed to show him compassion. Changing the subject he said, "How're the boys looking this year?"

"Great. Better than ever. Who's the kid?"

"Well, actually that's why I'm here. He's been my partner since we left Denver. Great kid, great kid! He's interested in Base-Ball. Thought maybe you might let him help you out as a ball boy. Strong as an ox this boy. What do you say?"

"Got me a ball boy already. Started last week. I couldn't let him go for no reason and I don't need two. I'm sorry."

"Come on, Sam. Give the kid a break. He's a mute and he's got nowhere to go. I can't take him to my sisters. You know how it is."

"I just can't do it, Orville. Sorry. Everyone has a tough luck story these days."

"Guess we'll just sit an' watch for a while then."

"Sure. Gotta get back to the club. Good seeing you again."

Orville had tried to explain the game but now seeing it, Bryon was able to easily apply all he had heard and the game fell into place for him. By the end of practice, Bryon's heart was palpitating, his hands sweating, there was a glow on his face that could only mean one thing; he had fallen in love with the game.

"Might as well go. There's nothing more we can do here. We'll figure something out if . . ."

The boy was running toward the manager, Sam Jenkins. Quick as a flash, he picked up the heavy canvas bag of bats Sam was reaching for and heaved it over his shoulder."

"Give me that," Sam demanded. "I told you I don't need help. See that boy over there gathering up the bases?"

Bryon saw the dark haired youth who appeared a bit older than him and nodded.

"He's my ball boy and I don't need two." He reached for the bag but Bryon stepped back and shook his head.

Sam frowned, turned his head and spit. "Fine, carry it then but I won't change my mind."

And he didn't. For three weeks. Orville had given up on trying to talk Bryon into leaving with him, wished him luck and was on his way east. Bryon had been waiting at the field every day when the club showed up and he worked hard to beat the other ball boy at performing every duty. Before and after practice he would find houses with big wood piles and chop wood until he drew attention. He was always rewarded with food. There were plenty of barns with warm haystacks to sleep in so his needs were taken care of.

A terrible day came when the players did not appear on the field for practice. The boy waited until dark before giving up. Bryon was back the next day full of hope and trepidation but once again no one came. He could not keep back the tears. He stood for a long while on the empty, green field.

Five days passed but he did not give up. There was nothing else in his life, nothing else he wanted. They returned the sixth day. Bryon's relief was so intense he again felt the tears stream down his face.

When Sam saw the tears on that pale, drawn face, his heart just could not hold out any longer. He had been sure the boy would disappear while the club was on a road trip but now he acknowledged that the kid had been bitten by the bug and there was no cure.

"All right. You're my second ball boy." He chuckled at the happiness that lit the boy up like a candle. "Didn't know where we were did ya?"

The boy's expression instantly turned solemn as he slowly shook his head.

"Sorry, kid. We were on the road. Took the train to Hamilton and Columbus to play some ball. We do that a lot but next time you'll be coming with us." He looked the boy over and added, "But first we'll get you some new clothes. I don't want to be seen with a ragamuffin."

A few days later Sam was sitting on the bench watching the team practice their hitting when he noticed the mute boy shyly pick up a bat and examine it.

Sam smiled with tolerant amusement as the boy lovingly caressed the pale ash bat. Bryon ran his fingers reverently over the wood grain then slowly lifted the bat to his nose and sniffed. A wondrous smile spread across his face. Sam thought all this was a bit odd yet the sweet look on the boy's countenance touched him.

The kid stood watching the players practicing as he rubbed his hands up and down his bat. He saw the careful way the hurler pitched the ball to give the striker the best chance of hitting it. The throw was underhanded, with both wrist and elbow straight and was tossed from a box that was level with the rest of the field and forty five feet from home plate.

The strikers used bats of difference sizes and shapes

95

according to their personal preference. Bryon lifted his bat to mimic the players' swing. Sam could not help himself as he walked over and helped the kid with his stance and swing.

"Hands together, that's right. Get your elbow up a little more, okay now follow through. Let your hips turn more . . . good. I'll toss you a few balls and you keep your eye right on that ball. Don't take them off at just the last second like most kids do. Ever hit a ball before?"

When the boy indicated that he hadn't, Sam told him, "Well, get ready to start living."

Sam stood close and gently tossed the ball. The boy's natural instinct proved to be uncanny. He felt a connection with the wood as if it was an extension of his arm, almost as if it were alive. When Bryon heard the crack of the bat and watched the ball dribble out onto the field, he felt as if he had conquered the world. Smiles blossomed on both the young striker and the old hurler's faces.

"Great job, kid. Let's see if you can do it a second time." He threw it again and this time Bryon hit it straight back to Sam. "Well what do ya know? You're a natural. Okay, a little harder now. Put those broad shoulders of yours into it. You're a big boy, you should be able to get it over my head easy enough." He moved back a few steps and threw it a little harder.

With each pitch, Bryon grew more relaxed and comfortable with the bat. The years of swinging an axe was the perfect preparation for this. He just needed a few reminders to keep his back elbow up. His chest was deep and his arms like iron for a twelve and a half-year-old. In addition, his hands were strong and coordinated from carving.

With a feeling of exhilaration, he swung hard at a faster pitch. Sam watched in surprised admiration as the boy connected with the ball. His mouth dropped open as the ball sailed over his head and landed almost one hundred and fifty feet out in the field. Bryon had a barely conscious thought that the bat represented good and the ball evil and he was driving the evil from him. This time it was good and gone. He dropped the bat and leaped up, shoving his fist into the air.

Rubbing the back of his neck, Sam stared at the ball a

moment then looked back at Bryon with suspicion. "I don't like it when people try to make a fool out of me, boy." He walked away in a huff muttering, "beginner my foot." But he watched him, week after week he watched him hit balls farther and farther as he and the other ball boy pitched to each other.

Sam watched the new boy shag balls for the players hours a day. They started using the mute boy almost exclusively since he never complained and showed no inclination to do so. He did not quit when he was tired like the other boy Lester. This did not sit well with the first ball boy who decided it was time to teach the upstart a lesson.

Lester caught Bryon as he was leaving the field after everyone had gone home. The beating was not too serious. Bryon was so surpriseded he did not even try to defend himself from the two solid punches that knocked him down. He lay in the grass staring up at the other boy in pain and confusion.

Seeing the question in the mute boy's eye, Lester explained. "You been horning in on my territory. First you got this job by being pig-headed. Now you're sucking up to the players and making them like you better than me. Knock it off or next time I'll knock your head off."

When he realized he had done nothing to deserve the beating, Bryon saw red. Scrambling to his feet he lunged for the older boy and met a hard fist.

In a silent growl, with his lips peeled back like a mad dog, Bryon again started to get to his feet but found a foot planted in his ribs before he could rise.

"My pa told me people like you were idiots but I didn't believe him 'til today. You're proving him right, little boy." With a shove of the foot for emphasis he warned, "You'd better stay down unless you really are a dummy."

Lester laughed when the mute boy turned away and buried his face in his hands. His laughter stopped and he felt revolted at seeing the shaking body of a boy obviously weeping but no sound coming out. "You *are* an idiot," he taunted as he turned for home.

Bryon was convulsed with grief; almost hysterical. *I forgot, I forgot. Maybe I am an idiot after all, that's what my papa always told me. I thought this time it would be different. If I worked hard enough and did good, I thought they would think I was smart. No one will ever think I'm smart 'cause I can't tell them I am. Oh, I don't know, am I? Am I? Oh, God, help me. Is there ever going to be a way to let people know what I am inside? Please, God, let me out of this trap,* the boy's heart screamed to the heavens.

Bryon did not knock it off as Lester had order. He was beaten up a second time for it but this time he got in a few good licks himself. Unbeknownst to Lester, Sam was watching that time. He decided to leave it alone, assuming it was a onetime problem but when a fight broke out between the boys the next week and the mute boy took a bad beating, he decided to do something about it. He knew if he tried to protect the younger boy, it would make things worse so he decided to teach him to fight dirty the way Lester did. He brought him home with him every day after practice, fed him dinner then took him out back for lessons. He had Bryon work with a sandbag to toughen his fists and worked with his stance and footing to begin with, just as he had in Base-Ball. He was no longer surprised when the boy picked up the rudiments with astonishing speed.

It just seemed natural when the boy began sleeping in the spare room at Sam's instead of in barns. He had already been eating breakfast and lunch with the team so now life felt settled.

It was ten days later when the big fight came. Lester was feeling big for his britches and wanted to show off a bit so he got reckless and tripped the younger boy as he walked from the field carrying the canvas base bags. Bryon skinned his chin on the rough dirt and got the wind knocked out of him from landing on a bag. While he waited for his breath to come back, he listened to the laughter above him. Finally sucking in air, he calmed himself as Sam had taught him and bunched his muscles beneath him. In one smooth movement, he spun off the ground and his right foot lashed out, catching the other boy on the side of the knee. With a yell of pain, Lester started to fall but caught himself with his hands and quickly pushed off the dirt and warily backed up.

The players had gathered around and were quiet as they sensed the intensity of the animosity between the boys. One of the men noticed the ugly scrape on Bryon's chin and asked, "Hey, kid, are you all right?"

Looking over at the man, Bryon nodded and that was when Lester came flying at him. They crashed to the ground and wrestled for dominance. The weight of the older boy gave him the advantage and realizing this, Bryon broke his hold and rolled away. Leaping to his feet, he crouched low and when Lester dove for him, he sprang to the right, spun around and using the boy's momentum, he gave Lester a good kick in the keister. He politely waited for the boy to pick himself up before he marched up toe to toe and offered himself as a target. Lester swung and Bryon ducked. The blow glanced off his ear and a return swing was on its way. He gave Lester a right jab that rocked him to his heels. Confidence blossomed and Bryon bore down, pummeling the other boy with both fists to the head and stomach. Lester collapsed to his knees and Bryon reached down and yanked him back to his feet for one last lesson. He put his full weight behind a right hook while holding the boy by the shirt with his left. Then he let go and watched him fall to the ground. Even then, he wanted to be sure the message was received. He knelt down beside Lester and pressed his forearm against his throat. Bryon heard some of the men protesting but Sam quieted them. "Don't worry, the kid knows what he's doing. Lester has it coming."

With his arm pressing the boy's windpipe, Bryon stared into Lester's frightened eyes. Lester saw those dark orbs boring into him and knew he was being warned of worse to come if he did not watch his step. He whispered hoarsely, "Okay, okay. Sorry." Bryon moved away and gave him a hand up.

Sam knew the boys would have no more problems. He pulled out his handkerchief and handed it to Lester and turned to Bryon. "How old are you, kid?"

He held up all his fingers and then two more."

"Twelve? That hardly seems right. Lester is fourteen. You're awfully big for twelve. Too much muscle. You sure?"

Bryon nodded with conviction.

Sam conceded the point with a shrug then looked thoughtfully at the boy. "You need a name, kid." He saw the expectant look in Bryon's face. "All right, let's try to guess. Is your name Stephen?" Bryon shook his head. "Matthew, Mike, Harry, Jack" he chuckled at the boy's grimace. After a string of twenty or so names, he gave up. "Guess I'm not too good at remembering all the names out there, so I'll just give you one. You look like a Luke to me."

Bryon's lips thinned and he determinedly shook his head. Sam grunted, "Well, I like it. It's a good strong name, so that's who you are, Luke."

The newly dubbed Luke shrugged his shoulders in defeat and walked away.

#

The next night Sam went outside to get a load of kindling and saw Bryon with his best hunting knife carving on some wood. Sam let loose and bawled him out good for using his knife without permission, dulling the prized weapon. "Put it back where you got it and don't touch it again."

That night, when Sam went to bed he noticed a wood carving setting on his nightstand. He picked it up and studied it in awe. The boy had been making this for him. The little carving was of a Base-Ball player in striking stance. After carefully examining it he called Bryon in. "Sorry I got so mad. I never knew you could do something like this. Handing it to him, he said, "You're good."

Bryon shook his head and handed it back. He pointed to himself and then to Sam.

"You mean you made this for me?" With Bryon's affirmation he said, "Maybe I'll pick you up your own knife one of these days."

It did not take long for an idea to pop into Sam's head. "Say, Luke. You know how I told you that you were on your own when the season ended?" When he saw the nod he continued. "I was just thinking. Maybe I could help you out. Get you some professional training with that carving hobby of yours. You could do chores around the place for your keep and maybe, you could do some more of that carving. What do you think?" Sam wondered what kind of price good carvings would bring him.

Bryon was over-joyed. He was even getting use to thinking of himself as Luke.

When the season ended, Sam arranged for Bryon to be trained from an expert in wood carving. The man had come from one of the famous Quebec wood carving families who carried on the great French tradition and style. Carving was losing some of its popularity but there was still a market for expert work.

For the first lesson, the carver asked Luke to show him what he could do. He gave him a piece of seasoned wood, showed him the tools laid out on the table and told him to feel free to create whatever he wanted.

As the carver watched the mute boy work, he became instantly riveted. After an hour of quiet observation, he marveled at the wild grizzly taking shape in the boy's hands. He tapped Bryon on the shoulder and spoke. "I have seen this style of work before. It was from the Northwest Indians. They alone rival my people for skill in this art. Is that where you learned this?"

Thrilled at having this part of his past unlocked, Bryon nodded enthusiastically.

"So, an Indian taught you?" Again a nod. "In Washington?" A negative shake was his answer. "Oregon?" He returned the boy's smile of affirmation. "You already have a remarkable start for one so young. I can't understand it, your hands shouldn't be able to create such detail at your age. Of course there is much I can teach you and the first thing is, you will need your own set of tools."

When Sam returned for his young charge, he was irritated when the teacher handed him a list of tools he would have to buy.

"Looks like you've doubled up on a lot of this. Why does he need both a square chisel and a bent one? Can't he bend the square one? And the same with those straight and bent gouges."

"Of course it is up to you, sir. But the boy cannot be a true carver without all these instruments. Make sure the mallet you buy fits his hand well. And don't forget the skew chisel and the bent V-tool."

Mumbling his thanks, Sam led the way out of the small workshop. "You better work hard at this, Luke. It'll take you carving some fine stuff to pay me back."

For three months, Luke went three times a week to learn from the Frenchman. At first the instructor was enthused with his talented student but after a few weeks, the boy's brilliant talent truly began to be apparent. Bryon's clever hands and innate feel for the wood intimidated his teacher. At the end of twelve weeks, the Frenchman became down right insecure, worrying that the student would soon surpass the teacher, and perhaps already had when it came to creating likenesses of wildlife. It just was not natural and he informed Sam that school was over.

"The boy is too young for me to teach him more. He doesn't have the maturity to learn the finer points of the trade so he should wait a few years before going on with his hobby."

Shaking his head in disgust, Sam clearly saw straight through the arrogant artist. The Frenchman was intimidated and offended that a mere boy would rival his own talent, which in Sam's opinion he now did. Bryon was disappointed to lose the opportunity to learn intricate design tooling for furniture, jewelry boxes and such but he knew he would always prefer carving subjects from nature.

By December, Sam had a number of beautiful pieces to sell to gift shops for the Christmas season. Not only did Luke carve ball players, he made a variety of animals that were amazing life like; especially bears. Indian peace pipes with intricate designs were a popular item as were the small boxes with nature scenes carved on top. The Northwestern Indians excelled not only at carving the finest totem poles, but at ornate boxes, bowls, pipes and masks and Bryon had learned some of all of it from Storm-That-Kills. On the bottom of every carving, he put his trademark bear claw.

Sam justified keeping the money to pay for Bryon's keep and because the team needed it. There was no professional Base-Ball and it was illegal to pay the players although almost everyone did pay their best men. The money would help him pay players under the table and he could increase his profits with a little gambling on the games. What was wrong with that? he reasoned. Lots of people were doing it.

During the off-season some of the guys still got together for a game when the weather permitted. They often invited Luke to play when they were short a man, and he improved and grew in confidence as a ball player and he began to see himself as a real person and not just a defect.

He learned a lot from the guys that winter but he sure wished Base-Ball players had some thick mittens or something to take the sting away when that ball was caught by ice cold hands.

The men usually needed someone for third base so that is what the boy learned. The first and third base players normally stood with one foot on the bag or a step or two out of bounds during play. They had to watch for the tricky fair/foul bunt. That is when a striker hits the ball and it lands inbounds then rolls out before it gets to either first or third. The rules allowed this as a fair play so the basemen had to be ready to chase those bunts hard. Fellows who were good at those, were highly valued.

The game had one umpire who usually sat in formal attire at a table by third base. He would not call strikes or balls unless either the hurler or striker wasn't doing his job, then he would give a warning and begin calling. Three balls was a walk, and three missed swings was a strikeout. Fouls didn't count as strikes. Often the umpire would ask the players or spectators to help him with a difficult call. That winter, the guys sometimes had a hard time finding someone to umpire for them, but the game of Base-Ball was so friendly there were seldom problems. Tradition demanded that the players act as gentleman toward the other team and the umpire. Only the team captain had the right to dispute a call and that was always done calmly.

Swearing was prohibited in the game as was spitting which irritated Sam.

The next season was a lot better for Luke who was accepted warmly as a part of the family. This year he was the only ball boy and he was treated like a cherished mascot. Sam allowed Luke to practice with the boys whenever someone was absent. Luke especially had fun learning to steal bases. In 1863, Ned Cuthbert had stolen a base, telling the surprised umpire there were no rules against it. Now it was catching on and Sam wanted his players to learn the skill. They had to be careful if they stole a base when the catcher was involved. Only if he muffed the ball could they run. That meant the ball wasn't caught in the air or after one bounce.

On Oct. 18, 1866, after their own season had ended, Sam took Luke to Ninth Street to watch a game between the two top clubs. Bryon was amazed at the level of talent among these two teams. At the end of an exciting game, the Cincinnati Base-Ball club won 53-21 over the Buckeyes. Harry Wright was the hurler for the winning team. Bryon thought he was a fine looking man with his neatly trimmed dark beard and strong bearing. For some reason the man stuck in his mind.

Chapter Ten

The smell of growing things brought back to Bryon the first time he had stood on a ball field two years ago. Base-Ball was in his blood and this was his favorite time of year. A lot was happening in the fast growing city of Cincinnati. That year they built a brilliantly engineered suspension bridge over the Ohio River greatly increasing efficiency in Hamilton County.

The afternoons were growing longer and Sam was getting more excited each day as the season approached. Except tonight at supper, he was acting plain weird.

Like a slow fuse, Luke's temper often took a long time to ignite but when it did, it blew. Shoving his chair back from the table, he jumped up and flung out his arms, palms up and gave Sam that look he knew so well. *What on earth is wrong with you?*

"All right, all right. Sit down. I know I've been staring at you. Got something on my mind is all. Been thinking about putting you on the team this year. You're fourteen and a half right?"

Bryon braced his hands on the table and slowly sat down as he stared in disbelief at his mentor.

"Now, don't go getting your hopes up about playing. You'll just be a substitute but you're good, Luke. Real good for your age. Still think you're mistaken about how old you are so we might as well say you're sixteen. Don't go shaking your head at me. Do you want to be on the team or not?"

#

The season was half over before Luke finally got his chance to play. Arnold Aster, the third base player for the team was drunk again. Sam had warned him but he knew the team only had two substitutes. Aster stunk with drink, but he knew the regular substitute stunk at third base, and that left the mute kid as the only option and he did not believe Jenkins would resort to that insult.

"Aster, you're on the bench today. Luke, you take his place."

The ears of everyone on the team perked up at this. Most of the men were fond of the mute boy and they admired Sam for putting his little (well, not so little anymore) mascot on the team. But to really play him? Were the dumb allowed to play?

The game was a shoe-in for Sam's team so Bryon was relaxed and having fun. The first time a play came his way, he scooped up the ball and it didn't even seem to touch his glove before it popped up into his right hand for a bullet throw to the hurler who quickly whipped it to first for the out. Luke loved the new gloves. Best thing that ever happened to Base-Ball in his opinion.

All the eyes on the bench turned in unison toward Arnold Aster, then looked away again as if on a string. They knew Luke played well but most had never taken the time to

105

notice how well. Sam swiped hard at his mouth to erase the smirk, set on a firm frown, crossed his arms and stared, heavy lidded at the pitchers mound. No one looked at Arnold again that game.

When Luke started the next game, Aster could not take the insult. He was waiting for the upstart after the game. Two years of boxing lessons came in handy that afternoon as the heavy limbed boy thrashed the shorter, slimmer man.

As Luke walked away from the beaten man, Aster called out threats through his smashed lips. "A freak like you won't last, kid. You're a flash in the pan who is too much of an idiot to keep up with the big boys." Luke ignored him but thought as he was walking away, *yeah right, I couldn't keep up with you, big boy.*

Seeing himself ignored the man yelled out one last threat. "If you aren't careful, you might find yourself on the business end of a knife one of these days, kid!"

He didn't know Sam was standing behind him until he heard his voice. "Guess I'll know just where to look if I ever find out anything has happened to that boy. Don't let me see your face around here again, Astor."

By the end of the season, both Sam and Luke knew his starting position on the team was secure. He had the third leading batting average on the team and his fielding was strong.

That fall, when the season ended, Sam found a supplier who paid more for Luke's wood carvings than the local stores were willing to pay him. Slowly, the boy's art began finding its way into fine establishments back east. The bear claw signature was making its mark.

At fifteen and a half, Luke had reached his full stature of six feet two inches and his bulk was solid muscle. His hair had darkened to a soft fawn brown with gold burnished ends when the sun had at it. Sam broke down and bought him his own razor since he was tired of sharing.

Luke felt the familiar rush and tingle the first day of the new season. The weather cooperated and indeed, all the blues were driven away.

One of the less gentlemanly players asked Sam if he had been able to find a permanent replacement for Aster. At the look of disgust the manager gave the man, no other negative comments were made about Luke. Indeed, he was soon treated almost normally, and for a mute boy in 1868, this was a miracle.

The club was having a good season and were feeling confident as they traveled to play the Cleveland farm team in July. Luke hit two doubles, the second one with two men on base to help win 18 to 13.

After the game, he was getting a drink of water when he felt a tap on his shoulder. Turning, he saw a young woman peering at him intently. "Excuse me. I was wondering if I knew you. You look so familiar." The woman saw the young man's expression lite with recognition. Her round, cheery face warmed with a smile. "So you do know me?"

Luke repeated the familiar actions of pointing to his throat and shaking his head.

The woman blinked and gasped. "Bryon! I can't believe it. Is it really you? How on earth could you . . . uh?" She looked a little ashamed of herself. "So, you play Base-Ball? Wow, that's incredible. I'm so proud of you. You were the best one out there."

Bryon looked at her in question, motioned with his arms and looked around.

"Oh, I'm in nursing school here in Cleveland. My father is going to about die when I write and tell him you're alive. He heard you escaped from the asylum but he was afraid they killed you. He was sick over it, still is."

As she was talking, an idea came to him. Grabbing her by the hand, he motioned for her to follow. She had a hard time keeping up with him and pulled hard trying to slow him down. They reached the manager of Bryon's team who had been watching them with interest. Bryon pointed to each of them and stepped back indicating they should talk.

Sam stuck out his hand. "Hello. I guess Luke wants me to meet the pretty girl he's been flirting with."

Betsy blushed and shook his hand. "Pleased to meet you, sir. I'm Betsy Carter, an old friend of . . . did you say

Luke?"

"Yes. That's his name. Gave it to him myself."

"But his name is Bryon. Bryon Hancock."

"You don't say? Well don't that beat all. You really know him then?"

"Since he was a baby."

"Why don't you come over to the hotel and have dinner with the team. I surely would love to hear all about this boy. Bryon . . . humph. I prefer Luke."

Betsy couldn't rest that night until she wrote her father. She started the letter with; "you'll never guess who I had dinner with tonight." She told him all about Bryon playing ball for some farm team and bragged about his talent. Sam had done some bragging himself about Bryon's gift with carving wood. He told her to look for the bear claw signature if she was ever in St. Louis, Chicago, New York or Boston. Those were the cities his distributor supplied. Betsy told her father to tell Storm-That-Kills about the carving, knowing full well what that would mean to the old Indian. After filling three pages front and back she was able to sleep knowing the happiness she would be giving her tender-hearted father with that letter.

The kindest thing she ever did for Bryon was to forget to add two important items to the letter; his new name and which team he played for.

#

I'll have to go back to the United States, Anthony decided as he re-read the letter from Oregon. It doesn't say which team but Ohio isn't that big. I can be there by June and I'll finally have that boy before the season ends.

#

Eighteen-sixty-nine was a red-letter year for America. The golden spike was driven at Promontory Point, Utah to connect the intercontinental railroad, and the first professional

Base-Ball team emerged in Cincinnati, Ohio. The year before, the newspapers had dubbed what had been known as the Cincinnati Base-Ball Club, as the Red Stockings after their flashy new uniforms. After years of managers paying players under the table, Harry Wright, manager of the Red Stockings was the first to pay his players over the table. Professional Base-Ball was born.

#

"Oh brother, here comes trouble again." Sam rubbed the back of his neck, turned to the bench and ordered, "Freddy, go in for Luke."

The substitute third base player ran out onto the field beaming at another opportunity, beginning to believe he might really have a shot at a permanent starting position.

When Luke was relieved by Freddy, he jogged up to Sam and stood in front of him, finally forcing the confrontation. This was the third game in a row he had been pulled early. Freddy was good but Luke knew the stats. He was the top hitter and the second best fielder on the team. He hadn't made one error these three games, the little he had been in, so why was Sam treating him this way? He was sixteen and a half and everyone believed him two years older than that. Was he finally giving into pressure about playing a mute? Luke knew Sam had always tried to get the team to keep it quiet fearing public opposition, but perhaps the news had gotten around anyway.

He planted his feet, thrust his fists on his hips and glared. It didn't help.

"Go sit down, kid. You look like you need a rest."

Luke didn't move.

"I said go sit down. I'm the manager, I make the decisions not you."

Trying not to lose control of his temper, Luke turned and walked off the field.

"Hey, get back here! Luke, don't you dare leave this game! Get on that bench, now!"

Home to Sam's house was not where he wanted to be

but at least the grouchy manager would not be there. He had not only been difficult at the games, the last few days he had been hard to live with at home too.

Growling low in his throat, Sam spit in disgust and yelled one last time, "That's just fine, you go on home. Act like a spoiled two-year-old."

He was halfway home before Luke noticed someone following him. A large man crossed the street toward him and lengthened his stride. Luke walked faster, feeling a little nervous. He hated to be approached by strangers and being forced to go through the motions to explain he was mute. It was humiliating and he feared he would never get used to it.

The stranger had increased his pace to a slow jog and Luke decided to get away altogether. He had just begun a full out run when the man's shout stopped him in his tracks.

"Wait, Luke. I can tell you why you keep getting pulled from the games."

Curiosity is a powerful force and Luke had his share. He turned and waited for the man to catch up.

Sticking out his hand, the man introduced himself. "I'm Harry Wright, manager of the Cincinnati Red Stockings."

If he hadn't already been mute, Luke would have been struck dumb. All he could do was stare. He didn't notice when Harry lowered his hand with a grin and said, "I take it you have heard of me?"

Luke nodded.

"Well, I guess some folks have been happy to meet me but I never made anyone speechless before." He smiled charmingly. "So how old are you, son?"

Ducking his head in shame, Luke wished this wasn't happening. Of all people to have to embarrass himself in front of, this was the last man on earth he would chose. This was the manager of the first professional Base-Ball club in history, and the best team on earth. Luke followed his club's stats fanatically. Sam read the paper to him and he remembered every word about this man and his players. Luke's shoulders heaved in a sigh as he raised his head and went through the motions showing he couldn't talk.

The manager tried to hide his shock but failed miserably. "Oh, I'm sorry. I didn't know. Amazing that something like this could be kept a secret. I thought in Base-Ball there were no secrets. Though I guess I understand why your team would want to protect you. People can be pretty ignorant can't they, Luke?"

Relief flooded his body and he nodded with a tentative grin.

"That's all right. I can still tell you why Sam isn't playing you and I don't mind about your, uh, your . . . problem." Harry looked a bit uncertain but he was fast getting adjusted to the news. "You see, son, I lost my third base player two weeks ago and my back-up just isn't up to snuff. I've been hearing great things about you so I've come to the last three games trying to catch a glimpse of what I've been hearing. Problem is, Jenkins knows me and obviously understands my need and therefore my interest in you. When I saw what happened today, I decided to offer you the job on the spot because if Sam Jenkins is trying that hard to keep you from me, I have no doubt you can do the job." Harry was a little concerned about the pasty color the young man had become and the glazed look in his eye but hoping it would pass, he pushed on. "So what do you think? Would you like to come and play with us?"

Luke opened and closed his mouth like a fish; as if something profound would actually come out of it if he could get his brain to function.

"I'm offering a contract of course. You'll be paid. What do you say?"

Glancing nervously in the direction of the ball field, Luke tentatively nodded his head, glanced away again and ended up shrugging in confusion. He simply did not know if Sam would allow it or if he had the right to go against Sam's wishes if he objected.

Harry patted his arm. "Now, don't you worry about a thing. I'll take care of Sam. He won't like it but he'll understand it is definitely the best thing for you. He won't stand in your way.

111

"It's absolutely out of the question. How could you even ask such a thing? I take it you know now the boy is mute?"

"Calm down, Sam. Yes, I know he is mute but it didn't matter to you so why should it matter to me?"

"Why should it matter? Are you crazy? You're big time ball. There will be reporters, lots of fans . . . how can you keep it secret about him being mute? If the public finds out, they'll throw a fit. They think mute people are mentally retarded. No, no for Luke's sake, I can't let you do it."

"Are we really talking about Luke's sake here or yours?"

"How dare you? That boy is like a son to me. I gave him my name. Of course I'm thinking about him."

"Then don't stand in his way. I'll take good care of him. I'll protect him. The boys will understand and they'll do same as yours did. Don't take this chance away from him, not when he wants it so bad." He stared hard at Sam who tried to stare back.

As his gaze faltered and his heart swelled with pain, Sam turned his head and spit. "Ah, hell!"

Luke was watching through the front window as the two men argued in the front yard. When he saw Sam rub his neck, he knew his mentor was extremely agitated. *He'll never let me go*, he thought. *He needs me for his team and he wants me to keep making money for him with my carvings. No use getting my hopes up; won't happen.*

When the door opened, Luke was sitting in a chair staring into the fire. He thought he was dreaming when he heard Sam say, "Guess you'd better get packed. Wright wants you moving into the boarding house where his bachelor club members live."

Chapter Eleven

"Listen up, boys. This is our new third base player, Luke Jenkins." Harry waited for the murmur of approval to die down. "I can see some of you have heard of him. He's been burning up the smaller teams. You can see from the shoulders on him that his reputation as a striker is well earned. I want you to make him feel welcome and show him the ropes. He's a bit nervous. Appears he's got our team on a bit of a pedestal but that'll pass once he gets to know you mugs."

When the laughter died down, he took a deep breath and launched into the hard part. "Oh, and there's one other thing. Luke was born with an impediment. He can't talk and so we . . ." He was unable to be heard among the loud grumbling questions being shouted at him.

"Come on, Harry. What does that mean?"

"Is he an idiot? Are you bringing an idiot to the team?"

"Is he deaf? Because I always heard dumb people are deaf!"

An angry shout from Harry quieted them down for the most part. "That's about enough from all of you. Shame on you, embarrassing this kid on his first day like this!"

"Don't look like no kid to us. Looks about twenty."

"He's eighteen, smart mouth. Now pipe down and listen up. Last I noticed, the ability to make a great speech out on the diamond wasn't a part of being good in this game. Luke is a very solid player and he has earned the right to be here same as all of you. After the childish way you reacted to that little piece of news, I'm a bit worried about telling you what I expect. Let me ask a question first. Do you men consider yourselves honorable people? Men of integrity?"

"Hey, what are you implying? Of course we are." Resentful affirmations were given all around.

"Okay then, that means you will help me keep a promise I made to Sam Jenkins. He's been protecting this boy, keeping it quiet about his, his, um . . . quietness. You can see from your own reaction that folks can be downright nasty about people who aren't just like us." He glanced over at his only Negro player, Ethan Brown who returned a tiny grin. "Anyway, I promised that we would keep it to ourselves about Luke. Someone asks you why he never talks, you say he's terribly shy. Hey, even better, let's say he has a bad stutter and never talks in public. That'll do it. Now, can all of you, as men of integrity, promise me to do this?"

Thoughtful nods were given, some reluctantly, others with conviction as the men got use to the idea and most just shrugged it off. They knew Harry was a softy. Just look at the slave boy he signed on. Harry had been an abolitionist so you had to expect him to have weird ideas about people.

"Thanks boys, now let's get out on the field and get in a good practice. We've got a hard game coming up tomorrow."

With a bad case of nerves, Luke stood at third base and kept looking around in awe at all the players he had been following since living with Sam. His head was turned toward Harry in center field when the ball hit him the stomach.

"Hey, Harry, I thought you said the kid wasn't deaf?"

"Shut up, Gould. Wake up there, Jenkins."

After that, Luke concentrated but he felt like he had too many fingers. Twice he fumbled the ball, each time blushing furiously. The players exchanged concerned glances and cursed under their breath.

Harry's brother George, the star player on the team walked over to his brother while waiting for his turn at bat. "So, Harry, did you actually see this guy play?"

Harry choked and coughed up the air he had swallowed then faced his brother. "Actually, I didn't but the stats don't lie. He'll settle down, George. Give him a chance."

When the manager called a halt to practice, Luke walked slowly from the field staring at his feet. He felt a hand on his shoulder and looked up. He had never had any personal experience with a Negro before. The man standing in front of him looked human enough. He had deep dimples and crinkles in the corners of his eyes when he smiled that made it seem as though he held some amusing secret to life. Luke had seen what a great player he was. Some of the stories that went around

114

about the African slaves were so absurd that Luke had just naturally dismissed every ugly rumor. Now he was glad he had. This guy looked like a solid man a fellow could depend on.

Ethan watched the thoughts run through the new guy's eyes and waited for his complete attention before speaking. "I thought I'd tell you to remember that these men all put their pants on one leg at a time, Luke. By the way, I'm Ethan Brown and I put both pant legs on at once so you can look up to me if you want but not the rest of these clowns. They all bleed when they're cut; I guess I have to admit to that weakness myself, and not one of these guys claims to be God."

The confused and doubtful look on Luke's face told Ethan he had more work to do. "All right. I'll give you some examples. See Mason over there? He chews his nails before every game because he's so nervous. And right behind him, Lloyd. He's twenty-nine and his mommy makes his lunch for him for road trips. Says she doesn't trust him to eat properly otherwise. Then there's Trumble but the less about him the better. The point is, you don't have to be intimidated by this bunch. From what I hear, you deserve to be here so forget about the guys and concentrate on the ball. And if you aren't having fun, go turn in your uniform."

A sigh of relief and a crooked grin told Ethan he had helped. "I'll see you at the game tomorrow, champ."

Head held high, Luke walked calmly off the field. He was stopped a second time by the right fielder, Donald Trumble. This message was a very different type.

"Listen, Jenkins. Thought I'd better give you the heads up. Stay away from Brown. He isn't our kind and if you cozy up to him, the others players will lose all respect for you."

Am I your kind? Do any of you really have respect for me?" Luke wondered as he listened to the young man.

"So if you want to be accepted by the club . . . you know, be our friend, then keep your distance from Brown. We're like a family here and I'm telling you now, my daddy never sired no . . .."

"Don't use that word, Trumble. I've warned you and this will be the last time."

"Didn't say it, Harry."

"You were about to. Now take off and quit trying to corrupt the new kid."

After the other man left, Harry put his arm around Luke's shoulders. "I don't know what he was saying about Ethan, but don't listen to him. Ethan is a good man and one of my best players. Some of the fans grouch about it but that doesn't bother me. Enough of that. I know you were nervous out there today but I want you to shake it off and play like you always have. My substitute isn't that great in the infield so I need you to step up and show me what you've got. See you tonight, kid."

Harry had Ethan and Luke over for dinner that evening to try and help the new kid settle in and feel like part of the team family. Harry Wright was the son of a very talented British cricket player. He was a fine looking man, and in superb shape for thirty-six-years old. His younger brother, George, was the club shortstop and the most valuable player for the Red Stockings. Harry had been the team hurler until this year and now he was playing center field. He had gotten his club uniforms the year before and the bright stockings had the newspapers dubbing them the Red Stockings and the name stuck.

"Welcome to my home, gentlemen. This is Aaron B. Champion. Aaron, meet Ethan Brown and Luke Jenkins."

When everyone was seated in his spacious parlor he explained Champion's presence. "Mr. Champion wanted to meet you both so I've invited him to dine with us this evening. He is responsible for putting together the group of Ohio investors that financed our club this year."

Aaron smiled at the humble manager. "Actually, I simply caught Wright's vision. Professional Base-Ball has a real shot at changing the game. If people pay to go to plays and concerts, they'll certainly pay for something as exciting and loved as our new sport. Since all the best clubs were already paying under the table, we are just making the game honest."

The enthusiasm of the two men was palpable. Harry rubbed his hands together. "With Aaron's expertise and

116

contacts, we have a good group of backers. Anyway, the committee was curious about both of you and this was a good opportunity to have you get to know each other." He looked nervously at Luke then glanced away. "I've told him all about you, Luke, so don't be concerned. He understands you have a problem stuttering and would rather not speak."

Giving a slightly uncomfortable but pleasant nod to Luke, Champion turned to Ethan. "So, Mr. Brown, I hear you were quite a sensation when you played with the Negro team in Buffalo."

"There are a lot of good players there, sir. I was lucky to learn from some great ones."

"What brought you here?"

Hesitating a moment, Ethan decided for Harry's sake to put aside his reticence to talk about personal things. "I learned that some close friends of mine, actually they're more like family, lived here in Cincinnati. Nathan McNair was like my father and now he's laid up with crippling arthritis. I figured if I was here, I could help out his wife, Georgia."

"So you played for one of the farm teams here?"

"That's right. They paid me enough under the table so I could help out the McNairs and feed myself."

Harry joined in. "Until six months ago that is. Aaron, I told you about the new ruling, right?"

"You did and I was sorry to hear it."

Noticing Luke's confusion, Harry filled him in. "On Dec. 11th, the National Association of Base-Ball Players voted unanimously to bar any club which may be composed of one or more colored persons."

"This is the first appearance of a "color line" in Base-Ball," Aaron commented. "But since we are now a professional team, we don't come under the association's ruling since they cover amateur Base-Ball. That's why Harry hired Ethan. It's his only chance to play unless he wants to move back to Buffalo."

Looking back and forth at the two men, Luke shook his head in astonishment. He was stunned that anything other than talent would be considered.

"And he deserves it," Harry added, "he's one of the best

out there."

They were interrupted by a plump and very cheerful housekeeper. "Mr. Wright, supper is on the table."

"Thank you Mrs. Cole." Rising, he waved his guests before him. "Gentlemen, I hope you agree with me that Mrs. Cole can make healthy food taste heavenly."

The other three kept up such a brisk conversation at table that Luke was able to relax and enjoy the meal. He was a bit surprised to find himself relishing the crisp vegetable salad and vegetable soup and the hot, hearty rye bread. For desert they had fruit compote that Harry assured them was sweetened with honey and not table sugar. His guests tried to keep a straight face when he waxed eloquent on the subject of health but he was so sincere they didn't want to offend him.

When the meal was completed, and cups of herb tea had been, somewhat finished, they went into Harry's office to sign their contracts. Neither player was literate and they struggled painstakingly to get their names on the paper. While they were finishing, Mrs. Cole knocked on the office door and informed her employer that two gentlemen wished to speak to him and Mr. Champion. When they left, Bryon wandered around the office. He saw a piece of paper lying on the desk but since he couldn't read, he didn't know what juicy information was before his eyes. He did recognize the name Luke penciled in at the bottom of the page since Sam had taught him to sign his name. It was the team roster.

Player:	Position:	Age:	salary:
Harry Wright	Centerfield	35	$1,200
George Wright	Short stop	22	$1,400
Asa Brainard	Hurler	25	$1,000
Douglas Allison	Catcher	22	$800
Charles Gould	First base	21	$800
Jolly Lloyd	Second base	21	$800
Fred Waterman	Third base	23	$1,000
Ethan Brown	Left field	19	$800
Donald Trumble	Right field	20	$800
Ray Mason	Substitute	19	$600

Luke Jenkins to replace injured Fred Waterman at third.

Reality finally was sinking in. He was actually a member of the famous Red Stockings. He felt such a euphoria, he didn't notice how subdued Harry and Aaron were the rest of the evening. Ethan noticed, however, and wondered if the visitors had anything to do with him being a Negro. He had heard some flack and knew it was just a matter of time before there was real trouble.

#

Running his hands over the bright, new flannel uniform, the reality of how big an opportunity this was, hit the new third base player. The Red Stocking's uniform was white with a big red C on the chest, red stockings and a black belt. Bryon slipped his white cap on his head and took a deep breath. *I'm really one of them. But can I live up to it?*

The players groaned good-naturedly as Harry called them together before the game for his traditional speech. Donald Trumble put his arm around Luke's shoulders and whispered in his ear, "Harry keeps his wings taped to his back so they won't show. If you do half of what he says, you'll be better than me, kid," Trumble winked. "Harry Wright is well known for being a health nut and he wants to make us nutty too."

"Okay, pipe down fellas. Now, I know most of you know my rules but we all need reminding now and then. You know it is very important to be in good shape if we want to be winners. You know my rules about not drinking and no tobacco. Good clean living is what we want to represent. The harder rule to follow is good diet but I want you to try your best and if you have any questions, just ask.

"All right, boys, we have a big game today with the Mansfield, Independents. Keep your heads and play our game and we'll give our fans what they come for. Oh, and don't forget the new rule on getting an out. Old habits are hard to break but remember not to let the ball bounce before you go for it. You have to catch it on the fly now to be an out. Good luck out there."

Bryon could not shake the self-doubt. He doubted not only his talent but his courage as well. The only thing he could compare the feeling to was when his mother was killed. He ran then and hated himself for it. He looked out at the crowd, swallowed hard and fought the desire to run. He found his brain shutting down from pure panic.

"Hey, kid, you okay? Need to come out?" Harry was truly concerned at the wild-eyed look on the boy's face.

Luke tried to look confident when he shook his head. The movement brought a wave of nausea. Suddenly he had to pee but there was no time.

The game began. He had crazy disjointed thoughts randomly passing through his mind as he stood a little to the left of the third base bag. The first crack of the bat sounded distant, like an echo in his head. He was terribly afraid he was going to be sick right here in front of everyone. *I'm a coward! I thought I had outgrown it. What a time to learn a thing like that*, he frowned as his knees turned to water.

The thought was interrupted by a crack and shouts. The ball came hurtling fast, bouncing ten feet in front of him. Instinct took over as his body calmly and without thought,

120

fielded the ball and whipped it to the hurler as the rules required. The runner was thrown out. Utterly amazed that his reflexes were working just fine, his breathing eased and the nausea lessened. Still, he felt as though he were standing beside himself watching someone else move. *Guess I know where that saying comes from now.*

He grounded out on his first up at bat. In the third inning it was his turn in the order again. Even though the ball seemed a little out of focus, Bryon was determined to drive the evil from him so he would be safe. After two balls, he caught an inside pitch right on the sweet spot and took off for first without checking where it had gone. The roar of the crowd confirmed what he knew when it left his bat so he turned the corner for second. Glancing out to the left field where his ball had gone, he saw the player had almost reached the ball that had flown over him. The thought ran through his head that if other teams would learn to relay the ball like Harry had taught them to do, he would stop at second. Bryon made his decision and headed for third, beating the throw by three steps. A triple was rare in this game and the crowd went crazy. After that he felt completely normal and began to enjoy the game. The Red Stockings won, 48-14.

#

"Luke, I mean Bryon Hancock could never have done the things you accuse him of. What I want to see is a warrant for his arrest if what you say is true."

"I don't have a warrant. I'm an attorney. I have been asked to look into the rumor that he is playing ball for you since I was going to be in the area."

"Oh? And who asked you to look into it, mister?"

"The Federal Marshal in Oregon. You see, I knew Bryon's family. I'm worried about the boy becoming violent again. He could get hurt. He needs to be taken to a place that is safe for him."

"Like the lunatic asylum you say he escaped from?"

"Exactly."

"If he did kill someone there, it was in self-defense. He's a good boy. Look for yourself. He isn't here."

"I know that. I've seen two of your games and I've been watching for him. Where is he, Mr. Jenkins?"

"Couldn't tell you."

"Can't or won't?"

"Hey, I'm not one who would ever stand in the way of the law. I'd surely do my duty if I knew where the boy was. He just up and left one day. I figured he was tired and needed a break. Wanted to do some traveling. I suspect he's riding the rails somewhere. Maybe he'll take up with some other farm team some place. He isn't all that good but some hard-up team might pick him up."

"I have a feeling you are lying to me. You could be in real trouble if you are. Obviously you care about the boy or you wouldn't have given him your last name. I'll find him whether he is going by Luke Jenkins or Bryon Hancock. And don't you try and interfere or you'll be buying more trouble than you can handle."

"Whew, for a minute there I thought you were threatening me. But since I don't know nothing, guess I don't have to be afraid. Good day to you, sir."

Sam wasted no time that day writing to Harry Wright suggesting that he get Luke a different last name to go by . . . immediately.

#

The season was a little more than half over when he first saw her. She was embarrassed when he glanced over at the stands and caught her staring at him. She blushed and looked away.

Pulling his attention back to the game, Luke tried to concentrate. It was hard. Between plays he snuck quick looks. She was always turning her head and flushing every time he saw her. She had a beautiful English rose complexion set off perfectly with thick chestnut hair that had a shine that could blind a man. Her small, delicate frame made Luke feel big and

122

clumsy.

That is exactly how he felt when a ball blew by him.

Harry exploded. "Luke, what are you trying to pull? Someone pay you to tank this one? Another stunt like that and you're out."

Luke was more embarrassed about the girl seeing his error than the manager. After that, he ignored her and concentrated solely on the game. Well, almost solely. He focused enough to hit a double with a runner on.

The next day they were off on a four game road trip. As he rode the rails, Luke wasn't seeing the scenery in the window he stared through. He was seeing the beautiful smile of a girl.

Back in Cincinnati, a young woman was sitting at her desk, trying to capture with her lead pencil, the man who had captured her fascination. Tall, dark blond, big, expressive eyes and a generous mouth that made her shiver. Closing her eyes, she tried to imagine what it would feel like to have those big arms pull her against his chest. Chiding herself mentally for thinking such immoral thoughts, she checked her calendar. She couldn't wait for the next home game.

#

Wracking her brain again and again, Abby tried to think of a way to get rid of her cousin LuAnne for a little while so she could try to meet her ball player after the game. Being new in town, she didn't know anyone who could introduce them but this was the fifth game she had been to and she was tired of waiting.

She cheered louder than anyone when Luke hit a double to bring in two runners and lengthen the final score to 32 to 15 in the ninth inning. As the crowd surged out of the stands, she turned to LuAnne. "I'm going to go shake the hand of that man who hit so well. I'll be right back."

"Oh, no you don't. Your father told me to never leave you alone in public. He thinks you're too head strong. I'm coming with you. Besides, he's gorgeous, I want to shake his hand too."

They had to wait behind a crowd of well-wishers and

123

before their turn came, Luke was rushed off by Donald Trumble and two of his friends on the club, Ray and Jolly.

"Come on, Luke, you'll never get out of there if you don't escape with us. We're taking you to my favorite restaurant to celebrate. You played terrific out there today. Good job."

Basking in the attention from his teammates, he let himself be swept along to Baywater House. He didn't notice a determined young woman dragging her irritated cousin behind her.

For a moment, Luke wondered if the reason Donald and crew were being friendlier lately was because they were trying to influence him to turn his back on Ethan. Instantly feeling guilty for that uncharitable thought, Luke determined to enjoy himself. He had heard of Baywater House and was curious. This was the first time he had ever eaten in a fine restaurant.

When they were seated, Luke suddenly wished he had not come. The snow white linen, crystal and silver, these were things he didn't feel comfortable with. *What if I shame myself? What am I supposed to do with three forks and two spoons?* Feeling like a bull in a china shop, he sat stiff and uncomfortable until he noticed a woman sitting two tables away. After that, he forgot to think at all.

Abby could see him out of the corner of her eye as she studied the menu. He was staring at her like a hungry animal. She could see his naked emotion before he turned his head in embarrassment. *Oh, I knew it. He feels it to.*

Leaning over, LuAnne whispered, "Stop staring at him. You're embarrassing me."

"I'm not staring at him, silly. I'm staring at my menu."

"Then tell me what you are thinking of ordering? Tell me anything that is on that menu."

Slamming her menu down, Abby glared at her cousin. I'm not very hungry. I'm just going to have the soup d'jour."

"If you want to meet him so bad, go over there and introduce yourself."

"LuAnne! I wouldn't dare. I'm a lady."

"Good grief. You were going to do it at the ball game."

"But that was to congratulate him and lots of people

were shaking his hand."

"This is ridiculous. Here's the waiter. Let's just eat and get out of here."

Luke watched her cheeks grow even rosier as she argued with her friend. *I wish I knew what she was saying. I wish even more I knew what she was thinking.*

He didn't notice when Donald ordered for him. When the food came, he did not recognize what was on his plate but he wasn't in the least interested in food. He forked down the tasteless meal without complaint as he continued to stare at the lovely girl. Occasionally she met his eyes and they would exchange brief, shy smiles before he would again look away. *Blue... her eyes are the same color as my favorite shade of bachelor button's.* He was not paying much attention when one of his friends asked him how he liked his food.

He looked at his fellow ballplayer and shrugged non-committedly.

"Sorry, Luke. I guess we should have ordered something else for you. Escargot is pretty fancy food. You're probably a meat and potatoes kind of man."

"Give it up, Jolly. He isn't paying attention to us or the food. In fact, I'd say the joke's on us. All he has eyes for is that dame. Maybe we should help him out, what do you say?"

Luke's ears perked up at this. He shook his head vehemently and reached out for Donald's arm but he was too late. He watched helplessly as his friend walked up to the girl and introduced himself.

"Hello there, miss. My name is Donald Trumble and I would like to tell you that my friend there, Luke, thinks you're beautiful. He wants to know what plans you and your friend have for the day?"

Her heart beating with excitement, Abby thought furiously. She didn't want Luke to think they were following him. Amazingly, her cousin came to her rescue.

"We are celebrating my cousin Abby's birthday. It was yesterday actually but she was busy and so I couldn't treat her until today."

In a move he thought was suave, Donald put his hand on

125

the back of Abby's chair and leaned over her. "Well then, happy birthday, pretty lady."

This man was making her nervous. Why wasn't Luke over here instead of this meathead? Manners never failing, she replied, "Thank you."

"Hey there, sweet sixteen and never been kissed? How would you like my friend Luke to change that tonight?"

"I am eighteen and this is outrageous. How dare you? How dare he?" Pushing the man's hand from her chair, she flung her anger toward Luke in a killing glare. Her temper died in an instant when she saw the horror on his bright red face. She watched him fling back his chair and storm from the restaurant.

Looking back at the rude ball player she spoke scathingly. "Some friend you are."

#

The atmosphere was festive but with a definite underlying tension the night before the big game. The last game of the season was being played against their arch rivals, the cross-town club, the Buckeyes. Harry had thrown a ball club dinner in his big home. He took plenty of razzing from his players about all the healthy food he served up. "Night before a game like this is no time to break down and ruin the body," he sheepishly told his boys. "Tomorrow night's the grand shindig if we win. Then I don't give a hoot what you eat or drink. For a few days at least."

After the dessert of fresh fruit pies was finished, Harry drew both Ethan and Luke aside. "I've been meaning to talk to you boys. "I've had a lot of pressure on me all season about you, Ethan. You know how darn prejudiced folks can be and now I'm getting some heat from our opponent about playing against you tomorrow night."

"But, Harry, I've earned that right! You know I have!"

"I know it and you know it, but some people don't care about the stats. They think you'll bring us bad luck. As if our perfect record gives them a leg to stand on. But the point is, there is such an uproar about it, that I'm afraid if I play you

126

tomorrow, there will be real trouble and then I wouldn't have you come next season."

"Folks I've talked to had no trouble with me playing!"

"I know. Most of the citizens of Cincinnati are fine about it. A few loud voices are the problem. One of our biggest investors is originally from Georgia and he brought his prejudices along with him. In fact, he showed up trying to make trouble that night you and Luke signed your contracts. I've been trying to keep him at bay all season but since the manager of the Buckeyes is giving us grief, the two have teamed up to make trouble. They say there is a lot of anger about you but from what I hear, most of the trouble is from the dock workers who aren't even local citizens. Base-Ball is how they pass their free time away from home and apparently they have too much of that since they're causing an uproar." Harry had a hard time looking Ethan straight in the eye. The only way he could justify this was knowing that if things went wrong, then Ethan would have to return to Buffalo.

"Cincinnati has become the Base-Ball capitol of the world this year and there is a lot of focus right now. I think if we can ride this out, then next season people will have gotten use to the idea and everyone will settle down. That's why I won't play you, and I'm sorry for it. Truly sorry."

Ethan dug his fists into his eyes then slapped his thigh. "I'm one of your top players. Why can't they see that? Don't answer. I know. I've known all my life even if it doesn't make sense. Harry, you're in a bad position and I understand. Just don't like it."

"Neither do I. Thanks, Ethan. That's one down. Now, about you, Luke. If we . . . I mean, when we win tomorrow, the press will be all over every player like ham on rye and there is just no way we can keep the secret about your, uh . . . you know." He cleared his throat nervously. "Anyway, with the hatred we've run into about Ethan here, I'm as nervous as a newborn babe about reaction to you. It makes no more sense than the attitude toward Ethan but it is just as real. Maybe someday the world will become more enlightened. I certainly hope so but until that happens, we have to be careful." He saw

127

the bitter frustration reflected on the mute man's face and squeezed his shoulder. "At least you can't argue like Ethan here." Harry sighed heavily. "Listen, I promised to protect you, son and I intend to keep that promise."

Harry nervously tapped the table a moment then added, "Luke, I didn't want to tell you this. I figured there was no need to worry you needlessly but now I guess I'd better. I got a letter from Sam telling me it was more important than ever to watch out for you but he couldn't tell me why. He said it was crucial that I give you a different name. I decided that Luke was common enough and changing it would raise too many questions with the club so that is the real reason I gave you a new last name. It was easy enough to tell the guys Sam had recently learned your real name so you were using that instead of Sam's. I saw how confused it made you but I didn't want to scare you. Castleberry is a good name. My mother's maiden name actually. Anyway, Sam wouldn't tell me what it was all about but he's a good man and I trust him. Tell you the truth, the whole thing gave me a funny feeling. I may be overly cautious but you're young. Just nineteen. You have years ahead of you. Both of you. Sometimes you have to pick your battles so let's be patient this time and hopefully the future will be better."

Chapter Twelve

Abby sat nervously in the stands awaiting the start of the game. She was nervous for more than one reason. She had finally decided to take matters into her own hands. She was tired of the stolen glances and bashful smiles. She knew Luke was painfully shy and doubted he would ever take the initiative since that terrible Mr. Trumble had shamed him in the restaurant last month. As soon as the game was over, she would act.

It seemed as if half the city had shown up to see the two rivals play. The Buckeyes had plenty of fans but the majority were rooting for the famous Red Stockings. Ray had taken

Luke's place at third and from the start; it was obvious he was not comfortable at that position. Normally he played outfield and his nervousness made his movements clumsy and slow. Again and again, the Buckeyes took advantage of this and sent the ball his way. In six innings, four bunts came toward third but bounced out of bounds and each time his response was too late to make the play. Most first and third base players stood a step or two on the far side of their bag to defend against this bunt but as many times as Harry yelled at Ray Mason to get over, he kept drifting back to the other side of the bag.

In the seventh inning, Harry had finally had enough. He pulled Mason and put Luke in. The crowd sighed in relief and cheered their encouragement for Luke.

The first time he came up to bat, he was too tense and swung early three times in a row, fouling to left each time.

"Settle down out there, Castleberry," Harry hollered. "Play your game."

Stepping away from the plate, Luke sent his manager an apologetic grin, rolled his shoulders and came back to the plate. He hit the next pitch hard but it wasn't square on and the ball grounded to the shortstop. The man bobbled the hard hit and it fell to the dirt allowing Luke to reach first and Donald Trumble was safely on second.

Asa Brainard followed with a great pop over the head of the man in right field, bringing in the two runners. Jolly Lloyd brought the inning to a close with a pop fly straight to the second base player and the Red Stockings were down by one point heading into the eighth.

The first Buckeye thrilled the crowd with a rare triple and even with the relay throw Harry had taught his players, the man was safe at third. Luckily, no one else was on base.

The next man up was picky about the pitches and finally the umpire had to warn him and started calling strikes. After the second one, the man got serious and swung at a poor pitch. The ball dribbled straight to the hurler who started to throw it to first, then snapped his head around toward the man on third. He held the ball and the runner was safe on first.

Hoping that Luke was no better at defending the

Fair/Foul bunt, the next Buckeye striker sent one toward third. It made a great hop out of bounds but Luke was moving the moment it hit the bat. He flung the ball to the hurler who threw it to first, beating the runner. The defender at first threw it to second to catch that and get the third out. The runner from third made it home but it didn't count.

Now it was time for the Red Stockings to close the gap.

Nerves were high and the first two strikers, feeling the pressure of the eighth inning in this crucial game, went down one and two. Groans and booing from the crowd did not ease the problem but luckily, Harry's brother George had nerves of steel. He put the ball between the center and left field for a nice double. Harry singled to first and suddenly the air was charged with excitement.

Trumble was cocky enough to keep the momentum going and his single to third, where George was already standing, loaded the bases.

The cheering was deafening as Luke walked up to home plate. He was not thinking of himself as Luke or Bryon, as a mute or an unwanted son as he faced the hurler in that moment. He was wearing the uniform of a Cincinnati Red Stocking and that was how he saw himself; a professional Base-Ball player. He could not wait to get his bat on that ball. The very first pitch was a beauty and Luke felt like he was moving in slow motion as he took his step toward the hurler and put all his bulk behind his swing.

The cheering stopped instantly and only a few gasps could be heard above the pounding feet of the runners. George crossed the plate followed by his brother and then a triumphant Trumble. The Buckeyes stood helplessly watching the ball sail so far over the head of the left fielder who was running for all he was worth, that they forgot to set up for the relay throw they had learned by watching the Red Stockings. By the time the player had reached the ball, Luke had made it home and the crowd erupted. A grand slam was almost unheard of in a game where a home run was an anomaly because of the large size and poor quality of the ball and the slow pitches. With no outfield fence, all hits were played.

The deflated Buckeyes were only able to score two points in the ninth and the Red Stockings won the day.

The revelry was exuberant and Luke was surrounded by well-wishers. Harry stayed at his side, explaining many times that Luke was shy because of a speech impediment and no one seemed to care. His hand was pumped repeatedly and he was sure he would have bruises from the pounding his back took. During the mobbing, he was given a note by the club's ball boy. He tucked it away and when the tumult had calmed down, he searched out Donald and asked him to read the note.

Trumble had apologized profusely for his actions a few weeks before and had gone out of his way to be friendly to Luke. It had taken awhile but Luke finally forgave him for his blunder, as Donald called it, and had accepted him and his two cronies again as friends. Donald took the note and read it, trying to hide the smirk on his face. "It's from some girl named Abby saying she'll be at the dance tonight." His mind started racing to come up with a way to have some fun with this without angering Luke. Donald was a typical bully who loved feeling empowered over those he called friends and this big, silent man was a curiosity to him. "So you're going right?"

Was it here? The girl he thought of as his English rose was at all the games. He lived for her gentle smiles and if this was who the note was from, how could he ignore it? Panic seized Luke. He wanted desperately to go but he had no idea how to dance. Identifying the problem, Donald asked, "Let me guess, you don't know how to dance, right?"

Nodding in affirmation, Luke shrugged as if it did not matter.

"Don't worry about it. Jolly and his wife love to dance. I'll set it up so you come by their house an hour before the party and she can show you how to do it."

Shaking his head, Luke thought this was too big of a step for him. And although he did not consciously admit it to himself, he didn't entirely trust Donald, Ray or Jolly.

"Come on, kid. You got a new suit and all. Just try it and at least come for the supper. It's our celebration after all. Then if you decide you don't want to dance, no problem."

Agreeing to this, Luke headed home to put on his handsome new suit.

#

The blue serge suit was stiff and uncomfortable. Feeling conspicuous, Luke stepped back and helped hold the wall up beside a potted plant. The Dennihy Mansion was even bigger than it looked from the outside if that was possible. He watched people come down the wide staircase that led from the entrance hall to the grand ball room where he was hiding.

He was right, it was her. There she was, with the girl who was always with her and a man who appeared to be her father. He took little notice of the other two. Abby was wearing a gold filmy dress and although Luke hadn't the slightest idea about fancy materials, he could see it made her look like an angel. The color set off her chestnut hair piled artfully on her delicate head. He wished her dress wasn't cut so low. He imagined every man in the room was staring at her and he didn't like it. Luke felt a primitive urge to threaten any man who came near her.

Just as he feared, she was noticed. Every dance found a line of hopeful males vying for her attention. Her dance card was filled within minutes so the unlucky ones had to settle for conversation between songs. Luke hadn't move from his perch and had watched in despair while her card filled, knowing his slow, awkward signature would repel her, therefore he had no hope of holding her in his arms.

The dance was half over when Ray's wife noticed the young man she had taught to waltz, secluded behind the big plant. She felt sorry for the handsome ball player. Apparently he had a lisp or something that made him too shy to speak. With a reassuring smile she approached him and cajoled him into dancing with her.

Luke was too stiff at first but with the patient encouragement of the woman, he soon relaxed and his natural rhythm and grace kept him from disgracing himself. When the

132

dance ended, the wife of another ball player, with a word from her thoughtful husband, asked Luke to dance.

So that's how it is done with a man too shy to ask, Abby thought to herself as she was whisked around the floor by another boringly polite gentleman. Squelching a feeling of guilt, she decided to ditch the next man on her card.

When the dance ended, Luke escorted the woman back to her husband, bowed politely to his partner and turned to leave.

She was standing right behind him, an inviting smile on her face, her arms held up to dance. The music had just begun. The Blue Danube Waltz sweetened the air as he took her into his arms for the first time.

Abby had been anxious to finally talk with him but now that she was in his arms, speech seemed like a burden. They simply stared at each other and all thoughts fled. She doubted her tongue would even work when all she could do was feel.

Irritated at the press of people around them when they needed their own world to move in, Luke slowly spun them toward the French doors. Abby was so lost in his eyes she didn't notice they were outside until he suddenly swung her into wide, swinging circles. She flung back her head and laughed at the freedom of flying with this beautiful man who looked at her with such heat.

Breathless and smiling, they slowed and his hand tightened on her waist. She watched in both horror and excitement as her fingers moved, completely of their own accord up his shoulder and wound into his thick, silky hair. She felt a rush of emotion when his eyelids slid lower and he pressed his head into her fingers and moved it back and forth.

When the music softened to a finish, he stilled, his arms tightening around her. They were in a far corner of the big patio, under the shadows of a sheltering dogwood tree. Slowly, he reached out and touched her hair, then drew a finger gently down her soft cheek in awe.

He wasn't surprised when he found himself entering one of his moments even though they came so rarely now, but he was stunned at the strength of it. The only other person he had

133

ever consciously touched with his gift was his mother. This was different. He felt the connection with Abby as if their spirits joined. The beauty of the feeling when he felt at one with nature was one thing; this joining felt as if beams of lights were wrapping Abby and him into each other. He experienced the hammering of her heart, the rise and fall of her breast, the emotion."

Luke watched her eyes widen as he touched her feelings, her very essence. She appeared almost frightened by what she was suddenly sensing. Never had she imagined that two people, two strangers could become so absorbed by each other that there was almost no separation of thought and feeling. Could he read her mind? Chiding herself for fantasizing, she decided to test her ridiculous suspicion. *Kiss me, Luke!*

His eyes immediately dropped to her lips. She leaned into him as if pulled by a magnet and they fell into what was the first kiss for both of them. She felt his lips soften against hers as the kiss deepened.

Luke had the sensation sinking, of actually falling into the kiss. *How can I feel like I'm melting and at the same time feel like I've conquered the world? Can you hear me as I hear you, Abby? Do you know what I'm feeling for you?*

"I saw her dancing with a ball player named Luke Castleberry." LuAnne said. "They went out on the patio I think."

Her uncle looked at her with disgust. "I've told you she is head strong and I have asked you to keep me informed of her escapades. Why didn't you tell me right away or go chaperone?"

"I'm sorry, I didn't think there was any harm. Other couples have been dancing out there since there is such a crush in here. It wasn't until the song ended that I became worried and told you."

"Do a better job as chaperone or I'll send you back to your mother in St. Louis. Maybe I'll send both of you. Louise could keep any girl in line." He hurried out onto the patio and looked for his daughter. There were a few other couples dancing but he couldn't see the gold lamee dress. She must have slipped back in, he decided. He was turning to leave when he saw the moonlight reflect on gold beneath a huge dogwood tree beside the far corner of the patio. His daughter was kissing a man.

Appearing calm on the outside, he strode purposely toward the unlucky couple. "Abigail, go into the house immediately." He watched with narrowed eyes as his daughter gasped then turned toward him, deeply flustered, hands flying to her cheeks. "Young lady, you have disgraced me beyond words."

Watching her flee into the ballroom he felt his anger grow and his fists clenched as he swung around on the culprit. The two men stood stiff and frozen staring at each other for an age. "Stay away from her or I'll have you horsewhipped. No dirty Base-Ball player is going to lay hands on my daughter if I can help it." Not waiting for an answer, he went in search of Abby.

Her father's anger couldn't really touch the thunder-struck young man. He leaned up against the fat trunk of the tree and looked out at the stars. He felt as if he were soaring. He folded his hands over his chest as if the intense feelings would fly out if he let go.

While her stern father went to bid good evening to their host, Abby watched for Luke. She grew frantic when he didn't come in. Starting for the French doors, she mentally stomped her foot when her father called her back. "Abby, we're leaving right this minute."

"I have to get my wrap, Father. One moment." Though she hated to do it, she couldn't think of any alternative so as she was tying her cloak around her shoulders, she moved next to Donald Trumble and quickly whispered, "Tell Luke to write me at school. Abby Peterson at "Boston Finishing School for Young Ladies".

"Sure, okay." Donald saw Mr. Peterson waiting impatiently and didn't ask any questions. He watched the girl leave with her father and wondered what had gone on.

After Luke calmed down, he went back inside in search of Abby. He searched everywhere but she was gone. *How will I ever find her again? Now that the games are over, she won't know where to find me. I don't even know her last name.*

Donald saw Luke searching the room and started for him then changed his mind. He decided to have a little fun with him instead.

As the carriage rolled down the tree-lined street, Abby remembered the foolish words she had spoken to her cousin earlier that day. "Don't worry so much about things, LuAnne. I just want to have some fun with Luke. I know he doesn't fit into our world. Father would never allow me to marry a man like him."

She closed her eyes and tried to recapture that strange experience. How could two people who didn't know each other, learn to love so completely in a moment's time? A thought came to her and she clasped her hand to her mouth but wasn't in time to completely stifle a nervous giggle. *Oh my word, I just realized, we haven't even talked to each other. After two months of looking and smiling, and now kissing and I haven't even heard the sound of his voice.*

Chapter Thirteen

After the phenomenal season, the Cincinnati, Red Stockings were scheduled for a victory tour of exhibition games in California. The completion of the railroad made the trip easy and fast.

As the train made its way across the endless expanse of prairie, Donald decided Luke had suffered enough. The poor kid had been morose the whole trip. Taking pity, he rose from his seat and strolled down the aisle. "Oh, Luke, I forgot to give you a message."

Luke looked back at him without interest, his eyes dulled with apathy.

"That girl, what's her name?" He wanted to draw this out and watch the mute man squirm with anticipation. "Let's

136

see, was it . . . Amy? Anyway, she gave me a message for you at the dance a couple weeks ago. You know, after the big game."

Luke's gut clenched but he tried to keep his face passive, sensing that Donald was toying with him. He nodded nonchalantly.

"I can see you aren't interested so I won't bother you."

He gasped when Luke grabbed him by the throat and stood up. He towered over Trumble and glared into his face. The implied threat was felt by the smaller man and he felt the fingers slowly begin to squeeze. He grabbed Luke's hand with both of his, to no effect.

"Geez, Castleberry," he rasped. "I was only teasing." He could feel the eyes of the other players seated around them. "I'll tell you," he whispered hoarsely. He was instantly released and took a moment to rub his throat. Swallowing, he said, "You have a problem with your temper, Luke. You need to work on that."

Luke knew that was true but at the moment he didn't want to hear it. He continued to glare at Trumble.

"Okay, okay. "Abby told me her last name was Peterson and she wants you to write her at school in Boston. She's at *The Boston Finishing School for Young Ladies.*

Feeling both joy and despair, thoughts raced through Luke's head. *She really does care for me. I didn't lose her after all, except maybe I have. I can't write. What am I going to do?*

It was easy for Donald to read the expression on the big man's face. Deciding that maybe his fun wasn't over yet, he made a suggestion. "Hey, buddy, I know you can't write so why don't I help you out with that? You can't let a pretty woman like her get away now can you?"

Scrounging up some paper, they began right away with Donald asking Luke to nod about anything he liked that Donald suggested. When Luke pointed to his throat and then to the letter, Trumble shook his head. "No, that isn't a good idea yet. First let her get to know you before she learns you're a mute."

Taking the man's arm in one hand, Luke pointed to his throat again and then tapped the letter firmly.

"Okay, okay, it's your letter. Luke had no idea that the friendly, simple letter he okayed, somehow turned into a flowery and romantic declaration of love. And there was no mention of Luke's defect.

The deceptive letter was posted in Wichita.

For a while, the club had a great time playing to the cheering crowds in California but over time it grew a little monotonous and the players looked for various diversions during their off-times. One night, in the beautiful young city of San Diego, Donald decided to have some more fun with good ole Luke. Gathering his two cohorts, they knocked on Luke's hotel room door. When he answered, they grabbed him by the arm and ushered him down the hall, talking as they went. "We've been worrying about you, pal. Looks like you and that girl are getting mighty serious from the way her letters sound. We figure you two will probably be getting married soon and we feel it is our solemn duty to make sure you're ready."

All kinds of possibilities went through Luke's mind. Engagement rings, wedding clothes, possibly a gift for Abby? He followed trustingly as his friends led him out of the hotel and into the night. A walk of a few blocks brought them to an elegant Victorian mansion. They were pleasantly invited into a lush and vibrant sitting room by a middle-aged woman in a red velvet evening dress.

It was a party of some kind. Luke tried not to look as shocked as he felt at the indecent dresses some of the guests were wearing. However, the men appeared upstanding and decent as they visited with the ladies so that was some comfort. Occasionally a couple would ascend the stairs and disappear. He decided there must be other activities offered at this party and wondered if they would partake in any of them. Perhaps there was dancing, he definitely enjoyed that.

His thoughts were interrupted as Jolly brought over three young ladies. "So, Luke, which one do you think is the prettiest? Just point."

Surprised at his rudeness, Luke shook his head and looked away embarrassed.

"It looks like I'll just have to pick for you then." Jolly looked the girls over carefully and pointed to a tall, willowy blond. "You'll do. Honey, you take our boy here on upstairs with you and show him what's what. He's a novice so go easy on him, oh and don't bother trying to talk to him. He doesn't like talking."

"He won't talk at all?" the slender girl asked.

"Nope."

With a shrug she reached over and tugged on Luke's hand. He quickly looked down at her and shook his head. He didn't know what was going on but he had a queasy feeling in his stomach that told him it wasn't good.

The young lady sidled closer and whispered in his ear. "Don't worry, baby. I'll take good care of you. There's nothing to be afraid of. My name is Sadie and I guarantee after tonight you'll never forget it."

Reluctantly, feeling sick and trapped, Luke rose and followed the woman up the stairs. She pulled him into a small room that reeked of perfume. His eyes flew to the unmade bed and he jerked back his hand. She quickly closed the door and ran her hands up his chest and began slipping his jacket from his shoulders.

Luke grabbed her wrists to stop her, understanding now the money he had seen Jolly give the middle aged woman. He was in a whorehouse. Finally he recognized the dark feelings for what they were, a warning. Shoving the woman away, he opened the door and fled. The cacophony died as the crowd below watched Luke race down the wide staircase. The wild look on the young man's face struck the crowd as hilarious and loud laughter followed him as he elbowed his way through the crowd to the door. He found his way back to the hotel and alternately sat brooding and pacing the floor in his room for most of the night. He was rooming with Ethan who was a sound sleeper so he didn't worry about his restlessness bothering him.

It was near dawn when he heard the obviously drunk threesome stumble down the hall past his door. After debating a minute, he quietly slipped out his door to go confront his so-called friends. When he reached the room Donald and Ray shared, he started to open the door when he heard the laughter from inside.

"Could you believe that idiot was too scared to go through with it?"

"Told you he wasn't man enough. Would have been a waste of money if you hadn't been so randy tonight."

"Ole Luke will probably have to ask me to take over on his wedding night." He guffawed and choked out the words, "as if there's gonna be a wedding night for a dummy like him."

Early the next afternoon, Luke was sitting in the lobby waiting for the rest of the club to assemble for the trip to the game. His head was leaning back against the high, leather chair and his eyes were closed when he heard Ray's nasal voice. "Hey, Luke. Did the little girl scare you away?"

The temper and sense of betrayal he had been trying to hold in snapped. He lunged at Ray, threw him to his back and started pounding his face. He felt himself grabbed by two pairs of hands. Donald and Jolly pulled him off their friend but quick as lightening, Luke swung and caught Jolly on the chin causing lights out for that man. Then he turned his anger on the real problem. He knew now Donald Trumble had never been his friend. He hated himself for his naiveté, and he was going to make Trumble pay for that.

The two men circled each other, Donald warily, Luke confidently. The heads of both men swiveled when they heard Harry Wright shouting from the top of the stairs. "You two knock that off. You know the rule about fighting."

The second string third base player was thrilled with what Luke did in the next ten seconds. One snap to the nose and the crack was easily heard in the silent room. As Donald began to fall, another fist gave him a cauliflower ear, another swing bruised a kidney, and that one lifted the poor man enough for a fourth punch to break his jaw. So as it turned out, both men were out of the game that day. One on the bench, one at the doctor.

"You must be an idiot after all, you know that don't you?" Ethan stood glowering at the benched man. "There

140

wasn't a player on this club who didn't know Trumble was playing you for the fool you are."

In his familiar gesture of despair, Luke clench his fingers into his hair and pulled, rocking back and forth as a substitute for yelling.

The agony in Luke's face cooled Ethan's anger. "Don't worry hotshot. I'll be your pal and I won't treat you like a pet dog like Donald did."

Life was calmer and definitely more peaceful for Luke after that. He sensed Ethan's respect and returned it. He knew the other players looked down on him for his friendship with the ex-slave but he no longer cared about their opinion. Trumble had cured him of his hunger for approval. The only drawback with Ethan's friendship was that he couldn't read and write so Luke could not continue his letters to Abby. Her letters continued to reach him almost weekly throughout most of the winter. He was too self-conscious to ask any to read them to him so he bundled them together and kept them tucked away.

Spring found the club back in Cincinnati, ready for another outstanding season. They were welcomed as conquering heroes and afforded every privilege the city could shower on them. That is, everyone but Ethan Brown. The furor over the Negro ball player had escalated while they were in California. Newspaper editorials and barbershop gossip had fueled the fire until Harry had no choice but to let him go. He knew Ethan's life would likely be in danger otherwise. The black man appeared to take it well much to Harry's relief. Only with Luke did Ethan reveal his true thoughts.

"You're the only white man I know who can understand what I'm feeling, Luke. You know it should be what's inside a man that determines how he is treated. My color offends the purty white folk and your silence does the same. What's a man to do?"

Ethan's pride made it hard for him to accept the concession prize from Harry Wright although he knew it was done out of respect. He became assistant manager. Harry told him just to use the word assistant so the pig-headed, hate-

141

mongers would see him as a servant and leave him alone. "Doesn't matter what others think, Ethan," Harry told him, "as long as you know I think of you as my right hand and I'm paying you like it too."

#

Maybe I'm moving around too fast for his letters to catch up with me, Abby thought. Or maybe he is jealous of me spending time with the blue blooded crowd. He probably thinks I'll fall in love with some aristocrat. She wished she hadn't written about all those dumb balls and soirees her father had been dragging her to. He knew she didn't want this European tour but would he listen? Does he ever listen to me? she asked herself. If she had her way she would have gone to college instead of that ridiculous finishing school. Abby already knew how to bow and scrape, she'd been doing it all her life. Does Father actually think I'm going to marry some Lord?

A big sigh from Abby earned her a nasty look from a nearby matron for interrupting the piercing soprano performing an Italian aria. And right here in Italy, no less. She wondered what her father would do if she cut her graduation tour short? Maybe I'll get sick and need to go home. Or maybe I'll tell him I simply can't live without returning for the Red Stockings second winning season. Sighing again, she pictured a tall ball player an ocean away and asked his image, do you still think of me?

Abby Peterson had been making a splash in all the fashion centers of Europe that year. London, Paris, Stockholm, and now in Milan, men were throwing their hearts at her dainty feet. Her natural English beauty and her elegant new wardrobe were certainly more than sufficient to attract the male species but there were a few others just as pretty and with the added attraction of titles. What made her such an original was her aloofness and bored demeanor. The cream of society worked hard to affect these traits but since she sincerely felt those emotions, she succeeded where others failed. Being unapproachable made every eligible bachelor and many who

142

weren't, want to approach her. Her father was thrilled at first then furious as she continued to turn down excellent offers for her hand. One morning at breakfast, he confronted his stubborn daughter.

"Abigail Peterson, you have to make up your mind!"

"But, Father, I already have. I don't want any of them."

"That isn't an option."

"You can order me to marry one of those fops, and you can write up the contracts but you cannot force me to say 'I do' at the altar and I most certainly will not."

Throwing up his hands in defeat, Peterson stormed out of the breakfast room of the rented villa muttering under his breath.

"Now maybe he'll let me go back to Cincinnati."

#

With their second season ready to begin, Harry looked back at what they accomplished that first year. His team had finished with an official record of 57 wins, 0 losses and that didn't include all the exhibition games they had won. The manager grimaced when he thought about the financial outcome of the grand experience of professional Base-Ball. The total profit for the year was $1.39.

The second season began as the last had ended. The famous club was burying every opponent. During a game against a poor Chicago club, two young black boys shyly introduced themselves to Ethan. "You're our hero, Mr. Brown. We're gonna play ball just like you some day." Little did the two brothers know how right they were. In 1884, Moses Fleetwood Walker and Welday Walker would play major league ball, some of the few Negroes to do so before the clamp down at the turn of the century of integrated play.

#

"It wasn't a complete victory, but at least I should get there before they've played too many games," Abby whispered to the pale moon as it hung over the endless ocean. She leaned out over the ship railing and enjoyed the warm night breeze that ruffled her hair. "And I'll finally find out why the letters stopped. I just know there is a good reason. He loves me. Oh, Luke, please still love me."

#

She's here or is it a dream? Maybe I wished this so often I'm hallucinating or maybe it is just a girl that looks like her. Frightened by that thought, Luke glanced again at the breathtaking woman smiling at him from the stands. He grinned and focused again on the striker. *No! No one else could look like her.* His smile grew and even though he tried to wipe it off his face, his excitement would not let him. He thought of the small carving he had carried in his canvas game bag all season in hopes she would come and his anticipation to be with her grew. Before Abby, he never dreamed he would find someone who could look past his handicap and see him as a whole person the way his mother had. Sitting in that stand was the proof it had happened.

Never had Abby wanted anything to end as much as that darned game. She was sure time had slowed. The crowd stood and cheered at the final out as their club won again. Abby hurried down the bleachers and shouldered her way through the crowd. In disbelief she saw him run off the field and disappear into the team quarters and her heart sunk. I was sure he would come right over and talk to me, she thought. Lifting her stubborn chin she marched toward the small building. Well if he won't talk to me, I'm certainly going to talk to him.

Her cousin had caught up to her. "Where are you going?"

"LuAnne, I'm going to go see, Luke. I'll see you at the house later."

"But, Abby, you shouldn't see him alone. It isn't seemly."

"It's broad daylight, there are people everywhere. Give

144

me a break here!"

"Okay, but your father won't like it."

Abby watched her walk away then went in search of her young man.

Luke rushed back outside looking for Abby. He saw her walking toward him and quickly hid the gift behind his back. When she reached him, he smiled shyly and held out his offering.

She took the carving and looked at the image of herself as she had appeared at the dance, the tiny wooden arms lifted for a waltz. Her breath caught and she stood dumbfounded, carefully examining the miracle in her hands. Blinking back tears of delight, she smiled warmly. "Oh, Luke! This is the most amazing thing I've ever seen. Did you do this?"

He nodded, his smile widening.

"I can't believe you never wrote me about this unbelievable talent. I have never seen a more beautiful work of art in my life. Thank you." She was a little confused when he didn't respond. Compliments must embarrass him, she decided. She didn't mind, she would help him get over his shyness. Hope blossomed full and rich when she looked into his deep brown eyes that shone with points of light so bright she was sure she could see into his very soul.

"I was wondering, why did you stop writing me?"

He didn't answer. The light in his eyes began to dull and the smile began to melt off his face.

"Did you write but because I was traveling the letters didn't catch up with me?"

He blinked hard and slowly shook his head helplessly. He watched her confusion grow and then the irritation came. His eyes widen in agony as the full import of his mistake crashed down on his head like a hammer. He had trusted Trumble to write what he had instructed. *She doesn't know I can't talk.* His knees buckled and he stepped back as the pain roiled through him. *Why did I trust Donald? I'm a fool!* his stricken mind wailed. *I can't go through my mute routine. I hate it, I hate it! Why do I have to be a dummy? Why can't I be normal so she could love me?*

145

His head bowed with the pain.

"Luke? What's wrong? Why won't you talk to me?"

Moving like an old man, he turned and walked away.

She stared at him in shock, her world rocking beneath her feet. "How can you be so rude?" she called out to his retreating back. "What have I done, Luke? Why won't you talk to me?" She continued to watch him as she blinked back the tears. Embarrassed and angry at being so easily taken in by this charlatan, she pulled her pride around her like a cloak and stomped off.

She came to the edge of the ball park and feeling weak, she leaned up against a poplar tree to steady her breathing. The hurt kept growing until she felt heavy with it. Abby looked at the amazing carving in her hand and shook her head. Nothing made sense. How could he have done something like this and then . . . and the way he looked at her; but he just walked away. She slid down and wrapped her arms around her knees and concentrated on holding back the tears.

"Well if it isn't little Abby!"

"Go away."

"That's no way to talk to the man who wrote you so many love letters."

Her head snapped up in shock. "Oh, Donald Trumble isn't it? What are you talking about?"

"Maybe you didn't like my letters. It's just that I'm not sure what kind of things a dummy would write, if he was smart enough to write but I tried my best, little lady."

"I don't understand you."

"Come on. Don't tell me you don't know by now? I saw you trying to talk to the idiot. You have figured out that he can't talk, right?"

She was embarrassed when she realized her mouth was hanging open. Her throat was tight but she managed to whisper, "What do you mean he can't talk?"

"He's mute, sister," he smirked. "Dumb as that tree behind you. You know, from your letters, I kind of thought you liked what I wrote. And since I can talk, and other things a man should know how to do, I thought maybe you and I could have

146

some fun? How about it?"

"Mr. Trumble, if you do not leave this very second, I am going to scream at the top of my lungs. And if I weren't a lady, I would tell you where to go this instant."

"Get down off your high horse, Miss high and mighty. If you're not too good for an idiot, you're not too good for me." When he saw her take a deep breath and open her mouth, he stuck his hand out. "Okay, okay. I'm leaving. Just an idea."

As soon as he was out of sight, she took to her heals and ran home. LuAnne tried to talk to her as she raced through the parlor and up the stairs but she was completely ignored. Abby locked herself in her room, threw herself down on her bed and expressed the anger and pain with hot tears.

She wanted nothing to do ever again with Luke Castleberry but she didn't know what to do with all those feelings. How could he be so cruel to keep such a secret? Abby focused on the sense of betrayal she felt at him keeping such a secret so she would not have to think too deeply about the real reason it was over. No proper lady could marry someone with a handicap such as his. It simply was not done. She was so crazy about him she knew it would be a monumental chore to get him out of her head. The clouds of dreams she had held to for a year burst into showers of tears and this would have no silver lining . . . no hope.

"Where is Abigail?"

LuAnne was afraid she would get the blame for whatever had happened to her wayward cousin. "She's upstairs. I'm not sure what is wrong but she has been crying for hours."

She was relieved when her uncle hurried up the stairs instead of interrogating her.

When she heard the door open, Abby wiped at her face and sat up. "Father!"

"What's the matter, sweetheart?"

She thought she would just die if he found out about Luke. "Nothing. I'm tired is all."

He walked over and sat beside her. "Please don't treat me as if I'm dense. Something is very wrong. Don't keep secrets from me, Abigail."

Knowing she had to tell him something, she gave him part of the story. "There was a man after the game who insulted me. He made a crude pass and I was ashamed. Leaving LuAnne was wrong and I'm just embarrassed about the whole thing."

Her father looked at her doubtfully. "Of course what you did was very wrong, and dangerous, young lady; but the daughter I know wouldn't let that tear her up so much. What aren't you telling me?"

"Nothing, Father. That's all."

He stared at her until he was sure she would not add anything more then stood to leave the room. His eyes fell on the small wooden carving setting on her dresser. Moving to pick it up he asked, "Where did this come from?" One look revealed a remarkable likeness to his daughter. "Abby, who gave this to you? This is you!"

"Oh, um . . . it, um, that man. The one who insulted me; he gave it to me. He said he had a friend carve it as a gift for me."

A sudden instinct gripped Anthony Peterson. Turning the statue over, he felt his world tip when he saw the bear claw signature. Six years ago, he had seen that same signature on a carving in Adrian Hancock's cabin. *I've found Bryon Hancock.*

"Tomorrow is the championship game. Abigail, you will introduce me to the man who gave you this."

"Why, Father?"

"Because the boy who carved it murdered a child in a lunatic asylum and then escaped. He is criminally insane and the public must be protected from him."

"No! It isn't true!"

He turned and pinned her with a penetrating stare. "What do you know of this boy, Abigail?"

"He isn't a boy. He's twenty-one."

"He is nineteen. How do you know him?"

"I . . . I don't. The man told me is all."

"Is the man a ball player?"

"No, of course not."

"Are you being a bit too adamant?" He walked very slowly toward his daughter. "You know the boy who made this.

148

I believe you are lying to me, girl!"

Abby had never seen such a look in her father's eye before. He didn't appear sane. For a split second she was sincerely frightened for her safety. "I never lie to you. Why is this so important? What does this boy have to do with you?"

"That is none of your concern. *Your* only concern is to answer my question, now."

"I'm sorry, Father. I can't help you. Maybe that man will be there and . . ." She reeled from a slap she didn't see coming.

"I've never laid a hand on you before so this should show you how seriously I take your betrayal, Abigail." He watched her scoot back on her bed and cower against the wall. "Tell me how you know the boy!"

"I don't," she whispered as her throat closed in terror. The man staring down at her was a stranger. His face was so twisted and filled with obsession that she actually now did fear for her life. "I'm sorry. I don't know him," she tried again to whisper but no sound came out.

"Tomorrow we'll settle this. Don't think we won't." He gave no more thought to his terrified daughter as he went downstairs, considering his plans for Bryon. He thought of LuAnne and followed her soft humming into the kitchen.

"I want to speak with you." He ignored her nervous start. "You left Abigail alone today. I've warned you about that. You'll have to go back to your mother."

"No, Uncle Anthony. I'll do better."

"Do better right now by telling me what you know about a boy named either Bryon Hancock or Luke Jenkins."

"I don't know a boy by either name."

"Abigail does, though."

"She does? I haven't met him. We do know a man named Luke Castleberry, though. He's a ball player."

Charles grabbed her shoulders, hurting his alarmed niece. "Does he speak? Tell me, can he talk or is he a mute?"

"What? Uh, well, he must be able . . . um, actually I've never spoken to him. Abby went to talk to him after the game today. Ask her."

"But you have never heard him utter a sound, is that right?"

"I guess so. Actually, you've seen him."

"What?"

"At the dance a year ago. He was the man kissing, Abby."

LuAnne ran to her room and locked the door when her uncle slammed his fist into the wall and began to yell.

Chapter Fourteen

Impatient to get on the field to warm up, Luke almost brushed by the couple who were approaching him expectantly, but at the last moment, recognizing Abby's cousin, he stopped.

Holding up her hand to stop him, she spoke quickly. "Luke, I wanted to introduce you to Abby's Father."

Taking the proffered hand, Luke nodded his head politely.

"Hi, young fellow. I've heard a lot about you. I'm Anthony Peterson. So, where are you from, Luke?"

Staring at his feet, Luke refused to point out that he was mute. *She must not have told them. I don't care if they think I'm rude.*

The pleasant smile on Anthony Peterson's face grew into malicious glee as he listened to the wonderful silence. Luke didn't see that look or notice the triumph in the smooth voice as the older man spoke. "You have no idea how very pleased I am to meet you, Luke. Good luck at the game today."

Peterson watched the ball player walk away then spoke gruffly to his niece. "LuAnne, go on up to your cousin. I'll join you shortly."

Rolling her eyes at the way LuAnne was kissing up to her father, Abby stuck her chin on her fist and stared at the back of the bald head in front of her.

"So, Uncle Anthony, do you want me to peel you

150

another orange?"

"No thank you, dear. I'm fine."

LuAnne hoped he was fine; fine enough not to send her back to her mother. She didn't want to live with a woman who was so vain she chose a city to move to that had her father's name, and almost hers. And she has to tell everyone we know, every time she sees them. Darn that Abby. If she ruins this for me, I'll never forgive her, LuAnne frowned.

While waiting for his turn at bat, Luke scanned the crowd. There she was, looking gloomy. He was even more discouraged when he noticed how pale and drawn her features were. *I hate myself for hurting her like that*, he thought.

Ten thousand people were there that day to see the historic game between the Brooklyn, Atlantics and the Cincinnati, Red Stockings. It was June 14, 1870 and after 130 consecutive wins, Harry's club was looking at a tough and determined opponent. Most games ended with high scores but it was apparent from the outset that this would be a defensive battle where fielding skills shone and set the mark for teams to follow.

From the start, Luke knew something was wrong with him. He had not been able to sleep the night before, seeing Abby's tortured face in his mind and reliving the wrenching truth over and over. *She doesn't want me because I'm a mute; inferior, a fraud. I should have found a way to make sure Trumble gave her the truth.*

Although he had not broken down emotionally, his eyes seemed to be slowly leaking. He kept wiping at them but they remained foggy and the lack of sleep and tension made his vision swim. He struggled to hold his own through the first half of the game and he struggled even more to care. It was more luck than anything that got him on base twice but he did not score either time before the third out came.

He let a ball get by him in the fifth and was grateful that Ray was there to back him up from left field but the runners advanced and the crowd booed. He glanced at Abby but his vision swam again and he could not clearly see her, though her head seemed to be down.

Harry did not give up on him, though Luke later wished he had. Neither club was able to gain an advantage and everything was tied up, seven all in the ninth so the game moved into an extra inning. Extraordinary hits were met with breathtaking fielding to end the hopes of both clubs to claim victory in the tenth inning so they moved to the eleventh.

Brooklyn buckled down and got some solid singles to move their runners at the top of the inning. They were on a roll and when a runner came in to break the tie, their fans went crazy. Brilliant fielding by George Wright set in action a double play to stop the Athletics and give the Red Stockings a real chance to come back. They only needed one to tie and two for a victory.

Douglas Allison and Charlie Gould both hit singles and waited anxiously while Trumble waited for his pitch. He hit a bunt so weak that no one was surprised when he was thrown out at first but he advanced the runners to second and third.

Rubbing his eyes, Luke blinked hard, swung his bat to his shoulder and strode toward the batting box. Once he got there, his movements were slow and he gingerly stepped up to the plate and squinted at the hurler. He didn't feel set when the first pitch came but it was so perfect, he automatically swung. Too late. He hunched his shoulders against the booing, shook his head to try and clear it and got set. The next pitch looked so fuzzy as his eyes watered profusely, that he actually closed them when he swung.

"Strike two!"

The crowd was on their feet, screaming and yelling threats and insults.

Stepping back from the plate, Bryon rubbed at his eyes again and held them shut for a few seconds. His vision cleared and he prepared for the third pitch. It was high and inside. He was glad he could see or he would have been beaned. He watched the hurler take his time. The man studied the ball in his hand and then looked at Luke. He bent low and brought his straight arm forward in his underhand pitch. The ball was a lot faster than normal and a feeling of unreality crashed down on Luke as his vision blurred. He gasped and swallowed air, stepped and frantically swung at the ball.

"Strike three!"

Luke was tempted to put his hands over his ears to shut out the roar of dismay and fury from the spectators but instead he closed his eyes. Swaying from a loss of equilibrium, he quickly opening his eyes again. Angry faces were everywhere. Without realizing it, he had dropped his bat so quickly he bent to retrieve it and hurried to the bench. Burying his head in his hands, he listened to the sounds of Asa hitting the ball high to center field. *If he gets the runners in, maybe they'll forget what I did,* he hoped.

The loud groan told him the center field player had caught the ball. The game was over. The Brooklyn Atlantics won, 8-7 in the 11th inning. The winning streak was over.

"Can you believe it? No way we should've lost to a team like that. What got into our guys, messing up like that?"

"I'll tell you what got into our boys. Someone who never belonged in Base-Ball to start with."

Abby's ears perked up as the complaining fans grew angrier.

"What you talking 'bout, Aster?"

"I'm talking about Luke Castleberry, only that wasn't his name when I knew him. Old Sam Jenkins gave him his own surname. Changed it I guess."

"You knew that clown?"

"Yeah, I knew him. Jenkins gave him my spot on the team 'cause the little idiot was making him a bundle whittling wood carvings for him. I've been wanting to teach him a lesson for a long time. Bet you don't know what the real problem with this guy is?"

His friends leaned forward, waiting.

"Good ole Luke is dumb. Can't speak a word."

"No way! You mean Wright put an idiot on his team?"

"That's exactly what I'm saying. And you all saw how it turned out."

"But that's the guy who blew the whole game for us. The idiot should be lynched."

Abby was relieved to hear another man speak up. "Don't

forget he was the best player in the big game with the Buckeyes last year."

Lots of people were turning to listen. "Bet that game was just a fluke. You all saw how bad he was today."

"Hey, that's a good one. Luke the Fluke."

"Yeah, Luke the mute fluke. That's him. I say we tear him apart. Who does he think he is mixing with normal folk?"

Not waiting to hear more, Abby bounded down the bleachers and raced to where she had seen Luke disappear with his team. She didn't even hear her father calling after her.

The club had gone into their dressing room and listened to Harry try to put things into perspective. Words like 'everyone has a bad day' and 'satisfaction in doing our best' fell flat. Nobody felt better afterwards including Harry. Ethan and Luke had just emerged from the building when Abby came flying up to them.

Taking Luke's hand, she shouted above the noise, "Follow me, quick."

He looked at her with question in his eyes and didn't budge. She tugged but it was like trying to move a tree. "You have to come with me, there's no time. I heard an old teammate of yours talking to a crowd of men. He told them you're mute and they're blaming you for the game. They're planning on hurting you. Please, we have to get out of here!"

Ethan rolled his eyes and shook his head at his stubborn friend who was looking around belligerently for the men who dared threaten him, Ethan took hold of Bryon's other arm and pulled. "We'll debate it later, Luke, right now run. I'm sure Abby is right and half the town wants to kill you. Our days with this club are done."

"I know a back way out in case they have guys waiting at the front," Abby told them as they began to run. The two tall men hunched over as they maneuvered through the crowd so they wouldn't stick out so much.

Reaching the bleachers, Abby dragged Luke behind them and they ran to the far side where there was a small gate.

"I was afraid you meant this way. It's always locked during games," Ethan informed the nervous woman.

"But we can't go back. They'll hurt him. We'll just have to climb over."

"You sure you want to come with us? We can do it easy but you, a woman and all? Why don't you go on back now and we'll take it from here?"

"No. I want to make sure he's safe. You go first and Luke can lift me over to you."

"All right. I just hope you don't get slivers." Ethan leaped up and grabbed the top of the wooden fence, his wiry body easily scaling the height. When he dropped to the other side he shouted back. All set. Send her over, Luke."

Luke boosted her by the foot, worried when her skirts caught at the top and exhaled with relief when she dropped into Ethan's arms. He quickly followed and the threesome walked briskly away from the ball field.

"Where is Abby?" Anthony Peterson barked at LuAnne. "I don't see her anywhere."

"Find her and get home. I can't worry about her now, I have business with some men." He went in search of his two new business associates, the only men there that day who seriously intended to kill the ball player. When Hancock did not appear, Peterson instructed the men to search the surrounding area if they hoped to collect their fee.

#

Setting down his china cup, Ethan glanced nervously around the quaint tea shop. He was surprised they hadn't made a fuss about having him there. He saw Luke covertly studying Abby as she daintily sipped her tea. "You could have gotten killed back there, pal."

Luke had become fairly adept at simple communication with Ethan using facial expressions and motions. He knew he was putting his friends in danger and he was determined to change that. He pointed at Ethan and Abby and shook his head. He then pointed to himself and made running motions with his fingers.

155

"It isn't just you, buddy, I've been hearing talk about them wanting only lily white people working for the team. My time as assistant manager was about up anyway so I'm coming with you. But I do agree that this lady here needs to get home so she isn't caught up in this mess."

Vigorously nodding his head toward Abby, he again pointed to Ethan and made a separating gesture.

"Not on your life," Ethan said as he flashed his big dimples at his friend. "You're stuck with me, like it or not. Base-Ball is over for us so we had better face that and make some plans."

Covering his face with his hands, a shudder went through Luke. Starting over was becoming harder. *Where to from here? And how can I live without Base-Ball? Now what will keep the blues at bay? How will I survive losing both Base-Ball and Abby?*

He remembered when he fought hard to earn respect as a ball boy and after getting beat up that first time, he thought he had become nothing again. *That is what I feel like now, a nothing. Maybe it would have been better never to try.*

With his face covered, he didn't see the two men who entered the tea shop. The other two had their backs to the door.

The waterfront thugs Peterson hired looked nervously around the crowded tea shop. There were too many witnesses in here. The leader, a short man with a barrel chest quietly spoke to his accomplice. "We gotta lure him outa here before we knife him."

The second man nodded in agreement. He was tall and muscular, most likely Nordic with his white blond hair.

They approached the table where their victim sat with his face buried in his hands. "Excuse me. Are you Luke Castleberry?"

Luke's head popped up in alarm. He glanced at Abby to see if these were the men she had overheard. She gave a small negative shake and shrugged her shoulders.

"Guess if you are, you can't answer us. Could you come outside for a moment? We have a private message for you from your manager, Harry Wright."

Both Ethan and Luke knew Harry would never send someone they didn't know to tell them anything important. Ethan turned to look at the men standing behind and to his side and from his angle near them, he saw the gleam of a knife stuck part way into the belt of the shorter man where his coat gapped open. The hair stood up on the back of Ethan's neck and without needing any more warning, he leaped to his feet, kicked his chair into their path and shouted, "Run, Luke!" The two men tripped over each other trying to get away from the chair and fell into a heap of arms and legs on the floor.

Forgetting that he was the only target, Luke feared first for Abby's safety. He leaned over the table and picked her up as if she were a doll. Tucking her securely in his arms, he rushed behind the counter, through the kitchen and out the back door. Setting her down, he took her hand and began to run. Since Ethan was the fastest man in Base-Ball, he soon caught up with them. They heard the back door of the tea shop slam open as their pursuers followed.

As they ran, Luke pointed to his two friends, shook his finger toward a side street they were approaching and then indicated that he would go straight.

Not liking it but recognizing that they had to get Abby away from the danger, Ethan agreed and taking the girl's hand, peeled left into the narrow lane.

The swarthy leader called out to the taller ruffian, "you're faster, follow the mute. I'll follow these two. We can't leave any witnesses."

Running easily, Luke glanced over his shoulder and was disappointed to see only one man following him. He assumed they would leave the others alone. He was crossing an empty lot when he faced front again, just in time to run full tilt into a third man. He started to push away when the man grabbed him by the arms. "Where you going in such a hurry? My pals catch up to you then?"

Even after four years, Luke recognized Arnold Astor. Understanding came immediately. This was the man Abby overheard starting all the trouble. Hearing the pounding of approaching footsteps, Luke tried to wrench free but Astor had seen Luke's pursuer and clung to him with surprising strength. Luke brought his knee up but before contact was made, Astor flinched away from one of man's worst nightmares. With his release, Luke decided he had one chance to come out of this and that was to eliminate this man immediately. He faked a jab with his right then rolled all the power of his considerable bulk into a left swing. Astor was unconscious before he hit the ground.

Whirling around to meet the original threat, Luke was unnerved to see the blond man already upon him, knife flashing with the dying sun. His hands came up to ward off the thrust but he was too late. The blade caught him in the stomach. He collapsed to the ground as a cold sensation immediately spread in all directions, the knife biting into muscle. The man threw himself on his victim to drive the weapon further in.

Luke's hands grabbed the man's knife hand to stop the thrust from going deeper. A fraction of a second later and it would have slipped to the hilt.

In a brilliant move, knowing his victim's strength was greater than his own, the man gave into the pressure of Luke's hands as he reversed his thrust, pulling the sharp knife up through Luke's left palm. Luke jerked his injured hand away and in that second the man again shoved down on the knife, this time with both hands against Luke's one.

Luke gasped in silent pain as the knife worked its way deeper, slicing away layers of thick muscle, searching for a vital organ.

The thug grew frustrated when Ethan and the woman outran him. The black man helped the woman run by holding her elbow and carrying part of her weight. The two were flying. Ethan shouted into her ear that he would find a place for her to hide and draw the man away.

"Be careful," she panted. "He has a knife!"

Rounding a corner, he pointed to a shed beside a small home. "Run behind there and when it's clear, get home to safety," he shouted.

She did as she was told, sprinting off behind the shed before the man came around the corner. As soon as she heard the man pass, she stealthily moved back to the road and watched Ethan turn right at another corner. I knew it. That'll take him right back to the street Luke is on, she thought. He's going back to find him and I'm not going to be left behind. When she saw the man turn out of sight, she ran to follow.

That's what I've been waiting for, Ethan thought. Just in front of him was a stout stick which he scooped up while barely slowing. He was coming out on the street his friend took but before he could help Luke, he needed to take care of this fellow.

Instead of turning left to search for Luke, he turned right and stopped behind the blacksmith shop. When he heard the man coming, it was a simple move to pretend his stomach was a Base-Ball that needed to be hit. Ethan swung the stick hard and the beefy man doubled over and fell into a shoulder roll. As the man rolled, he pulled out his knife but Ethan was already there. His foot slammed down hard on the hilt, snapping the blade clean off.

The man wasn't out yet though. He grabbed Ethan's foot and giving it a twist, he threw him onto his back. It was no accident Anthony had hired this man. He had been fighting all his life and he feared no one. He leaped to his feet, quick for his size, and reached for his opponent. Both men froze as the shriek of a woman racing past startled them.

"Ethan," Abby drew out his name with desperate terror. "He's killing him!"

The men spun around and stared at the empty lot. One man's fear, the other's hope had them racing toward the sight.

Luke's vision was swimming in and out of focus and turning black around the edges. Nausea and weakness rolled over him like waves. He felt the knife slip farther into his body and knew he couldn't hold on. He closed his eyes and concentrated on an image of Abby, wanting her face to be the last he saw as his vision tunneled narrowed to a pinpoint.

He was hardly aware of Ethan hurtling out of nowhere, pulling the blond man off him. The knife went with him and was thrown by the impact when the men hit the ground, rolling over and over together.

Ethan had sped past Abby but she was still ahead of the second man. Spotting the knife, she pushed herself to reach it before the man caught her. She imagined his hot breath on her neck. From the pounding feet she could tell he was almost upon her. Scooping the knife up, she spun around and held it up in defense.

As if in a dream, Luke reached up his right hand and grabbed the ankle of the man running after Abby and the all important knife she was picking up. He watched from a calm distant place deep inside as the man struggled to free himself from the hand and stumbled forward, tripping and falling onto Abby, knocking her to the ground. Then the darkness claimed Luke.

Hearing Abby's low moans of terror, Ethan doubled his efforts to finish off his man. A kidney punch followed by an upper cut to the chin laid the man out cold. Rushing to the woman, he choked in fear when he saw her covered with blood, lying under the bulky street thug. He shoved the limp body away and helped Abby to her feet.

"Are you hurt?"

"No, help Luke. Hurry? Oh, Ethan, is he alive?"

Seeing the shallow breathing, he reassured her and together they lifted him over Ethan's shoulder and made their way the three blocks to the office of the team doctor. Leaving Abby to explain things, Ethan decided he had better collect their possessions from the boarding house in case there were more people who wanted Luke dead and might go there to lay in wait.

The proprietor assured him no one had been there except a ball boy who had delivered both men's bags from the ball field. Ethan paid her for both bills, quickly packed and returned to the doctor's office.

Having completed the stitching, the doctor warned them against moving his patient. "This man has lost a lot of blood. I'm afraid the knife pierced the lining of his pancreas and the stitches may not hold if he is moved."

By this time, Abby was wondering if there wasn't more to the attack than the angry men from the game. She thought of her father and his unreasonable obsession with finding Luke and decided they must hide him at all costs. Without going into details, she told the doctor Luke was in danger and this would

160

be an obvious place to look for him.

Sitting on the edge of a straight-back chair, unable to tear her gaze from the unconscious ball player, Abby finally forced herself to face a hard truth that had haunted her for years. Something was wrong with her father. It felt almost too surreal to accept the likelihood that he had sent those murdering thugs after Luke but she prided herself in honesty. It had been easy to hide from the truth because most of the time her father was a respectful man and often a loving father. The flashes of what she now understood to be insanity were few and far between. For the first time Abby analyzed the bigger story. It seemed obvious that his episodes were more severe whenever Luke was in the picture, or he was focused on a long-term search for some elusive person that had turned out to be Luke. What she didn't know was how to handle this new reality.

Another thought occurred to the concerned young woman. "Ethan, that man I killed, what if they try to pin that on you or Luke? That would play into the hands of your enemies. We have to get away where neither of you will be found."

Ethan was leaning against a wall with his arms folded. "I'm afraid you're right but you shouldn't be involved in this. You go on home now and I'll take care of our boy here."

"No."

He laughed at her stubbornness. "Okay, stick your chin back in. You can help me get him to safety but the longer you're away, the more complicated it becomes for you."

"Fine. But at least I'll know where he is."

The doctor wagged his head in concern. "I don't like it but if you're that sure he is still in danger, at least I can help. I'll have my assistant take all of you wherever you want to go in my carriage and then return Miss Peterson to her home."

#

Trying to hide her reaction to the appalling poverty in this section of town, Abby kept her head turned away from Ethan. They pulled up to a rundown shack almost exactly like its neighbors. Luke was conscious again, propped up on pillows on one side of the carriage. The two worked carefully to help him down without pulling his stitches out.

A tall, proud, white haired black woman answered the door and lit up at the sight of Ethan. "Why, it's my boy, and he's got him some friends, Nathan," she called back into the house. "Come in, come in. Y'all are welcome here, though you be the first white folk who's crossing our threshold."

"Aunt Georgia, this is Abby Peterson. Abby this is Georgia McNair, and this fellow I'm holding isn't drunk, he's been hurt and we need a place to stay for a few days."

"Shore, shore, y'all come right on in."

As Ethan helped his friend over the threshold, he explained that Luke was mute and couldn't speak. "He's a good man, though, Aunt Georgia. And he's my good friend."

"Well, he don't need to talk to me so long as he eats my food." She took another look at the big white man. "Maybe he needs a little time before he tries my cooking at that. He looks all but dead, he do. My, my, he's even taller than you, Ethan. Bring him in and be quick."

She soon had Luke lying on a freshly changed cot against the far wall. There was another bed against the back wall with a permanent occupant. Georgia's husband Nathan was completely crippled from arthritis. He had been forced to work in the cotton fields long after his arthritis already had a firm grip on him.

"Nathan here gave me my name," Ethan told the others. "He almost named me after himself. My papa was sold before I was born and so when my mama died birthing me, these two raised me up. We left Tennessee shortly after the emancipation proclamation and I won't ever step foot back there again."

Georgia looked fondly at the strong, handsome man she thought of as a son. "This boy is all we have in the world. He gives us money even though I tells him not to. We would get by with my sewing and washing, though it helps, it surely do." She gave Abby a shy smile. "Listen to me gabbing when you two must be half starved and you need to get cleaned up. I'll bring you hot water, soap and a cloth so you can wipe that poor dress down. And if either o' you are wishin' to tell me how this boy got hurt and why this pretty little lady is covered in blood, I

162

won't be stopping y'all."

It was well into evening before the cleaning, eating and storytelling was through. Luke had sipped a little water with laudanum but refused anything else.

Abby and Ethan pulled their chairs up to Luke's cot to discuss plans for the future. Ethan was the only one with a plan of any kind so he spoke first. "I know about this school that Luke could go to. It's the Ohio School for the Deaf and Dumb." He saw his friend's face flame red with anger.

Luke was remembering what happened in the asylum. He had an image of the school enforcing laws to castrate the deaf. It smacked too much of an institution. He shook his head hard but the dizziness knocked him back on the pillow. His face went from red to deathly white.

"Oh, Ethan, no. He doesn't want to. Look at him!" Abby's heart ached for the poor handicapped young man.

"Calm down, Luke. I know you aren't deaf but you need what they have at this school. There is this new science by some French guy, Le Clerc, I think is his name. Anyway, it's a way for people to learn to communicate who can't talk or hear. The school is a good place and they'll treat you well. Harry introduced me to the administrator, Charles Proctor. He worked with Harry's dad during the war helping with the underground railroad. Great guy."

When Luke gave him a perplexed look, Ethan understood and answered. "Harry and I have been talking about maybe asking you to check the place out. Seriously, buddy, I think this is just what you need."

"But what about you, Ethan?" Abby asked.

"I'm going with him."

"But how? You're not deaf!"

"What? Speak up, can't hear ya."

"You have got to be kidding!"

"I have to be getting . . . getting what?"

"I said kidding, not getting."

"Well, lip reading is a tricky art. Get mixed up sometimes, sorry."

"Oh, stop it. You aren't deaf."

"Says who? I can pull this off. I'm not leaving Luke."

"He's lucky to have a friend like you." Squirming uncomfortably, she began to speak, then hesitated.

"What is it?"

"I was just wondering . . ."

"If they accept Negros?"

"Well, yes. I understand there is some trouble with that kind of thing."

Ethan guffawed, "Some trouble? You could say that, Miss Peterson. But don't worry. Charles Proctor is a great guy. He'll let me in and fight to keep me there if he has to."

"I don't understand," Abby said. "Why would you want to do something like that?"

Ethan took a deep breath and looked down. "It's complicated. I guess you could say I want to be Abraham Lincoln."

Drawing her eyebrows together, Abby slowly said, "Okay," which was her way of encouraging Ethan to go on.

"You see, Abe gave everything he had to free my people. We were trapped in a life that we couldn't get out of." Ethan rubbed to back of his neck, hoping he didn't sound as stupid as he felt. "It's kind of . . . well, I guess youcould say I want to free Luke. He's trapped in a place that he needs help getting out of. He's come to mean a lot to me. Like a brother, you know? And I guess I don't want to start all over again. I'll be with Luke and be close enough to help out here too."

Abby was deeply moved. Reaching out she touched Ethan on the arm and said, "Well, Abe, you're my hero."

"Now none of that. The real truth is I'm just too big of a baby to want to cut the apron strings." He looked at Luke with an embarrassed grin and reached out and took his friend's hand. "Don't make me cut those apron strings, mama. I wanna come with you."

Luke tossed Ethan's hand away and rolled his eyes, but finally a big grin spread over his pale features as he nodded his head.

"All right," Abby said, "that takes care of that. There is one more thing I was thinking. Change Luke's surname to

164

Smith or something so he isn't so easy to find."

"Do you really think people will try that hard?"

"Something tells me, they will never give up."

"Do you know something I don't?"

"Give me more time to look into it. I'll tell you some other time."

"Okay, I'll wait then." He saw Luke's eyes start to glaze over. "This all work for you, buddy?"

Luke nodded weakly, hardly aware of what was being said. Floating from the laudanum, Luke looked at Abby's lips and stepped back in time one year ago tonight. The memories soothed him and kept reality at bay as he slipped into unconsciousness.

Sensing that he finally slept, the woman allowed herself to gaze on his face. She held her hands tightly clasped to resist the overwhelming temptation to brush back his hair and stroke his brow.

Seeing the yearning in the young woman's eyes, Ethan ached for these would be lovers with a social gulf between them that seemed impossible to bridge. "Abby, the driver is waiting to take you back home. Your father will be worried."

You have no idea what my father will be, Abby thought as fear of the coming confrontation grew in her belly.

Chapter Fifteen

"Are you aware of the time, daughter?"

His voice coming out of the darkness of the parlor made her jump. Her father was sitting in a wingback chair near the cold fireplace. Quickly composing herself as best she could, she answered calmly. "I know it is late, Father."

"Where have you been?"

His tone was even, maybe it would not be so bad after all. "Forgive me, I can't tell you that."

Softly he replied, "That I will not forgive, child."

"So be it."

165

"I'm afraid you have no choice. You will tell me where you have been and you will tell me where the lunatic is and you will do it this minute."

"Lunatic? He's mute, Father. Nothing more, just mute."

"Will you be reasonable, or will I have to take stronger measures?"

"Apparently you'll have to kill me because I'll never tell you!" She stood tall and defiant.

"Oh, I don't think it will come down to that in the end."

The chill in his emotionless voice spoke volumes. She was prepared for this and fully intended to lie. She had even done her homework to prepare for the lie. "Okay, all right . . . fine!" She sighed and turned away, hugging herself as if this was a grim betrayal. "I helped him on a train but they didn't want me to know where they were going for my own safety."

"What train and when did it leave?"

"It was the 7:40 headed to Chicago. But that wasn't their final destination. They want to disappear."

"I'll be leaving in the morning for an extended time. I want you to consult with my banker and hire a ladies maid immediately. You are to go nowhere without her."

"But, Father, Annie can . . ."

"Annie is the housekeeper. She has her duties and needs no more. There will be no argument. When I return home, we will discuss your future."

After waiting a cautious two weeks, Abby volunteered at the school where Luke and Ethan were now living. She began learning sign language from a handsome instructor named Randolph Fitzgerald. She did *not* engage a ladies maid.

Abby tried to cheer Luke up the day the local paper, the Gazette, put out a negative article about the Red Stockings. "The Base-Ball mania has run its course. It has no future as a professional endeavor," the paper reported.

Fans stopped coming to the games because of their single loss. Luke blamed himself for the failure of the club and suffered from melancholia for weeks when he heard that Harry was moving the club to Boston. It didn't help his mood that

Abby was spending so much time with one of the teachers. Okay, he admitted to himself, she was spending time with a very charming teacher and that was the problem.

Catching Roger's enthusiasm for teaching the handicapped was the balm Abby needed for both the fear her father had instilled concerning her future and for her thwarted love for Luke. Randolph looked a bit like him, dark blond with a tall, dignified stature and an easy going nature. He didn't have Luke's bold looks or strong frame but Abby liked his sweet nature. She enjoyed having his friendship and often had him over for supper. Occasionally she would invite Ethan and Luke also and the four enjoyed conversations that became more interesting as Luke mastered sign language and could more fully participate. During one of these evenings, Luke made a startling declaration.

"By the way, my name isn't Luke," he signed. Watching their reaction with amusement, he went on. "Sam Jenkins gave me that name since I had no way of telling him who I was. My name is Bryon Hancock."

Silence reigned until Bryon signed, "What happened? Did I shock you all dumb?" The laughter released the tension of surprise and everyone started talking at once.

Although she had known about this from her father, Abby was the loudest to complain. "You have been able to write and sign well enough for months to have told us something that important," she indignantly complained. For some reason it irked her that he would not share something so personal and crucial as his name. She didn't tell him that she had already known his real name because she wanted to keep her father's obsession a secret. "Don't laugh at me, Bryon Hancock. I can pout if I want to." She ignored him the rest of the evening and showered attention on Randolph who was a grateful recipient.

When her father returned after six months of travel, he appeared exhausted and thinner than she remembered. Time had softened the memory of his strange anger and hatred toward Bryon and she no longer feared him. He seemed genuinely happy to see her and as far as she knew, the problems had

167

blown over.

What she did not know was that he had her followed by a detective in his absence. "Tell me where she goes and what she does."

When the detective gave his first report, he told Peterson that his daughter was volunteering at a school.

"What kind of school?"

"I didn't go inside. It looked like a regular school. I saw kids playing outside."

"That's fine then, keep an eye on her when she isn't at that school."

One of the first things the strict father did was engage a ladies maid after gently chastising Abby for disobeying him on that count.

Anthony checked her mail, both what she sent and incoming. After a time, he was satisfied that she wasn't corresponding with Luke Castleberry or seeing him. She didn't seem interested in anything these days except that school. Well, that was harmless enough.

\#

After being at the school for eight months, Bryon began feeling sorry for himself. *God, why did You have to take Base-Ball away from me? Seems I never get to hold onto anything. Even my name keeps changing.*

It was strange after being called Luke for so many years to go back to being Bryon. He remembered when Abby tried to correct the spelling of his name.

"It is spelled: Brian," she insisted.

He told her, "No, my mother told me she didn't want me to be ordinary and so she spelled my name in a special way." His dark mood worsened. He tried not to think of his mother and at times when he felt low, memories of her were very painful. He wondered if he would ever get over his sense of loss. *I had forgotten until I learned my letters that she used to hold my hand and trace my name." Why did she have to go? What would my life have been like if she was still alive?* He

168

asked himself. Besides his abandoning her to her death, there was one other clear memory he had of that terrible time. She had wanted to tell him something that had happened to her when he had been born. He remembered the look on her face and he knew it was important. Whatever it had been, with the shamble his life was, he was certain that if there had been a plan for his life, he had ruined everything.

The moon had set by the time he fell asleep. He was unaware that he slept, believing himself fully conscience. It didn't seem strange to him that his grandfather Peter was walking with him. He was slightly surprised to find he could talk. It felt so wonderful to hear his own voice. It was deep and rich but at the moment that voice was complaining.

"Why did I have to lose Base-Ball, Grandpa? It was the only thing that ever made me happy."

"Is it *really* the only thing that ever gave you happiness, son?"

"Yes, Grandpa."

"Truly?"

Bryon began to reaffirm his answer then hesitated. "Well, no, not really. My mother made me happy but I can't think of that. It hurts too much. And I let her down. I left her to die alone."

"That wasn't your fault, Bryon. I'm sorry it hurts but I need to ask you why she made you happy?"

Thinking back, Bryon tried to pinpoint a memory that held the answer. There wasn't one specific moment, it was more a feeling that he always had with her. "I guess it was because she knew what was inside me."

"That's right, son. No one else has ever really understood what was inside you. You asked to be released from that trap. You wanted out of yourself, remember?"

A memory of that first fight with Lester returned. It had been buried with a pile of similar pain but now it lay exposed and ugly before him. "I remember."

"If you had stayed in Base-Ball, you wouldn't be released from your trap. Don't be angry, my son. Reach out and take what you asked for. Sometimes when you are imprisoned and you need a way out, first you have to work to make the necessary tools to free yourself."

Bryon thought of the bent spoon secured in the back of his top drawer. He had always held onto that precious tool. He remembered the patience it had taken to free the stones and nails to pound the hole through the spoon's handle. Now he needed patience to learn to free himself from his silent prison, patience to learn about the world and free himself from ignorance. "Thank you, Grandfather," he whispered in his dream.

The light of morning awakened Bryon. It took long minutes for him to accept that it was only a dream. He was sure it was important, though, so he rose and wrote down every detail of the dream. That very day, he began to soak up knowledge and sign language skills at the same amazing pace he learned Base-Ball, astonishing his teachers and his best friend. Day after day, week after week he dove into the world of knowledge and swam like a fish.

"Boy, why are you killing yourself like that?" Ethan complained. "Learning is great but there's more to life."

Bryon signed his answer. "Exactly. There is so much more to life than I ever could reach and now I have to learn fast so I can experience it all." He smiled up at his friend and issued his challenge. "Join me, Ethan."

With that gauntlet thrown, the race was on. The two young men competed at a frantic pace. It became a game; an exciting, fulfilling game. Learning became more than fun, it became an obsession for them both. They knocked at the door of the world and it opened. They discovered that their teachers loved hungry minds and determined workers.

One of Bryon's favorite past times was reading about Base-Ball in the papers. It almost broke his heart to learn that the Red Stockings were forced to fold after the 1870 season because of the financial strain. The year 1871 saw other teams turning professional, however. More rules were added in the coming years and slowly the professional sport developed. It became illegal to play games on Sunday and no beer was allowed in the ball parks. Strangely enough, the spectators had fun anyway.

#

After the first year, money became a problem for Ethan and Bryon. They ran out of funds from their Base-Ball savings and tuition was due. The embarrassed administrator talked to Abby, asking her if she knew of any means the two young men might have to take care of their financial obligation. She worried over the problem for days until remembering what that awful man at the championship game had said about Sam Jenkins making money from Bryon's carvings. The school was slowly filling up with beautiful wood sculptures that Bryon had made in his spare time so she arranged for a buyer to come and look at them. Much to her and Mr. Proctor's relief, the buyer was familiar with the bear claw sign and informed them that there had been disappointment when the artist's work had disappeared from the market.

"The value of his work has increased over the last year or two as available carvings became rare. I believe you will be pleased with the contract I can arrange."

Everyone was more than pleased and the money solved all financial problems with more than enough surplus for Bryon to gift a generous sum to Ethan's friends the McNairs. When the boys delivered the good news to Ethan's foster parents, Bryon brought another gift and placed it into the hands of the gracious old woman.

"My, my, look at this, Ethan!" She caressed the dark mahogany carving with loving fingers. "You caught my boy exactly." Ethan's long, lithe form glowed in the well-polished wood, his dimples beaming from the likeness.

Trying to hide his embarrassment, Bryon accepted the hugs and pretended not to notice the tears. It seemed to him that the grand old couple appreciated the carving more than the money. This carried them even higher in his esteem.

Wishing all his problems were so easily solved, Bryon struggled to accept what was generally understood by his

171

second year at the school; Randolph Fitzgerald was officially Abby's beau. Everyone expected an announcement at any time. Randolph was perplexed at not arriving at the sticking point himself. Every time he approached the subject, Abby became flustered and changed the subject firmly enough to discourage him. She felt guilty about avoiding the commitment and this guilt actually bound her more to him than her heart did. He was so sweet and thoughtful, he didn't even get angry the time she slipped and called him Luke when he kissed her. If he wondered about a past relationship between her and Bryon, he kept it to himself and was always the gentleman.

Needing to work off his frustrations, Bryon suggested to Ethan that they start playing ball again. A few of the students wanted to join in and Base-Ball soon became the favorite past time at the school. Bryon had read in the papers, news of some of the hurlers back east experimenting with various pitches. It had always been a gentlemanly understanding that the hurlers throw the ball slow and easy to help the striker have the best chance. One hurler shocked the Base-Ball world by throwing fast pitches. He was able to snap his wrist in the prescribed underhand throw in a way that it could not be detected. Another ingenious hurler was developing something called a curve ball. Candy Cummings from the Brooklyn Excelciors was frustrating a lot of strikers.

Bryon began practicing these new styles making everyone but Ethan afraid to catch for him. And no one would bat when he was acting so ungentlemanly.

One afternoon after Ethan had hit a number of perfect fair/foul balls, Bryon asked him why he didn't join the new Negro league in Tennessee.

"Not even for Base-Ball would I step foot in that state. I'll never willingly return to where I was a slave instead of a man. Especially not now."

"What do you mean?" Bryon signed.

Ethan looked down and cleared his throat. He started to speak, took a breath and waited. Then looking away he quickly spoke. "Nathan's dying. Georgia told me last weekend that the doctor said he doesn't have much time left. It's what they did to him in Tennessee that's bringing him to an early and painful death."

"I'm sorry. What will Georgia do?"

"I don't know but she's a strong woman and she works hard. Actually, it will be easier physically for her, and I'll help out."

Study became an escape for both men. Bryon threw himself into three things that became his world. The first was reading everything he could get his hands on. The second was Base-Ball and finally, his carving. It was only while creating beauty in wood that his emotions felt some relief from the constant pain of loving Abby and watching her care for another. Two years passed in this unsettled condition but the young man finally learned to find satisfaction by believing he was growing and expanding his world.

On a windy October afternoon as the shadows began to fall, Ethan complained that Bryon had never really learned to have fun. "You are what is commonly referred to as a fuddy-duddy. You probably think you would turn into a pillar of salt if you looked cross-eyed at someone. We've got to loosen you up and I'm going to take up the burden of being your coach. Lesson one in learning to have fun starts tonight. Halloween is coming up and I found out from some of the boys that last year, the High School Boarding Academy had some pranksters that tipped over our outhouses. Now, I'm thinking we ought to encourage them to do that again, what do you say?"

"Ethan, what are you up to?" Bryon signed.

After curfew that night, the two young men climbed out their window and headed for the academy. The moon wasn't full but it was bright enough to light their way through the trees and across three small side streets until they arrived at the high school. Staying to the shadows, they made their way back to the four outhouses at the edge of the yard. For half an hour they argued over the three potential victims that came one by one to use the facility. Two were girls and one was a boy who appeared to have a stomach ailment judging from the moans

173

coming from the latrine.

After showing mercy to the three students, they were paid in spades. "Well, lookee there, my friend," Ethan whispered. "It's the big man himself. Our stars are aligned right tonight."

Mr. Jedediah P. Armbruster, principle of the school and vocal critic of the School for the Deaf and Dumb, sauntered across the back lawn whistling a cheerful tune. The guys waited until he had been in the outhouse a full minute before placing their shoulders against the back wall and heaving together. With a groan, the building resisted for a few seconds, then rapidly tipped forward revealing their cursing victim struggling to pull up his pants. He was twisting around at the same time, trying to catch sight of the perpetrators and this action brought about his downfall...straight onto his nose. By the time he was in a presentable state and could confront the hoodlums, the young men were two streets away. He ineffectively shouted into the empty night, "I'll have you in jail for this, you criminals!"

Jogging into the woods, Ethan swung his arm around Bryon's neck and gave it a squeeze. "That should insure they come visiting on Halloween, and we'll be waiting when they do. So, Mr. Smith, how did you enjoy your first foray into the life of crime?"

Giving his friend a playful shove, Bryon signed a question. "How did you get your surname?"

Ethan struck a thoughtful pose, put a finger to his chin, and broke into an animated original song complete with dramatic motions.

One fine day, I thought I'd get a name,
My master's name was stupid
So I didn't want the same,
I looked around the town,
I looked up,
Then I looked down,
Imagine my surprise
When I saw my feet were brown
So instead of choosing white

Or something dumb like clown,
I like the name I found
Just plain ole Mr. Brown

Shaking with laughter, Bryon clapped Ethan on the back and signed, "I can see you've put some thought into this."

"Darn right. A name isn't something to take lightly like you do. Changing your name every time I turn around," he mumbled. "It's enough to make a man crazy. Why don't you do us both a favor and chose something that will stick. Something that describes you, like; how about Mr. Pasty Face, or Mr. Ghost?"

As a thank you for his suggestions he got tackled and the two friends engaged in a competitive wrestling match until they tired and headed for home.

Four days later, on Halloween, Mr. Proctor warned the students to be on the look-out for pranks. When he asked if anyone would volunteer to secure the outhouses, Ethan quickly raised his hand. "Luke and I would love to take care of that, sir." Ethan and Abby still called him Luke in front of others to avoid questions.

"Wonderful. Let me or the janitor know what you need."

As it turned out, they needed very little, just a rope. When night fell, the young men muscled the two outhouses forward a few feet then found a comfortable spot behind some bushes lining the school building. They waited in the shadows for their victims to show. Eating raisins and peanuts they had borrowed from the kitchen, they relaxed and waited until finally, they saw movement in the trees behind the outhouses.

The two men stood and made a show of needing to use the facilities, one entering each small building. They heard whispering and soft laughter as the boys moved toward the one Ethan was in.

A loud yell came from behind the outhouse, and one second later, another yell joined the first. Bryon brought the rope from his outhouse and together they helped the two boys out of the deep putrid hole. Their companions were long gone

175

so these two had to walk back to their boarding school covered in shame and other things.

The next day the school had a visit from the principle of the academy. Mr. Armbruster stormed into the entrance hall and looked around, waiting for someone to help him. He spotted two young men coming down the stairs and waited, tapping his foot impatiently.

Ethan and Bryon calmly waited for the irate man to march up to them. They listened politely to his question. "Where is your administrator?"

Turning to his friend, Ethan cocked his head. "Maybe I need some practice with my lip reading. Either that or the academy has a pest problem just as I always suspected. I believe he just demanded we share our exterminator. Should we look for the janitor for him?"

"Administrator, not exterminator," the red-faced principle shouted.

"Terminator?"

Suspecting he was being played a fool, he answered curtly, his voice dripping with disdain. "Anyone ever tell you what a creep you are?"

"Why would you tell me how cheap you are?" Ethan looked the proud man up and down. "Okay, maybe your suit is a bit tacky, but I wouldn't call it cheap . . . exactly."

Charles Proctor saved the embattled principle from probable apoplexy. His arrival rescued his stuttering colleague from the clever tongue of his student.

"Jedediah, what brings you here?"

"I am here to demand a formal apology and you are going to give me satisfaction in a general assembly of my students."

"Calm down, now."

"Don't you dare tell me to calm down, you—you--! I was in our outhouse when it was tipped over!"

Serenely, Mr. Proctor questioned, "And you think I tipped it over, Jedediah?"

"Don't be absurd. Your deviant students did. But now, after what you did to two of my boys last night? It isn't to be born!" he shouted.

"What did I do to two of your students last night?"

"You, I mean some of your students moved an outhouse forward and they fell into the hole. They came back reeking and we had to pour buckets of water on them and have them strip before they could come into the school."

"What were they doing here?"

"It was Halloween. They were doing what kids always do, I suppose. Horsing around."

"I see. And I suppose you believe it was unsporting of us not to let them tip over our outhouse?"

"I demand an apology, Proctor and you know I can get it. Your board of directors has many of the same men on it as mine does. I am an important man in this community. You've chosen a dangerous enemy this time, Charles."

As it turned out, Mr. Armbruster was right. Charles Proctor humbly offered his apologies in front of the boarding academy in order to save his job. Seeing how it stuck in his craw, Bryon and Ethan confessed their crimes to Mr. Proctor and apologized themselves.

"Don't blame yourselves, boys. I asked you to take care of the problem and I actually thought you were rather clever in how you did it. Who could have foreseen the hissy fit old Armbruster threw? I will never understand why the board knuckles under to him. Do me a favor though. Stay out of trouble after this so I can keep my job."

Ethan felt like throttling his bullheaded partner. "Stop shaking your head. I see you already."

"Then get it through your own head that we don't help Mr. Proctor by getting him into more trouble."

"Do you have so little faith in me to think I can't pull this off without getting caught?"

"Pull what off?" Bryon signed.

"I don't know yet but it will be perfect."

"No!"

"It is a serious matter of honor to redeem ourselves and

177

avenge Mr. Proctor for having to apologize. You know we have to do something, Bryon. No way can we leave it like this. Armbruster can't win!"

That very night the two followed the mean-spirited principle, hoping to overhear something that would give them an idea for revenge. It was Saturday night and they knew that he often went to the symphony so they waited outside for the concert to finish and then stalked him down the dim streets of town. They were surprised and hopeful when the esteemed professor slipped into the less than reputable Paper Doll Saloon.

"You go in there and see what he does," Ethan told his buddy. "Use that brain for more than holding your ears apart and help me come up with a plan. Tonight may be our best chance."

Trying to look relaxed and inconspicuous, Bryon wandered into the bar. He saw Armbruster playing cards and sipping a bourbon so he leaned up against a wall and watched. He found himself staring at a fancy pair of gloves lying on the table next to the man's elbow and suddenly, a fully formed plan was sitting deliciously in his mind. He pushed off the wall and nonchalantly walked by the card table, slipping one of the man's fur lined leather gloves into his pocket as he went by.

Taking his trophy back out to Ethan, he received approval for his plan and began studying the boardwalk. He found what he was looking for, a knothole, in the best place possible, near the end of the walkway bordering a side street. Checking to see if anyone was about, he took his knife, handle side down, knelt and slugged out the knothole in the wood. Bryon quickly enlarged the hole with his sharp knife while Ethan kept watch. When the hole was of sufficient size, he and Ethan scooped out the soft dirt under the boardwalk until they were confident he would fit. Recent rains had washed away a good foot of the dirt leaving two feet of leeway beneath the end of the boardwalk. It was a tight squeeze but Bryon was able to scoot himself completely under the walkway and conceal his big body by tucking his knees to his chest. After testing his plan, he crawled back out and hid around the corner of the building while Ethan leaned against a post and kept an eye on the principle through the window. These preparations had taken almost an hour but the two were determined to see this through and they both settled in for what could be a long wait.

Their patience was tested for two more hours before the great man called it a night and made his way to the door. At Ethan's signal, Bryon crawled under the boardwalk, tucked his knees and put on the glove. He slipped his hand through the hole he had made. Holding his hand limp as if the glove was lying part way folded over, he waited.

When the principle walked outside, Ethan waylaid him and pointing to the glove, he politely inquired, "Sir, is that your glove?"

"How on earth? Did you put that there?"

"No, sir. You must have dropped it going in."

"Must have." Peering through the dark at Ethan, he asked suspiciously, "Don't I know you?"

"Oh, lauzy now, Massa. I's is jes a poh slave boy who wouldn't be knowin' the likes of a great man like you, suh. Ain't it so we's all looks alike anyhow?"

With a glare of suspicion and a grunt of disgust, the man bent down to retrieve his glove. When Bryon felt the tug he held fast to the principle's hand and gave it a firm jerk. The dignified scholar slammed to the sidewalk and immediately blacked out.

The next day, the local paper ran the story that Mr. Jedediah P. Armbruster passed out in an inebriated state in front of the Paper Doll Saloon, Saturday night. There was no comment from the school board but one of his students, a Mr. Ethan Peabody, (not his real name and speaking from the safety of an enclosed carriage) told our reporter today, that he and his fellow students have been trying to keep their principle's alcoholism hushed up and regrets the public is now informed of Mr. Armbruster's little problem.

The esteemed principle maintains that he had dropped a glove and while retrieving said item, his hand became somehow caught in the glove and he was yanked to the boardwalk, losing consciousness by the contact. As a community, we owe it to Mr. Armbruster to give all the credence to his story it deserves.

#

Late March 1872 brought a heavy snowfall to Cincinnati. Abby had invited Randolph, Ethan and Bryon over to sample her latest efforts at cooking. She had given Annie the night off so she could play hostess and create without interference.

Lately, Randolph had been keeping some distance from his girlfriend hoping she would move to close the gap. He worried she had been feeling too much pressure so he made his excuses and did not join the party that evening. He may have subconsciously felt a twinge of jealousy when he suggested to Bryon that because of the snow they all postpone the event but his mild suggestion went unheeded.

After a delicious meal of grilled halibut in a rich French sauce, Abby proudly brought out her first attempt at a favorite American dish; apple pie. The boys had helped her churn the ice cream before supper so now she scooped out a big helping for each steaming piece of spicy pie.

"Now you're a real American." Ethan teased. "The English put apples in tarts, not pie."

"Hah! That is a myth. You Americans like to take credit for everything. We've been making apple pie for hundreds of years except when Cromwell banned them along with other treats."

"Well, they taste better with American apples," Ethan teased. "You won't be American until you stop talking so funny."

"Until I lose all my culture you mean?"

The three friends teased and chatted with the comfort that comes from close association and had a marvelous time. After the dishes were cleaned up, Ethan took himself off to the parlor to give the other two time alone. He knew Abby had no intention of renewing the romance between them but Ethan didn't believe for a moment she loved Randolph. He saw the way she looked at his friend and he did all he could to bring the two together. "I think Bryon wants another piece of pie, Abby. Don't starve the poor fellow."

The two were left alone at the kitchen table, Bryon eating pie while feeding her ego with compliments of her culinary talents.

Watching him fondly, Abby signed, "Watch it fella, you keep eating like that and you'll get fat." When they were alone together she usually signed instead of speaking.

"There isn't an ounce of fat on me, woman," he signed back.

"There will be if you keep sitting still studying so much. That's all you ever do anymore."

"Not true. I play some ball and I carve."

"Even when you carve you're sitting down so watch out or you'll get a fat butt."

"Abby Peterson, don't use that kind of language."

"What kind of language?"

"You know good and well what I mean."

"Well, you use that word all the time."

"That doesn't mean you can. You're a lady and you'd better speak like it."

"Hah, I wasn't speaking. What will you do, wash out my mouth with soap?"

"No, I'll wash your hands off with soap."

Abby acted highly offended, "Don't use that tone of hands with me, young man."

Grinning, Bryon warned her, "You just be good little girl, or else."

"Or else what? You'll paddle my fat butt?" She jumped up and ran but Bryon was quicker. He caught her before she reached the parlor door and threw her over his shoulder. Marching in the other direction, he took her out the back door, went up to a snow drift and threw her in. Scooping up a handful of snow, he held her down with one hand while smashing the snow into her mouth with the other. Satisfied she was well punished, he turned to go back inside but before he took two steps he found himself falling flat on his face as she lunged for his foot and tripped him. Quick as a cat, he grabbed her and they went rolling in the deepening snow. They could hardly see each other through the heavy snowfall but neither noticed the cold.

Tired of losing, she whined, "Stop being such a bully

181

and let me win sometimes!"

Bryon went completely limp and allowed her to flip him onto his back and barely pretended to resist when she ground a fistful of snow onto his mouth. Delighted with her efforts, she grabbed two more handfuls for more punishment but he was done being the victim. He flipped her over and pinned her wrists so she couldn't smash the snow into his face. He was piercing her with a fierce stare in what she knew was a mock threat. She tried to glare back just as fiercely but dissolved into giggles instead, her gaze softening under his. She watched in fascination, and something more as his pupils dilated and his breathing grew ragged. She felt his hands loosen on her wrists and his palms slide against hers. Her fingers loosened and twined tightly with his as her eyes slid shut against the blaze of his own stare. She felt his warm breath on her lips and the slightest hint of his lips brushing back and forth over her own. Much stronger was the strange and wonderful sensation she had come to believe had only been her imagination. Like three years ago, she felt him reaching into her with his powerful essence, enveloping her, heart and soul.

"No!" She turned her head to the side and tried to hide her tumult. Joking her way out of this was the only option she could think of under the circumstances. "Randolph is going to kill me if I get his star pupil sick. It's freezing out here. Obviously my wits are already completely frozen. Let's get inside, Luke. Sorry, I mean, Bryon."

Squeezing his eyes shut hard against the unbearable closing of her emotions against him, Bryon drew on all his strength to pull back, first mentally, then physically from the flustered woman in his arms. To accomplish this he had to withdraw completely from her and therefore was unhappy to learn from Ethan upon entering the house that the weather was so severe that no hackneys were working that evening.

Feeling both relief and consternation at Bryon's emotional withdrawal, Abby briskly rushed about, getting them blankets and pillows. She then hurried off to remove her wet clothes and to take herself off to bed.

After a short fight over who would take the floor, Bryon

won and Ethan slept on the comfortable sofa while Bryon bedded down on the rug in front of the fire. He took his soaked shirt off and hung it on a hook on the mantel to dry and wrapped himself in the cozy quilt Abby had given him.

In the small hours of the morning the wide awake mistress of the house gave up trying to sleep and wandered through the rooms. When she entered the parlor she stood indecisively then made her way carefully to sit in the wingback chair next to the man sleeping on the floor. She watched the fire reflect on the strong planes of his beautiful face and his sculpted chest while trying to hold back old remembered hopes.

Slipping from the chair, she knelt down by his head and softly ran her fingers through his hair. "Oh, Bryon." Sighing heavily she whispered softly, "My Luke, my Luke." Randolph's innocent and scholarly face popped unbidden and unwanted into her mind and she guiltily pulled her hand back. Indulging in one last lingering gaze, she sniffed and watched a tear drop from her cheek to his. Holding her breath, she backed away and quickly returned to her room where she was finally able to cry herself to sleep. The last conscious thought she had was, until I met you, Bryon Hancock, I almost never cried.

Abby's tear slipped to the corner of Luke's mouth. His eyes opened as he tasted her sorrow on his lips and he stared into the fire.

Chapter Sixteen

"Stubborn mule." Bryon covertly signed this message to Ethan as Abby flitted around nervously from occupation to occupation.

"Miss Peterson, tell Mr. Hancock not to sign insults to me in your home."

Bryon stood up and stomped over to his friend signing, "Keep your mouth shut you darned idiot!"

"Being deaf doesn't make me an idiot," Ethan laughed. "Although that is the prevailing notion, I thought you knew better." He laughed as Bryon gave up in defeat and slumped in his chair again. Ethan looked thoughtfully from his friend to Abby. "Why are you two so nervous?"

Abby glanced over and watched Bryon sign, "Because we should have been out of here hours ago. We could have walked. We didn't need to wait until the conveyances were running again."

"Didn't want to get my feet wet, ole boy. Besides, I wanted to eat the noon meal here so I could finish Abby's apple pie and ice cream. If she had let me eat it for breakfast like I wanted, then maybe I would have braved wet feet." Ethan looked back and forth between his two friends thoughtfully then said to Bryon, "Okay, I know why you wanted to leave. You just can't stand being around pretty women." Ethan turned his curious attention to Abby. "So why do you want us gone so bad? You've been twitchy as a cat all day."

"I'm sorry. I didn't mean to be rude. It's just that I'm expecting my father today and he can be . . . well, unfriendly to strangers."

"You mean he might want to put me out in the kitchen with Annie? Or in the stable with the horse?"

"No, it isn't that . . ." She flew to the window upon hearing the rattle of a harness. "Oh no, he's here. Oh, hurry! Go out through . . . no, that won't work. Annie's there and if she sees you running out the back she'll say something to Father."

The two men stood in alarm at her obvious panic. Something unusual was definitely going on here.

"Abby?"

"Get in the coat closet, hurry, there's no time." She forcefully shoved them both and picking up her fear, they rushed in and closed the door seconds before the front door opened.

"Hello, Abigail." Anthony Peterson was glad to be out of the cold weather and pleased to see his daughter waiting for him. "Give me a kiss, girl. It's good to see you."

Kissing her father's cheek, she smiled pleasantly. "Welcome home, Father." She had to concentrate on looking him straight in the face and not glancing at the closet. "Why don't you come into the kitchen and have some pie and ice cream?"

"Not right now. I'm expecting someone. Maybe later, sweetheart. Right now I'm going to enjoy this fire and relax a bit before my guest arrives."

The two men in the closet slumped in disappointment. They knew she would be frantic until she got her father away so they could slip out. What they couldn't puzzle out was why she was so terrified. As the afternoon grew long, they both at times considered putting an end to the farce and facing whatever wrath would be forthcoming, but respect for Abby's feelings held them back.

After a while, they managed to maneuver in the small space enough for one of them to sit on the floor, with arms wrapped around their knees while the other plastered himself against a wall.

They heard the rustling of paper for a while and occasional mutterings from Abby's father as he read his mail. For a time there was silence, then Ethan had a hard time stifling a laugh when he heard the loud snoring from the parlor. He started wondering if this was their chance to escape but before he could decide, he heard a knock on the door that interrupted the sonorous sleeper and soon they were entertained by conversation that grew more interesting as the men sat to table in the formal dining room that opened into the parlor.

"So Denver was a bust?"

"I'm afraid so, Mr. Styles. Your colleague was certain he was the one, but he apparently isn't quite the detective he believes himself to be." Peterson gave Styles a stern glance.

"Sir, we have a whole country to look in. One man is hard to find if he is determined to hide."

"It shouldn't be that hard. There aren't that many men fitting his description that are mute. Usually these freaks are both deaf and mute."

Hearing this conversation, Ethan squeezed Bryon's shoulder lending support at the shocking information they were hearing. Neither of them doubted who was being discussed.

"Mr. Peterson, you have been searching a lot longer than we have without luck. Our detective agency is one of the best in the country. If he can be found, we'll do it."

After supper, the two men made their way back into the parlor. The detective sat on the sofa and squirmed uncomfortably as his unhappy client stood over him.

"Maybe I can give you a suggestion, Mr. Styles. There was some mail awaiting me that held pertinent information. Adrian Hancock sent me a letter telling me he had heard his son may be at a school for the deaf and dumb. He could be going under another name so you need to personally send someone to each school with a description of the man. I want you to start with the Ohio School for the Deaf and Dumb which I believe is right here in Cincinnati.

"Right, sir. I'll go first thing in the morning."

Bryon jerked in shock at these words. His elbow hit the wall behind him, making a soft thud.

The detective looked around at the noise. "What was that?"

Rising from his chair, Peterson looked toward the closet next to the stairs. "Must have been Abigail. My daughter is upstairs in her room." He walked to the fireplace and leaned against the mantel. "At least she is no longer involved."

"If you don't mind my asking, what has this man done? I've never seen a person as determined as you to find someone."

"I told you, he killed a child and escaped from an asylum in Oregon."

"Of course I remember that but why is it your responsibility to spend years and what amounts to a small fortune to find him?"

"That, my friend, is personal. Just stick to your own business. If you'll pardon me a minute, I need to excuse myself. The wine you know. While I'm gone, why don't you look at this list I've started of the schools that I've heard about. Obviously, you will add to the list as you do your research."

Bryon heard Ethan cursing under his breath. They had both begun to wonder if the man would ever relieve himself. It was their luck it had to happen while the other fellow was still there.

It was another two hours before Styles took his leave.

Abby, frantic with anxiety for her friends, came downstairs. "Father, aren't you going to bed?"

"Not right now. The fire feels good and I have a lot on my mind. You go on though, it's late."

"Who was that man you were with so long?"

"Just a business associate. I'm sorry you couldn't join us for supper but you would have been bored with our discussion and business is really best kept from feminine ears."

Rolling her eyes, Abby mumbled a defeated good night and retreated to her room. Anthony watched her go, amazed that she was such a grown woman now. His thoughts traveled back to when she was a toddler left to his care when his wife died. He really had tried to be a good father. In his mind that meant giving her everything earthly possible for she was truly meant to be a queen. Would he ever get to keep his promise to her? The stunning image of Ivy Downs popped into his mind. Who knows how high she could marry if he could only secure that enormous estate for her! Certainly a lord, maybe even a duke may find her alluring with that kind of wealth. Leaning his head back he closed his eyes and wished he knew where Bryon Hancock was hiding.

The two men in the closet, besides being cramped and sore, despaired of beating the detective to the school in the morning.

Wondering how to solve an increasingly serious dilemma, Ethan decided to kill two birds with one stone and grinned in the darkness at the surprise insult he was about to deal out to the man who was somehow Bryon's enemy. Quietly, he picked up one of Peterson's boots and relieved himself into it. He offered Bryon the other boot which was gratefully accepted. After that, they settled in as best they could for a long night.

Abby came downstairs near dawn and saw her father dozing in his favorite chair. "Didn't you go to bed at all?"

"No. Wasn't sleepy."

"You look so drawn, Father. Why don't you try lying

down for a while and see if you can't get some rest."

He chewed on his pipe and shook his head, then changed his mind. "Maybe I will lie down for a bit."

As soon as he ascended the stairs, Abby went to the closet. Upon hearing her father's door close, she softly opened the closet and urged the two stiff young men out. "Hurry, he might not stay up there."

Ethan leaned close to her and whispered, "Now I know your secret. We overheard your father talking to a detective last night. He's been tracking Bryon for years. Why?"

Bending her head in shame, she admitted, "I have no idea. I'm sorry I didn't tell you before. I'm so ashamed by the whole thing. He has changed so much since we came to America and for some reason he is completely obsessed with finding Bryon."

Confused and amazed, Bryon started to sign questions but Ethan stopped his hands. "We have no time now. Abby, the detective is going to the school first thing this morning to ask for any mute answering Bryon's description. We have to beat him there, warn Mr. Proctor and be gone before we're found. Can we use your horse?"

Clamping down on her horror, she whispered, "Of course. Leave him there at the school and I'll take a conveyance and bring him home this afternoon. I'm sure my father isn't going anywhere today." Pushing them toward the kitchen and through the back door, she whispered instructions. "Get word to Mr. Proctor about where you are and your plans. I won't rest without knowing how you both are."

She watched as they slipped a bridle on the mare and led her out of the small stable and through the drifts of snow to the road. Mounting double, they both waved as they cantered off.

The students were just rising when they reached the school. They found the administrator and where ensconced in his office within minutes. After the story was related in abbreviated form, Mr. Proctor sat back and studied his hands in silence. He sighed then tapped the desk nervously. "The timing is interesting. I didn't want you boys to know this but I've been under rather a lot of pressure lately. It seems my job has even been brought into question again. The board has been increasingly unhappy over my allowing a Negro in our ranks. I want you to know, Ethan, I wouldn't have compromised my values, but since this trouble has come to you, it will allow me to keep my job. I love these students and I would hate to leave them just as I am going to hate you both to leave me. Since we don't have time to debate options right now, why don't you gather your belongings and go stay with Mrs. McNair. I'll put some thought into this and come see you in a day or two. In the meantime, I'll call the school together and nudge the students into forgetting the existence of one tall, handsome mute fellow. Now, let's move, gentlemen."

Hearing a carriage pull up, Ethan hurried to the door and waited impatiently for Charles Proctor to enter. It had been four days since they had left the school.

"Good afternoon, Ethan. Looks like you are anxious to see me."

"Did that man show up?"

"He sure did. About an hour after you left. You would have been proud of what good actors your fellow students were. Maybe they weren't quite as convincing as a certain man I know who has people believing he is deaf, but they did the job."

He turned to address Bryon. "He left, convinced that you were never there. He sure painted you to be a desperate fellow, though. I feel it is best to get you far away from here and as soon as possible."

Bryon nodded and signed. "But Ethan and I stay together."

"That's what I figured. I'm sorry to have taken a day or two longer to get back to you but I have been sending and waiting for telegrams morning and afternoon and finally the details are worked out. You both have a job if you are interested. I have a good friend I knew back at Yale, Roy Bingham. He is one of the finest scholars I have ever known. He was a professor of Philosophy at Yale for years before giving it up to become the administrator of the Nashville School for the Deaf and Dumb. I've bragged about how brilliant you

189

both are and Bryon, he has offered you a teaching position and Ethan, he has a job for you as his assistant if you're interested."

Bryon was watching his friend warily and felt his heart sink when Ethan spoke. "I'm sorry to do this to you when you have gone to so much trouble, sir, but I won't go to Tennessee. I was a slave there and I've sworn never to go back. Bryon has to go, this is a fabulous opportunity for him."

Shaking his head firmly, Bryon signed, "I won't go if you don't, Ethan."

"Don't be a fool. You've told me you were thinking about becoming a teacher. You know you want this. I thought I had taught you better than that?"

"If being a fool means I don't want to be alone again, start from scratch with nothing familiar, then I am a fool just like you were a fool to come to school with me."

The administrator spoke. "Listen, you two discuss this and get a message to me within the next few days. I have to get back to Roy before long."

The next morning when Bryon awoke, he found a letter by his pillow.

Bryon,

I'm afraid if I stay here you will continue acting the fool. I have other plans for my future so I am off to follow them. After you are in Nashville, I will write and let you know where I am. Go to Proctor today. Get your white arse out of Blacktown today. Without me there to hold your hand, you're in sorry shape.

You are going to be a great teacher. Do it, buddy.

Ethan

Two days later, Bryon left for Nashville.

#

Bryon was so lonely on his arrival in Nashville that letters became his lifeline for a while. He and Abby wrote constantly. Betsy Carter had kept up a correspondence with him so he wrote, letting her know his change of circumstances and location. He also sent a letter to her father, who normally wrote two or three times a year. Harry Wright and Sam Jenkins were regular correspondents also. In his letters, he asked everyone to keep his location in confidence for the time being. They all knew by this time about the story circulating that accused him of killing a boy at the asylum in Portland and they knew he was trying to avoid the people pursuing the story.

Pale lemon-yellow began to paint the eastern horizon when Bryon woke to a loud voice shouting, "I'm coming, George. I'll keep my promise to you, I'm coming!" Mental confusion was slow to fade as Bryon looked around him, trying to remember where he was. Nashville. And the shouting voice had been his own, the voice he remembered from his dream with his grandfather. He liked to believe he would have really sounded that way if he had been able to speak. Maybe he would have been a great orator like Ethan. Sighing, he allowed himself a moment to think of George with his pleasant, elfin features. How could he keep his promise when the boy was surely dead? Perhaps he could go back someday and try to locate his grave. The least he could do would be to pick some wildflowers and lay them on his resting place and maybe purchase a nice headstone. That would discharge his promise. Bryon hoped there was a heaven because it was beginning to seem that place would be his only hope to hanging onto friends and family. This life was tearing him away from everything he loved.

A lot of his tension eased when he finally heard from Ethan. He had gone to Chicago to work on the docks for a few weeks to make sure Bryon really took the job. Now he was back staying with Georgia and working at the docks along the Ohio River. He said in his letter that he was still reading in his spare time and asked Bryon to write the titles of any books he would recommend. The stimulating discussions by letter would bring them both great enjoyment in the future and fill a lot of the emptiness Bryon dealt with.

After the initial few weeks, he began overcoming his shyness as a teacher. He gained confidence as he realized that though his schooling had been short, he had learned enough to be fully qualified to help the youngsters in his charge. The children slowly began worming their way into his heart and the loneliness eased a little when he was with them.

He had just passed his second month there when a letter came from Abby that made him both fear and hope. Her father was pressing her into returning to England for a year before committing finally to an engagement with Randolph. She wrote of her confusion and indecision and this gave Bryon the courage to do the unthinkable.

Late one Saturday evening, in a moment of loneliness so intense Bryon lost his normal bashfulness, threw caution to the wind and wrote to the girl he desperately loved. The big man gazed out the window at the Milky Way spangled across the velvet night and allowed himself to be carried away on the romantic river in the sky. Emotions swelled and drowned out common sense and self-doubt. His mind wandered back to a snowy night and a snowball fight as waves of longing crashed over him. Picking up his stylus, he began to write.

Dear Abby:

I received your last letter and am concerned that you are going back to England when it clearly isn't your wish. You are twenty-one now and should be able to make your own decisions. Fearing I am making a fool of myself as Ethan always tells me I do, I would like to put forth a suggestion, another option for you to consider. It seems that you have been hesitant over committing to Mr. Fitzgerald. I believe this is because you have never lost your feelings for me. Having been a student these past three years, I wasn't in a position to offer you anything. Now that I am a teacher, and also I nicely supplement that wage with my wood carving, I am prepared to support a wife. You know you have always had my heart and I now lay it at your feet.

192

I am so lonely for you, Abby. I'll be in agony waiting for your answer so don't make me wait long.

All my love,
Bryon

The moment the letter was posted, the fog lifted and he suffered excruciating anxiety over what he had done. She had made it very clear she wanted nothing more than friendship since she learned of his impediment. *How could I have forgotten that?* he tortured himself.

At least she had the kindness to hurry her answer. When the letter arrived, he set it on his desk for two days before he had the courage to open it. He tried not to hope, told himself not to but it was impossible to be completely objective. Slowly, he unsealed the envelope and drew out the single sheet of lavender stationary.

Dear Bryon:

Please do not ruin our friendship by forcing something that isn't there. You know I am practically engaged to Randolph. Just think, if I had never met you, Randolph and I would never have found each other. I think it is hateful that Father is making me wait a year but sometimes we have to sacrifice what we truly want in life in order to observe societies strictures, so I will honor my father in this. I return to England with him.

Your friendship is important to me. I will write to you as soon as I arrive in England and hope to have a letter waiting from you.

Sincerely, your friend,
Abigail Peterson

Yes Abigail. You have to make sure you keep all those important 'society strictures', like staying away from freaks like me. I always wondered if people like me really belonged outside the human experience. Almost like a different species. Sorry, Miss Peterson, you will not have a letter waiting from me when you get to England, or any other time.

He viciously crumpled the letter and threw it in his waste basket. Lying down on his bed, he curled up, clutching his heart as if to protect himself against the cutting grief. Not wanting to be broken, he gathered to himself the anger he had struggled with since his mother's death. It began filling up the empty places, stiffening his spine until he was able to finally sit up without physical pain. If there was darkness inside instead of light, well that was a side effect of what it took to survive.

He learned over the next few days that his ability to carve was gone. After two frustrating attempts, he packed away his tools and focused on teaching. He wasn't as shy as he had been but it was harder to get through to the students now. They sensed his withdrawal and his coldness and stopped responding to him. When this condition continued for almost a month, Roy Bingham decided to step in and invite him to join him for his evening tea.

"How are you getting along here, Mr. Hancock?"

Bryon wondered how it was that he was a good eight inches taller than the slim administrator but the other man seemed like a giant to him. "I assume you have heard from my students or I wouldn't be called to your office, sir."

"It is true that I have observed a change in your demeanor. The first few weeks, you were shy. Now you have become an introvert. There's a difference. Don't look so concerned, Mr. Hancock. I am not angry with you. We all struggle in our own ways with change and from what I understand you have had all too many in your life. I thought it might help to talk about these changes together."

"Yes, sir," Bryon signed unenthusiastically.

"Would you do me the honor of sharing some of your history with me?"

"You want to hear about my life?"

The insightful administrator readily saw the young man's fear. "I am hoping very much you will share it."

"It isn't a very pretty story, Mr. Bingham."

194

"Pretty stories can be very boring. I assure you, I am most interested and will treat your confidences with the greatest respect and discretion." Roy Bingham was a fastidious, well-dressed man in his fifties, dark hair slicked back with a neat moustache that was waxed into a twirl at the end. Yet in spite of his strict demeanor, there was a warmth that shined through. Bryon discovered that he trusted this man and leaned on the lifetime of wisdom that stemmed from a well of experience.

So began a nightly ritual that lasted for weeks. Boring was the last thing that described the story that poured like pus from the suffering young man.

Roy Bingham was highly skilled at the new science called Natural Philosophy that delved into the human psyche and helped put together patterns of thoughts and behavior to explain and ease psychological distress of the patient.

Thanks to the Laurent Clerc, his newly developed form of communication called sign language was supplying a better option than the more popular oralism (lip reading). This enabled Bryon to share long suppressed memories and emotions to the quiet, dignified administrator.

"Let's go back to when the ball boy, Lester first beat you up. You were angry to have your hopes raised, hopes of being accepted as somewhat normal only to have them crushed by this boy's thoughtless words?"

"Right. I decided it was better not to try. But I didn't completely give up. I still had enough hope to plead with God to release me from being trapped alone inside myself."

"I see. So if I remember right, this would give your dream about your grandfather a powerful meaning?"

"Do you think it could have been an answer to my prayer?"

"What do you think?"

Bryon hated when he did this. He felt like saying, 'I asked you first' but never had the courage to question the kind but austere administrator. "It seems to have been an answer."

"And if you had stayed in Base-Ball, you would never have escaped your silent world. Isn't that right?"

"Probably."

"But that didn't take care of all the problem did it, Mr. Hancock?"

"No, I guess not."

"You are still trapped, are you not?"

"Yes."

"That is because you are afraid there is nothing worthwhile inside you to let the world see or to share with others."

Bryon gasped and the breath caught in his throat. *How does he know that?* he wondered. Suddenly he felt threatened. He had never been exposed like this and it was all he could do to remain in the chair. For the first time in his life he thought it might be better to hide alone in his own little world, free from the danger of being exposed.

"You think it is better to keep it inside so no one sees the ugliness?"

"It wasn't always ugly, sir. But God waited too long to help me. Everything inside got shattered."

"So you think God did this to you?"

"No, but he didn't stop it."

"Then he should have taken personal choice from everyone around you?"

"I guess not but I needed more help. I'm broken, no good anymore. I could have helped people, could have made a difference. I had a tender nature as a child. I had this . . . this gift I guess you'd call it; empathy or some such thing. The ability to see and feel inside living things. But now it's too late. I've lost that ability."

"And you don't think there is a power strong enough to put back the pieces?"

"No."

"You read a lot, Mr. Hancock. Have you read about the second law of thermodynamics?"

Bryon shook his head, disinterest showing in his attitude.

"The law is that everything is in a constant state of breaking down. But there is something working against that law. Scientists don't know what it is but it is real. An organizing

196

principle in the universe that brings order out of chaos; keeps things from breaking down. Let it work in you. Let it repair you."

"I don't know if I can."

"How can you live with yourself if you don't try?"

The next evening, Mr. Bishop set down his tea cup and quietly asked Bryon if he had thought about what they had discussed the previous night.

"That's all I can think about. I want you to be right but I don't know how to find myself."

"Did you find yourself playing Base-Ball?"

"No. It just kept the loneliness at bay. I was told once that Base-Ball keeps the blues away. It did for me, but after it ended, I learned the blues were waiting patiently for my return. As long as I was playing ball, hitting that ball hard, I was keeping evil away. Now I can't keep it at a distance. This probably sounds foolish but I feel it getting closer."

"What evil?"

"I don't know. But I can't stop it from coming."

"Then let's have you start a team here."

"But that is just an illusion. In the end, it won't be stopped."

"If it gives you a sense of control in the meantime, you will have more confidence to face your fears when they do come."

It was hard for Bryon to believe he had just spouted his worst fears and Mr. Bingham hadn't belittled them or tried to point out how ridiculous they were. "I've never been a manager. I don't think I would be very good. You've seen I'm not so great with the kids."

"I have a feeling Base-Ball will change all that."

#

The street urchins were so emaciated and filthy sometimes it was hard to believe they weren't part animal. As

197

Abby observed the slums of London out the window of her father's carriage, she noticed a slovenly woman furtively glance around her then disappear into a novelty shop. Twisting her head around to see if she could catch a glimpse of the woman through the big plate glass window of the shop, Abby was surprised to see her come outside almost immediately. The woman shuffled in the same direction the carriage was going and Abby was able to watch her pull a china doll out from under her shawl and caress it lovingly.

I wonder what makes so many people living in these conditions feel no obligation to keep society's strictures? Her own words struck her with a sudden and terrible realization. I used those very words with Bryon. Did I make him feel as if he was not a genuine part of society like so many of these people feel? If someone believes they are excluded from society, do they question why they are required to keep the rules and do those of us who look down our noses at them, contribute to their moral breakdown? No wonder I haven't heard from Bryon. I categorized and separated him almost into a different species or a lesser form of humanity. I'm certain, being so intelligent, he picked up on my subtle excuse for rejecting him. Societies strictures demand I marry someone whole. Someone normal and upstanding like my father? She shook her head in disgust at herself. If only I had the courage to stop caring what others think. Oh, Bryon, what have I done to you? How do I apologize for so great an affront?

Chapter Seventeen

Watching Bryon and his friend Betsy Carter through his office window brought a rare smile to Roy's face. Maybe this would help lift the young man from his melancholia. Base-Ball was helping but it wasn't enough.

A small notebook with an attached pencil was Bryon's constant companion in all social situations except playing ball. He and Betsy easily communicated through this means. She was spending a week in Nashville, keeping a promise to her father to visit with Bryon and see if he was all right. The two had enjoyed sight-seeing and long walks through the beautiful woods surrounding the school. Bryon patiently listened to her endless stories about her patients and the doctors she had worked with. He was touched by her gentle heart and her dedication to easing pain and suffering in others. He found himself opening up to her more and more as the week progressed and as he did this, the heaviness in his heart lightened. The sight of her freckled nose and thick cinnamon-brown hair pleased him more every time he saw her.

The evening before, he had taken her to dine at Anna Bell's, the finest steak house in the city. Her round, merry face was wreathed in smiles the whole evening and he began pondering the powerful ability she had to ease his emotional pain as she eased the physical pain of her patients. The thought of her leaving brought a mild sense of panic to him. He had felt that same panic when he was six and was forced to leave her to return to his father. *But now I am old enough to do something about it.*

As they strolled back into the reception hall of the school, he wrote a suggestion in his notebook and held it out to her.

Betsy, why don't you learn sign language? We could communicate much better.

She read the note and frowned. "Oh, Bryon, nursing keeps me so busy and I wouldn't have much use for it. And I'm so slow at learning anything that doesn't relate to my job, I would probably make a mess of it."

I will help you. I know you'll do fine, he wrote.

"But I'm leaving tomorrow to go back to Oregon and begin working with my father. When will we ever see each other?"

"Mr. Hancock! I have your mail," the secretary interrupted the couple. "You'll be happy to hear you have three letters today. I know how much you love getting them."

Taking the mail from her hand, he nodded his thanks and glanced at the envelopes. His heart always lifted to see

Ethan's neat scrawl. There was a letter from Charles Proctor and the third . . . a letter from Abby. He resented a feeling like a cold fist in the stomach that told him he hadn't been successful at erasing her completely from his heart. He had not expected to hear from her again, did not want to. He looked up at Betsy's warm, open face and felt the pain lift. Slipping the first two letters into a pocket inside his jacket, he tore the third one in two and dropped it into the fire place, then he motioned for Betsy to accompany him back outside. He needed some fresh air to give him the courage for what he was about to do.

"Who was that letter from, Bryon?"

No one important, he wrote. *I have something to ask you.*

"All right. You know you can ask me anything." The kindness in her green eyes showed her tender nature. He just hoped the tenderness was for him as a man and not as a person who wasn't whole.

I was hoping you felt that way. I know you love nursing and there is a good hospital in Nashville. Betsy, would you consider marrying me and living here? Before he heard her answer, he saw it as the roses in her cheeks faded and her mouth fell open in shock. Her freckles stood out sharply as her skin paled. He folded his arms tightly against his chest and stared at his feet.

"Uh . . . I . . ." she sighed and tried again. "I don't think of you like that, Bryon. You've always been someone I, well, that I wanted to help. Your life has been so hard and . . ."

He held up his hands to stop her. The fierce look on his face did silence her and she nervously watched him write. *I am not a tragic figure to pity. I am a real person who is unique. I can see now that you think of me like one of your patients. The little mute boy who you could never see as a man. Now I know. Don't look like that, it isn't your fault, it is mine. Sometimes I forget what I am and begin to believe I am normal. Forgive me.*

"I'm sorry, oh please don't hate me! I care for you, truly I do. So does my father. He has always thought of you as a son. Can't we go on like always?"

Certainly. Forget it ever happened. I intend to. I am

sorry but my lessons aren't prepared yet for tomorrow so it would be best for you to return to your hotel. Since you leave in the morning, this is goodbye.

"Bryon, please don't stop writing me. Your letters are so entertaining and I really do value your friendship."

He agreed with a nod and accepted her brief hug. The unwanted thought slipped in that he could continue to write this woman who rejected him but he would have nothing to do with another who had done the same. He refused to question why that was.

Roy Bingham laid his head back against his chair, sick at what he had witnessed through his window. He knew how desperate Bryon was to ease his sense of being alone. It was obvious what had just taken place. *Now what am I going to do to help him?*

#

"Who is that little girl over there?" Bryon signed to Mr. Ogleby, a fellow teacher who often assisted him with the Base-Ball team.

"She's new. Her name is Jenny McGrath. Sad case," he spoke in a hushed tone. "Her mother died a few years ago and it appears she was severely abused by her father. Roy put her in my class for those with special challenges. So far she hasn't made any progress. She shrinks from me if she thinks I might touch her. Quite frankly, I have no idea what to do with her." Ogleby was a dedicated teacher who was gifted with the troublesome children. He wasn't deaf but his sensitivity impressed Bryon. Half the teachers were 'normal' like Ogleby. They could have made more money elsewhere but each, for reasons of their own, had chosen this dedicated path in life.

"She seems to like Base-Ball. I've seen her watching like a hawk every day." Bryon watched the little girl follow the play with bright eyes. She had beautiful soft brown eyes that tipped down at the ends like a fawn. Her curly dark brown hair bobbed up and down her back as she jumped and clapped when the runner came in home.

201

"Well, look at that," her teacher exclaimed. "This is the first time I've seen any emotion in her."

They both jumped when they heard their boss's voice right behind them. "That was just what I was thinking, Mr. Ogleby. Interesting isn't it?"

"Um, yes sir. Encouraging I'd say."

"Encouragement, yes. Something she needs desperately, to have courage infused in her. Fascinating word, that. Of course you both can see the obvious solution?"

They both looked blankly at Mr. Bingham.

"Come now, isn't it clear that Base-Ball is the answer?" When he continued to meet with silence, he spelled it out. "Mr. Hancock, you will train Jenny to be a ball boy. It's just the thing to bring her out of her shell and give her hope. You know, keep the evil at bay?"

Bryon resented him using his own words against him to force this preposterous idea. "She is a . . . she is . . ." His fingers were getting tangled up in frustration as he tried to sign. Slowly he formed each word. "She is a she!"

"Yes, a she. A seven-year-old she. A female in other words. Have you something against females?"

Recently, the answer to that had become yes but he dutifully shook his head.

"Good. Begin training her immediately. Since it would be better for her to form a bond with only one teacher to begin with, I'm transferring her to your classes, Mr. Hancock. She is now your special project and I expect a weekly report on how she is doing. Any questions?"

With a hard look, Bryon asked, "Just what are you trying to do, sir?"

"Mr. Hancock, I am trying to help a broken seven-year-old child."

It was midway through the season when he began managing the team. A lot of the boys had already been playing for fun with some of the teachers helping them. Bryon was surprised to discover some serious talent on the team. Two of the boys, Snap, nicknamed after his irritating past time, and

Chris, could bat hard and consistently. They were in their twenties and had the full strength of men. A lot of the students were older, coming to school to learn the new skill of sign language. The catcher, Tom was the best player on the team, almost never dropping a ball and the left field player was almost as fast as Ethan. Horace struggled on first base and Slim was a disgrace at right field but the rest of the team was fairly solid.

Bryon decided to put together a practice game with the neighborhood teenagers who played almost every day at the sandlot a half mile down the road. When the game ended with the school on top fourteen to twelve, a friendly rivalry began. The neighborhood boys came twice a week for games that increased rapidly in skill and savvy.

The players hung on every word that came from their manager's hands. Bryon did not notice the admiration on their faces or how hard they worked hoping to please him. He still lacked confidence as a teacher and this colored his perception of everything around him including his relationship with the little ball girl. She was underfoot constantly at practices and games. She had tried a number of times to carry the ball bag but the other ball boy kept that honor for himself. She had tried a couple of times to tug at Bryon's sleeve and get him to let her carry it but he would shake his head and then ignore her.

Roy insisted he spend time alone with her every day but that effort did not seem to be paying off at all. Both of them kept to their own silent world as they walked through the woods or wandered the neighborhood.

Knowing he needed to take more of an effort with the child, Bryon tried to think of a way to interact with her. She was making little progress with her signing and real conversation wasn't yet possible for the deaf and dumb girl.

It was a hot, muggy evening in September. They often walked after supper and tonight they were sitting on some boulders by the creek at the bottom of the big hill just south of the school. She was extra still today and he could see thoughts churning in her pretty head. As he was racking his brain for a way to reach her, she turned to him and haltingly began to sign her first sentence. "Teacher, why you . . ." Her brows furrowed in concentration, "sad like me . . . always?"

Excitement at her breakthrough was mixed with embarrassment that he had failed so completely to help her. *She needs someone else,* he thought. *Someone who can cheer her up and make her happy.* "I am sorry," he signed. "I will try and act happier."

"No!" she signed emphatically. Thinking hard, she searched for the signs. "The teachers . . . they make happy. I no happy. I no want . . . play happy."

"You mean, you do not want to pretend to act happy when you do not feel that inside?"

"Yes," she smiled.

He took her small hands in his and helped her form the word pretend. "Now sign the words, 'I will not pretend to be happy'".

She tried to pout as she formed the words but her lips kept twitching.

"Do not smile, Jenny. You have to act sad."

She giggled and searched for more words. "You and me, we sad . . . together. This make me happy." She giggled again when she saw her handsome teacher's shoulders shake with silent laughter.

"I ball boy. It make me happy."

"Jenny, I'm sorry I haven't let you do more. Starting tomorrow, I will let you carry the ball bag for me every day, okay?"

Her eyes lit up with joy. "Okay, teacher, okay," she signed exuberantly.

When practice ended the next day, Bryon told the male ball boy to let Jenny carry the bag. The boy argued but couldn't budge the manager. The boy glared in anger at Bryon's back as he was walking away. He kicked viciously at the grass with his toe. When Bryon disappeared through the trees that led to the school, the disgruntled boy had a word with a few of the younger players he was friends with.

"She isn't supposed to carry the ball bag, that's my job," he signed. "If we let her get away with it, next thing you know, girls will be playing on the team."

The indignant group was waiting for the little girl when she came out of the equipment shed. Five angry boys dragged her across the field, and over a hill to the pond, pulled her into the water and shoved her into the deep part. The boys crawled up the bank laughing and punching each other.

"You'd better learn to swim even if you are just a dumb ole girl," one boy signed to her as she flailed frantically and swallowed the muddy water. When the water covered her head and she didn't come up, they were suddenly struck with the seriousness of what they had done. Frantically signing to each other to determine who could swim, they discovered only one of them could. That fifteen year old boy dove into the water and began searching desperately for the child. When she finally surfaced, gasping and flailing in terror, her would-be rescuer was under the water searching. She slipped under before he came up. The other boys tried to point and signal where she was but to no avail. After three tries, the boy was losing strength and he began swimming back to shore.

The ball boy was shaking and crying, wondering if he would be hung for murder. His friends slowly backed away from him, indicating by their action where they hoped the blame for her death would be placed. Time moved in slow motion as they watched the boy swim toward them. He had just reached the muddy bank and had begun pulling himself up when the sun above him was blocked for an instant by a large object hurtling over his head. The boy was soaked by the splash from the manager hitting the water.

All the boys stared in shock at where Mr. Hancock had disappeared under the surface of the large pond. The ball boy jerked when he felt a hand on his shoulder and looked up to see Mr. Bingham give him a concerned look then stare gravely at the water. Everyone held their breath in unconscious sympathy until, as if in a dream, they saw Mr. Hancock rise out of the water, the limp little girl held firmly under one arm.

Roy Bingham took the child from Bryon at the water's edge and laid her on the nearby grass.

The boys could see she wasn't breathing and her face

was white. "She's dead," they signed to one another.

Turning her over, the stoic administrator pressed rhythmically on her back until her body expelled the water from her lungs. It was obvious that she was gone. The students looked at one another in embarrassment as their normally dignified principal worked on the little girl. Her eyes were closed and her mouth slack. They were all stunned when she jerked and took a shaky, tortured breath.

Watching in fear, Bryon stood next to his boss, water dripping from his clothes. Jenny opened her eyes, turned her head and saw her teacher bend over and peer into her face. When Bryon saw the pitifully frightened child reaching out her arms for him, he could practically feel his hard heart begin to thaw. He clutched the little girl and pressed her to his breast. Besides his kiss with Abby, this was the first time anyone had hugged him since the day his mother died. They were both warmed from the cold from the water and from life that day as they clung to each other.

Relief overwhelmed the administrator as he rose on shaking knees. He was grateful for his tendency to stare out the window while he pondered the day's problems. He had seen the group of boys carrying the girl over the rise toward the pond and feared the worst. As he rushed toward the disaster, he had caught Bryon entering the school and together they had raced to the pond. Bending his head, he offered up a silent prayer of gratitude.

For the first time since the snow and Abby, Bryon experienced one of his moments with Jenny. Bryon understood it was made easy by her need to reaffirm life by connecting with a person she trusted and loved. The feelings he absorbed from the child were intense and covered both ends of the spectrum. He felt the scars of abuse that were her constant companion but he also experienced the sweetness and virtue that are the attributes of innocent children. He cradled her head into his neck and pressed his cheek against hers as he sensed the adoration she had for him.

I never knew, he thought. *If I am half the man she believes me to be, maybe I'm not worthless after all.*

There were three very nervous boys in first period class with Mr. Hancock the next day. The other two boys involved in the incident with Jenny were in Mr. Ogleby's class and he knew they were being lectured in front of their peers just as these three were about to be.

"We had an incident yesterday at the pond which we will discuss before the lesson," Bryon signed. "Actually, I hope this is the most important lesson any of you will receive today." He pinned the three boys with a forceful stare. "I'm sure by now everyone knows who was involved and as a part of their punishment, Mr. Bingham wanted this lecture to be public and not private." He saw the other students warily studying the three boys. "Haven't you boys learned anything from the way others have treated you? Some people think we aren't human. Actually we should be more human, if anything, than the average person with our understanding. We know that it is what is in the heart that counts. Having been the victim, we should be more humane, more empathic to the feelings of others."

He walked up to the boys and instead of anger, they saw pleading in his face as he signed. "Do you hate her? Is it because she is a girl? Do we hate girls if they dare love something we don't believe they should love, like Base-Ball? Is it because she has already been the victim of hate and we can sense that and so we know she is an easy target? Because she is small?" He rubbed his hand across his face as if tired, hesitated, searching for the right words, then began signing again. "If we treat others as if they are less than us, then that is often what they become. You and all handicapped people, should fight that tendency with all your soul."

The impassioned teacher signed with great energy, his powerful shoulders rolling with the effort as he leaned toward his students. "Let us become more than human. Let us portray the attributes of angels. Perhaps that is what we really are if it is true that we aren't quite the same as those around us. I have noticed that those of us with handicaps often have gifts that remind me of the famous words of Wordsworth. 'Trailing clouds of glory do we come from God who is our home.' I

207

believe you trailed more clouds of glory with you to help you cope with your challenge and not only that but to bless others. Some of you have the gift of loving more deeply and purely, some have a spirit of peace so profound that all around you are calmed. Others, have intuition, empathy, hope, that is above the normal dose met out to ordinary people. These gifts aren't just to help us cope, perhaps we have, in fact, an obligation to others to share ourselves with them, to teach those around us that we can rise above this plodding existence and experience a brighter world. And if there was ever any hope of accomplishing this, it is here in America, the land of freedom and opportunity where I expect to see this change take place. Help me work for it. As a school, let us begin to shower mercy, kindness and a helping hand to any who need us and in this way we lift ourselves far above what the world thinks us to be."

Wary eyes had become shining eyes. Hope filled every wounded heart in that class room that day, which included every heart, and spilled over to fill the whole school within hours of Mr. Hancock's famous speech. At least it was famous at the Nashville School for the Deaf and Dumb.

Bryon became a great teacher overnight, finally believing he had something worthwhile to say. He had feared that because of what he'd been through, he was unworthy to help others, but he now realized that it was precisely because of what he had endured and overcome that he found himself in a unique position to help. The students responded and the school became a genuine place of safety for every student there. The love Bryon received from those he taught healed much of what he feared was permanently broken including his ability to control his anger.

Life became full for the new hero as Jenny, the shy, introverted child blossomed into a chatty, bubbly chatter box. Her hands were constantly moving. Bryon's eyes often glazed over as he watched her share her decided opinions on everything including the deaf teacher who had a crush on her Mr. Hancock.

"Miss Johnson has a crush on you," she informed him one day.

"You just think that because she keeps stats for the team and we have become friends."

"That's what *you* think. She is always watching you when you don't see. Do you like her too?"

"Of course I like her."

"But, do you like her like . . . you know!"

"We are just friends, nosy."

They were on their way to a game in Nashville and Jenny was riding in the surrey with Mr. Bingham, Mr. Ogleby and her Mr. Hancock. Behind them was a buggy with Miss Johnson and a few other teachers coming to see the team play their first official game. The state champion Nashville Athletics had agreed to play them and take in donations for a fund raising activity for the deaf school. It was all in good fun and no one expected a close game but Pitcher Delaney, the player/manager for the Nashville team, told Mr. Bingham they would take it easy and play their two substitutes a lot of the game.

The popularity of the sport was exploding in the south. The beautiful city of Nashville had a number of smaller teams but the school was playing the Athletics Base-Ball Club who had formed in 1867 and were the state champions. Excitement was in the air that day. Some of it was from Base-Ball but there was also a sense of optimism in the city itself. Although there was a depression that year, their economy was holding on and a stunning new college named after the railroad magnate, William Vanderbilt was being dedicated.

Jenny twisted her head around to spy on Stella Overson. The deaf teacher was a strong woman with brown hair and hazel eyes. Tapping the preoccupied manager on the knee, the little girl signed, "If you look real quick, you will see her staring at you again." She giggled when he rolled his eyes.

The wagon carrying the team pulled into the lot by the beautiful ball field. The excited boys jumped out and began warming up. The first hint of trouble came immediately, much to Mr. Bingham's dismay. He expected the top tier clubs to demonstrate the highest gallantry. In Tennessee the top clubs were; Chattanooga, Memphis and Nashville. The famous southern hospitality was missing from the team they now faced.

One of the Nashville players strode up to Horace who was struggling as usual at first base. "So, what do ya have to say for yourself?" His lip curled in disdain as the young man watched him warily. "Cat got your tongue?"

Mr. Bingham hurried over and stuck out his hand. "Good afternoon, sir. I'm the school administrator." Since his hand was ignored, he lowered it. "Is there anything I can do to help you?"

"Just trying to be neighborly. Can't say these boys act too friendly, though."

"Are you aware that they are Deaf and Dumb?"

He snickered then straightened his face. "Well, actually I didn't know they were deaf but . . . anyway, I'll just be going. Oh, by the way, are you deaf and dumb too?"

"Good day, sir."

And that was only the beginning. Things turned downright unpleasant when their manager/hurler, Pitcher Delaney, recognized Bryon and approached him. "Saw you play up in Cincy. Yeah, was quite the debacle, losing to Brooklyn like that. I read what the papers said about you. 'Luke the mute fluke', that's what they called you. They said it was a fluke that you played so well in the big game with the Buckeyes the year before. After you brought them down, the whole club just folded. Had to move to Boston. You were the biggest mistake Harry ever made, you know. How'd that make you feel, Hancock? Pretty bad, huh? Maybe your boys will redeem you here today. Good luck." Knowing there would be no reply, he walked away whistling a cheerful tune.

A flush spread over Bryon's cheeks and his fists clinched so tightly that his nails bit into his palms. He understood that no mercy would be shown that day. Horace was so rattled that he missed more than half the balls thrown to first. The opponent also found out that Slim was a weakness in right field and took frequent advantage. Even strong players like Tom and Snap had an off day, sensing the animosity of the other team. The game ended, Nashville, fifty five, The Nashville Deaf and Dumb School, nine.

Chapter Eighteen

Bryon was watching Jenny instead of the carolers. Her eyes were huge with wonder as she swayed with the choir of children from the local Baptist church. The children had worked hard to learn the sign language which accompanied the sweet strains of Silent Night. Although Jenny couldn't hear the song, she sensed the rhythm and moved as she saw the carolers moving. She was completely captivated by the spirit of the season. It was Christmas Eve and fairies were definitely dancing in this little girl's head. He winked at Stella and she gave him back a shy smile.

After the singers left, the teachers ushered the excited children to bed. About a quarter of the students were left there for the holidays and the staff was trying hard to furnish Christmas cheer. Bryon went to his room to retrieve the special surprise he had planned for his child, for that is how he now thought of Jenny.

A small parlor sat off the large reception room and served as an intimate setting for family visits. Tonight, Bryon built a cozy fire and hung up two large, bright red stockings from the mantel and began filling them with the gifts he had bought for Stella and Jenny. All the children would find a stocking filled with candy and trinkets on their beds in the morning but he wanted Jenny to have more. He needed to give her more.

Stella waited an hour for the children to drift off to sleep, then spirited Jenny quietly out of her bed and brought her to the parlor. She thought Miss Johnson was taking her to the outhouse. Her mind was foggy with sleep until she saw teacher grinning at her as he leaned against the mantel in the parlor. This was a room she wasn't allowed in. Her eyes widened as she tried to take in the fact that not only was she in this beautiful, forbidden room, but her teacher had planned this time just for her. She ran and threw herself in his arms, not even noticing the bright stockings with peppermint sticks peeking over the top. When teacher held her tight, she was safe and loved and she wanted for nothing in the world. Secretly she thought of him as her daddy and she would have been surprised if she knew he was privy to those private fantasies and shared in them.

Bryon turned her so the stockings would come into her sight and put her down when he heard the squeal. She looked up at him expectantly.

"I saw this jolly character coming out of the parlor and asked him what he was doing. He said he had brought something extra for a little girl named Jenny because she had been so good this year."

Hopping up and down in excitement she signed back, "It was St. Nick, it was St. Nick. And I'm Jenny!"

She opened her presents, delighting in everything but when she pulled what she thought was an orange out of the toe of the stocking, she immediately lost interest in the candy and toys. There lying in her hand was the gift that validated her tomboy heart. A snowy, white Base-Ball. She reverently lifted it to her nose and sniffed the tangy, new leather.

Hit by a sudden realization, the child signed, "Now I can be like you when you pitch to the strikers. If I learn good, can I pitch sometimes in practice?"

"You bet, sweetheart. Your ball is a magic ball. It has special powers. As you practice, there is something I want you to remember. Every time you throw that ball, you will throw away some of the bad things with it until all the bad things people have done that still hurt, will be thrown away. Someday you will be able to throw it right past those big ole strikers and they will look around and say, 'where did that darned ball go to'?"

She giggled when Miss Johnson gave teacher an exasperated look. Jenny signed, "Teacher always tells me magic stories. I like the elf ones best." Her small fingers flew as her Christmas cheer bubbled out of her happy heart.

Seeing that the child's emotions were too overwrought to go back to bed, Bryon held out his arms to her. He was sitting on the floor in front of the fireplace leaning against an overstuffed chair. She came to him, clutching her new ball and he cradled her in his arms where she finally settled into sleep.

212

Bryon stared into the fire as he stroked the soft cheek of the angel curled in his arms and soaked in contentment like a drug.

He didn't notice Stella's jealous glances as he lost himself in dreams of a future with a home of his own and this child as his daughter. He glanced at Paula who was sitting in the opposite chair, her gifts lying in her lap. He was well aware by this time of her feelings for him, and for a while, he indulged himself in a picture of the three of them as a family sharing many Christmas Eves together.

#

Spring brought more excitement to the school than normal. Bryon had received inquiries about practice games from a few towns in the area. It seemed that news of the Nashville Athletics' poor sportsmanship had ruffled some feathers. The team managers all assured Bryon that their clubs would act in a gentlemanly manner to redeem the sacred game of Base-Ball in the great state of Tennessee.

The school's team barely resembled the bunch who had played for fun a year before. Bryon was proud of his players and believed they could be competitive with some of the smaller clubs so he agreed to play all four of the towns who had written. Over the next few weeks, his players worked hard and showed intense dedication. The neighborhood boys had a lot more respect for the team and provided good scrimmages for them.

Bryon felt a deep responsibility to his boys as he finally understood what a pedestal they had him on. He was their hero and they were doing this for him.

The team traveled south for their first game with a club from Murfreesboro. This town had become well known during the civil war as a result of a fierce battle fought there. It was a beautiful place with a quaint town square and friendly people.

There was a good crowd out for the game and both the spectators and Murfreesboro's club showed good sportsmanship even when the game came down to a tight last inning. When Snap hit a double, driving Tom in home and tying the game, the local fans applauded his effort. The catcher patted Tom on the back after he crossed the plate. This was the way the game was normally played and it was so refreshing to the school's team that they hardly felt the sting when in the bottom of the inning, Murfreesboro scored twice for the win.

Franklin was their next opponent. Their team came to the deaf school and showed good sportsmanship when they lost, thirty-two to twenty-eight.

A victory over the club from Cookville made the local papers. The students were beginning to seriously believe in themselves.

Local reporters showed up in McMinnville when the deaf school came to play. The town club upheld the state's reputation for hospitality and genteel behavior even though they were obviously embarrassed to lose twenty-six to nineteen.

Before heading back to Nashville, the team had a picnic on the field with the opponent. It was customary to share a meal after a game. The players enjoyed baskets of chicken, boiled eggs, oranges and muffins that satisfied their hearty appetites. An air of celebration sharpened the enjoyment for the deaf school.

Noticing that Jenny had energy to burn and thinking of the long trip home, Bryon challenged her to a race. The two ran across the green, past the town hall and down the street a few blocks where he had seen an ice cream parlor that would be the perfect finishing line.

After winning the race, Jenny signed her choice of ice cream to her teacher who wrote down their orders on his small notepad. She had one scoop of peppermint and one of chocolate. Bryon had a scoop of spumoni and the two happily licked their cones as they began walking back up town.

"Hey, if it isn't Luke the mute fluke."

Bryon's head spun around and there stood Pitcher Delaney, the manager/player from the Nashville team. Ignoring him, Bryon took Jenny's hand and they continued walking.

"What's wrong? Don't you want to *talk* to me?" he drawled. "I saw your freaks play today. They're a little better than last year but your team never had any business playing ours. It was an embarrassment to be on the same field with your kind."

Squeezing Jenny's hand tighter, Bryon continued down the street until Pitcher grabbed him by the arm and spun him around. Bryon's elbow caught Jenny's arm causing the little girl to drop her ice cream.

"Too good to give me the time of day?"

Jenny reached out with both hands and clung to Bryon's arm. With that anchor to give her courage, she leaned around him and stuck her tongue out at the frightening man.

"Keep that nasty tongue in your mouth, you little idiot or I'll make you use it for what it was meant for; licking the dust from my shoes like the dog your kind are."

Bryon pulled free from Jenny and launched into Pitcher. Tumbling into the street, the two men wrestled in the dust for position. Pitcher swung at the man above him but Bryon easily blocked the punch and slugged him twice in the jaw and had his fist cocked for a third swing when Pitcher lifted his hand in defeat.

"Enough." He grimaced and grabbed his aching jaw, wiggling it back and forth. "Okay, so you're stronger than me. That doesn't prove anything. On the field is where it counts and that's where I'm on top."

Jenny signed defiantly into the prone man's face. Bryon backed away from Pitcher and pulled out his note pad. *She says our team is better now and you wouldn't stand a chance against us.*

"Right." He picked himself up from the dirt and brushed off his pants. "The only way we'd play a bunch of losers like you would be if when the game is over you freaks lick the dust off our shoes in front of the entire crowd."

Bryon lost him temper and his wits and wrote, "Works both ways."

"Great. Write it up and sign it for me and then write another one and I'll sign it for you. Make sure you put down that only students at your school play, no teachers."

#

"You what?" Mr. Bishop stared in horror at his employee.

"I lost my temper."

"You lost your mind, Mr. Hancock."

"That too," he admitted sheepishly.

"Well, sir, I will let you break it to your team."

Waiting a few days to give the players the news didn't make things easier. Finally taking the proverbial bull by the horns, Bryon gathered them together after a practice and related the bet and the story behind it to his boys.

Although indignant at the Nashville manager's rudeness, the ball players were shocked and furious that their manager had gotten them into such a mess.

"We don't have a prayer of winning. That club smears all the clubs we played."

"And none of us want to go through the humiliation of how they treated us last year. Why didn't you ask before committing us to something like that?"

Taking his shirt off and getting whipped would have been easier for the embarrassed manager. With his chin tucked low, he continued to watch the hands of his players as they made their feelings clear.

"This is going to cause us shame and you have been telling us we shouldn't put ourselves in situations unnecessarily that will embarrass us. Other people do that enough without our own manager doing it."

That comment hurt worst of all because Bryon knew it was true. The school's new attitude had made a huge difference and heads were held higher, self-confidence growing in the blossoming students. What would this do to their emotional progress? Would they listen anymore to his encouragement and council?

He thought of backing out of the bet but that would bring worse shame to the school so he did the only thing he could think of. He worked the boys harder than ever and complimented them on every inch of skill gained. Some of the boys grew surly and he had a hard time reaching them. Tom was the worst. He had shined that season and it showed in his erect posture and improving grades. He didn't want to face the humiliation he knew would be heaped upon them in the coming contest.

The big game was scheduled to take place a week after the regular season ended. Two weeks before the game, Tom reached his boiling point when Bryon corrected his stance while catching a throw to home.

The frustrated young man got right into his manager's face and signed with wild gestures. "It is so easy for you to stand there and tell us to be perfect. You aren't the one that has to go out and play at the mess you got us into. You had no right to speak for us."

"Settle down, Tom. Everything will be all right if we work hard."

"Be all right? Maybe you're an idiot but I'm not. I know what's going to happen!"

Growing angry himself as Tom snarled into his face, Bryon pushed him away. It was not a hard shove but the young man could not take this final insult.

Bryon saw the swing coming and in a lightning decision, he decided to stand there like a man and take his lick. He knew he deserved this. The right hook caught him squarely in the jaw and knocked him off his feet. The pain eased some of his self-hatred and the terrible guilt that had been eating at him.

Rising slowly, he rubbed his sore jaw and signed, "You are absolutely right. I'm sorry, Tom."

The players stood with aching hearts watching their hero slowly walk away. Bryon made his decision as he went to Roy's office. Without knocking, he entered the room, came up to the desk of the waiting administrator and signed, "I quit!"

Chapter Nineteen

"What!"

"I quit."

"The team or your teaching position?" The administrator

217

was trying to keep his voice steady but it seemed to want to squeak all by itself.

"I shouldn't be teaching here, I don't know enough. I need to go back to school, Mr. Bishop." He looked at him significantly, "Immediately."

Understanding dawned and the administrator's face lit up. "You know, now that you mention it, you're a little weak in your history. I recommend you start class tomorrow. Just one class though. You need the rest of the time, now that you're not teaching, to work with the players one on one. I'll let each of them out of one class a day to have the extra time."

The press had gotten wind of the bet and the story flew across the wires all over America because of the strangeness of the bet and the rumors of the previous unpleasant match-up between the teams. Some of the write-ups were kind to the school, some were not. One widely published article was especially derogatory, saying it must be true after all that deaf and dumb people were stupid if that manager could not remember the stomping his team had taken the year before. The reporter termed the coming game 'The Dog Fight', equating the two teams to a tiny, yapping mongrel taking on a large, noble pure bred. The term stuck.

That article got under the skin of an old friend of Bryon's and worked on him until he could not resist the plan that lodged in his head. A train and a hansom cab brought him to the school.

"Ethan, it can't be you. Unless I'm mistaken, this is Tennessee and you swore you would never return here." Bryon was smiling for the first time in weeks.

"Well, friend, you've gotten yourself in a terrible mess here and you need your ole buddy to save your . . . "

"Watch your hands. No cussing in school." The friends grabbed each other and pounded backs. "Welcome back to the land of the learning."

At the first practice with their new player, Ethan impressed his teammates so much they inundated him with questions about himself, their manager and Base-Ball in general. Tom was especially excited and curious by this hopeful

218

turn of events. With both Bryon and Ethan playing in the big game, they stood a real chance.

As soon as Bryon called the team in from warm up to begin a practice game, Tom jogged up to Ethan and signed, "You know, Mr. Brown, you play just as well as our manager."

"No sirree, I don't play as well as your superb leader here. How could I when I don't have a handle half as long as his. Why, this is the famous Mr. Bryon, Luke, Hancock, Jenkins, Castleberry, Smith, Pasty face, Ghost!" He ignored the fierce warning Bryon threw his way. "Why, little ole me, I'm just plain Mr. Brown Peabody come to do my poor best to help you all." He struck a dramatic pose and continued with reverent intensity. "And this here Mr. Playbody will now pee for ya' all. No, no, no, what I mean is, Mr. Peabody will now play ball."

As the whole team doubled over in laughter, Jenny signed to Bryon, "he's funny."

Giving his girl a quick kiss on the cheek, he signed back, "He's smarter than a firecracker is what he is."

Every day during the last week of practice, Bryon grew more grateful for his friend. Ethan kept the team from feeling the pressure or taking themselves too seriously. After one practice he said to the boys, "I kind of hope you all play terrible against Nashville. I've been concerned that my diet lacks minerals and I understand there are plenty in the dirt around here so I'm looking forward to dining off our opponents' fine footwear."

Perhaps the greatest gift he gave the team was his work with Horace at first base. "Don't think of it as a ball, Horace," Ethan coaxed. "This is a baby. He's tender and needs careful handling. You can't catch a baby with your ham fisted palms. Use your fingertips and reach out for the baby. Grab him firmly but gently and carry him in to your stomach so you don't drop him."

Amazed at how well Ethan understood the sensitive young man, Bryon watched in amazement at the instant transformation in Horace's game. The team's biggest handicap became a solid part of the infield.

Just when things were looking up, they got a scare. Two

days before the game, the school had a visit from one of the Base-Ball officials accompanied by Pitcher Delaney.

Mr. Bishop was with Bryon watching the team practice and trying to learn the basics so he could fill in as the team manager. In reality, Bryon would direct play and Mr. Ogleby would stay close to Mr. Bishop in case of emergency.

Pitcher Delaney strode briskly up to Ethan and said, "I know you. I saw you play in '70. You're Ethan Brown."

"Thank you so much, sir," Ethan posed, flashing his dimples, his sparkling eyes crinkling at the corners. "I keep forgetting who I am and need constant reminders."

"Very funny. I'll have you know, I'm well aware that you aren't deaf or dumb, Brown."

"I could say two of those things about you."

"What?"

"You aren't deaf or brown."

Pointing an accusing finger at Ethan he whined to the official, "See, he could hear me."

"Actually I can't hear you. I can see you though, whoa is me."

"What are you talking about," Pitcher screamed.

"I don't know, what are you talking about?"

"You aren't handicapped. What are you doing enrolled in this school?"

"I'm deaf."

"Are not."

"Uh oh, this conversation is deteriorating fast."

Turning to the official, whose head had been pivoting back and forth as the conversation flew, he said, "You can see for yourself he isn't deaf."

"Sorry, Mr. Brown. I'm afraid Mr. Delaney is right. That's the way it looks to me. And I thought deaf people who could speak, sounded different."

"I had a great elocution coach."

"I follow Base-Ball and I heard all about you," Pitcher sneered. "You were thrown out after the first year for being a Negro."

"Tried to give it up but just couldn't seem to break the

habit."

"If you were deaf I would have heard about it."

"Wish I could have heard about it but I'm deaf you see. So stop making fun of my handicap. I kept it a secret knowing how prejudice people were against the deaf/mute folk. I tried to keep being a Negro secret, even practiced being white but I just couldn't get my nose up high enough in the air. Guess it gave me away."

The official, trying not to laugh warned him. "This isn't a joke. You can't play on the team unless you're deaf."

"I told you, I'm an oralist. I read everything you say by watching your lips."

"Okay, then I'll just mouth something and you tell me what I am saying." The man slowly and carefully mouthed some words.

Ethan appeared shocked. "I understand how you feel but you really should not say such nasty things about this man. His mamma loves him." He smiled sweetly at Pitcher.

Roy Bishop stepped up to the group and broke in, "There is an easier way to do this. If he wasn't deaf, he wouldn't know sign language. He sure isn't a sign language teacher now is he?"

Pitcher offered, "If he knows sign language I'll eat my hat."

Both Ethan and Bryon were surprised to hear the circumspect administrator say, "Would you like me to get you some salt?" He then signed to Ethan instructing him to sign back as fast as he could. When he did so, the official looked impressed.

"He faked that," Pitcher Delaney snarled.

Mr. Bishop politely asked the official, "You are aware that Mr. Hancock is mute, right?"

He nodded warily.

"All right then, if you write something on this pad here, I'll have Mr. Hancock sign it to Mr. Brown and in turn, Mr. Brown will tell you what you wrote. Fair enough?"

The official quickly jotted something down and handed it to Bryon. He signed to Ethan who went over to Pitcher, took

221

his hat and handed it to Bryon.

The official looked disappointed and shook his head. "No, that isn't right."

Ethan said, "I'm sorry, I know you told me to give this clown his hat to eat but it's a good hat and I thought Bryon might like it."

The official burst into laughter. "I guess this is all settled then."

"No, I still don't believe he's deaf. Sure, Hancock could have taught him how to do that hocus-pocus but that doesn't mean he's deaf."

"That's true." He turned hopefully back to Roy Bishop.

Bryon signed to the administrator who looked relieved and told the official; Mr. Hancock suggests you wire the Ohio School for the Deaf and Dumb in Cincinnati and ask them if Ethan Brown was enrolled as a student from 1870 to 1872."

"Was he really? That should definitely take care of the problem. He gave Pitcher an impatient glance. "We'll be leaving then. Sorry to have bothered you. Good luck at the game."

Pitcher glared at Ethan and gave what he thought was one last parting shot. "You may think you've won but you'll learn. If any of your kind can learn.

"Yes, suh, massa. I'll try my best, Suh Itcher."

"Pitcher not Itcher."

"Don't feel bad. Lots of athletes get that embarrassing itch. That where you got your nickname?"

"It's Pitcher. Watch my lips, see them come together? Pit...cher."

"I think I've got it now, but why would you call yourself something so crappy?"

"Why am I wasting my time on someone who's both dumb and crass?" He began to walk away until Ethan's next words stopped him in his tracks.

Ethan pretended to sound offended. "Now why on earth would you call yourself a dumb ass? This is a school. You should watch your shocking language, Bitcher."

Bryon grabbed Ethan's shoulder and squeezed in an

effort to keep a straight face while Pitcher stared in confusion, shook his head as if clearing it then hurried to catch up with the other man. As soon as the two visitors rounded the corner, the two friends, who had been holding their breath and fighting for composure, broke. One silent, the other with loud guffaws, they collapsed against one another in helpless laughter. Even Roy could not help letting a small chuckle escape.

#

The night before the game, neither Ethan nor Bryon could sleep. A cot had been brought into Bryon's room so they could stay together. The moon shining through the window was bright enough for Bryon to sign. "I hope everything turns out all right."

"Never thought we'd play together again."

"This time tomorrow you might be regretting it."

"What's this?" Ethan gently chided him. "We can take them, buddy. I remember how scared you were that first day with the Red Stockings. It's just nerves. Instinct will kick in tomorrow and it will be smooth sailing."

Seeing the discouraged look on his friends face, Ethan went on. "I've never seen a more dedicated or loved manager. They'll come through for you. I don't know anyone who has more courage than you. They feel that and lean on it."

He inwardly flinched at the word courage. Not even Ethan knew about his lifelong conviction that he was a coward. A courageous son would never have left his mother to die the way he had. He kept his face expressionless. "And I thought you knew me?"

Ethan grew very serious. "I do know you, Bryon Hancock. Ole' Roy may know your head but I know your heart. I knew it even back in the good old days when we were playing ball and you let those jerks like Trumble lead you around by the nose. You were too good for them and they made you feel like dirt."

He saw Bryon's look of surprise. "You know, Hancock, you aren't the only one with empathy. I've got some of that

223

stuff too and a lot of what I went through on the plantation as a kid, and the loving embrace of society since then," he mocked, "has given me more."

"It should have ended with the war."

"War doesn't end hatred, it fuels it although there are times it's justified. And was Lincoln's war ever justified! But still, in some ways the hatred toward my people has been worse sense then. Just shows there's important work to be done after the guns are put away. Senseless hatred is everywhere and I doubt I'll ever understand it. What I have to do is make sure I don't hate back. If I did, I don't know if I would have this empathy. Does that make me a wimp?"

"What you are is a man. A real man, Ethan and the best friend I'll ever have."

"Uh oh, we're getting maudlin. Time for sleep, pal."

Both men lay quietly in the dark with their thoughts. A soothing warmth spread through Bryon's veins as he thought about this man who knew all about him, was a part of him and didn't think he was broken. He was safe sharing the deepest parts of what made him unique because Ethan knew his weaknesses and loved him anyway.

With that realization, he felt most of his anger and frustration melt away. What began with Jenny, grew with the love of his students, fully matured tonight as he connected with Ethan. He wasn't lonely anymore.

Hoping his roommate wasn't asleep, Bryon touched his friend's shoulder and signed, "Ethan, I don't feel angry anymore."

"You mean I don't have to be afraid you're going to explode all over someone and get us expelled?"

"I'll try not to."

"Good. I'll admit it now, I was a bit worried about you doing just that in the game tomorrow. Everything will go just fine if you keep a cool head."

Chapter Twenty

It was Ethan who needed a cool head the day of the big Base-Ball Dog Fight. The morning paper revealed the frightening news of a band of hooded horsemen who had broken into the Gibson County jail during the night. They bound, gagged, forcibly removed and then lynched sixteen colored people. They were in a furor over a Federal Civil Rights Bill that was coming up for a vote so they took their anger out on some hapless victims.

"I knew I shouldn't have come here."

Bryon was thinking the same thing. "A ball game isn't worth you taking chances. Some people won't like watching you play today with feelings high like this."

"No, I'm sorry, I didn't really mean that. I'm glad I came, Bryon. Just make sure if you see people with pillow cases over their heads, you give me a holler. Wait, how do hands holler?"

Nothing could have prepared the school for the crowd that showed up at the game. There was an estimated 5,000 people at the park that day, plus reporters from around the country. The "Who is going to take a 'licking'", bet had grown into a media phenomenon. Bryon suspected Pitcher Delaney had spread the story to the press to bring his team into the spotlight. What Pitcher did not realize was that the underdog would win the sympathies of the day not only with the media but with their own fair minded Nashville fans.

Ethan was covering the school's weakness at short stop and Bryon was at his usual third base position. The game began with the Nashville Athletics at bat first, scoring a respectable four runs. When the school got up to bat the rules of courtesy held for most of that inning until Tom hit a solid double driving in the three men on base. The rally continued until the score was eight to four.

Now things began to turn ugly. Elbows began flying, and insulting talk flew. The third out came when the Nashville second base player shoved Horace off the bag as the ball was being thrown from the hurler. Horace was called out and a few

Nashville fans, hating injustice, voiced a few noisy complaints to the official.

The umpire, who was wearing the traditional tails and top hat, was sitting at his table near third base. He looked up into the crowd and shrugged his shoulders helplessly with the innocent attitude of; 'I don't know what you're upset about, I didn't see anything.'

In the third inning, play took a dangerous turn when Chris hit the ball into left field and took off for first. The rules demanded the ball be thrown to the hurler before being thrown to a base player but instead of staying in the hurling box, Pitcher committed the disgraceful act of running in front of the second base to wait for the throw. Chris rounded first and sprinted toward second. The left field player threw the ball to Pitcher who quickly tossed it to his teammate behind him. Chris was barreling toward second when Pitcher made the toss. Pitcher swung around the far side of the base and deliberately timed his move back to his box so that he would be in Chris's path. The collision was heavy and no one clearly saw Pitcher's knee make contact with Chris's groin, but the groan of the collapsing man was audible throughout the park.

Accusations and threats flew back and forth between Ethan and Pitcher until the umpire threatened to throw Ethan out of the game if he didn't shut up.

When it was the school's turn at the plate, Bryon gathered them together. "It seems pretty obvious that the Athletics have no intention of playing fairly and what is really disturbing, the umpire seems inclined to support them. It's up to us to play so well they can't stop us. In my opinion, we are the better team, gentlemen. I believe in each one of you. Let's go show what we can do!"

The boys caught fire and every striker got on base until Slim came up to the plate. He was their worst striker so the team leaped to their feet in excitement when he connected with the ball and sprinted toward first. The ball, more by accident than design, hit the dirt a dozen feet in front of third then crow hopped out of bounds. This was the valuable fair/foul that was so hard to defend but the third base player was ready and caught the ball on the second bounce. He threw to Pitcher who was standing close to first base and had already hurriedly given the player behind him whispered instructions.

Some of the crowd cheered loudly as they could see the ball would be behind the runner. Slim put on a burst of speed, spurred on by the spectators. The first base player reached out as if readying himself to receive the ball then seemed to lose balance as he leaned too far. He waved his arms and one leg as if to catch himself and suddenly his leg shot out toward the approaching runner, catching Slim squarely in the stomach with his shoe. Slim's velocity coupled with the force of the kick more than knocked the wind out of the poor runner. He fell to the ground and doubled over. After his breath returned, he began retching violently. His teammates ran to his aid and when he had emptied his stomach, they carried him off the field. This was too much even for loyal fans. Their club should not win this way. The crowd was going crazy, screaming at the umpire to throw the first base player out of the game.

Roy Bishop had been little more than a figure head manager in his stiff collar and black suit. With his hands clasped behind his back and his erect posture, he was something of a joke to the crowd, but now he was truly angry. Holding his hands up to quiet the spectators, he asked if there was a doctor among them. Immediately two doctors came forward and together they decided to take the young man in to give him a thorough check.

After Slim had been taken away, Roy marched up to the umpire and demanded to know why he was allowing this travesty to go on.

"Now, Mr. Bishop, you just don't understand Base-Ball. It's an intense game and the players can become excitable. It was just an accident. You saw the man lose his balance. He was falling and couldn't help kicking your boy."

"I saw a carefully executed farce. It was a deliberate attempt to cause bodily injury to my student. I am holding you personally responsible if anything else happens in this game to one of my players and I am holding that player responsible for the medical charges to Slim. Watch your step, sir, or you may

227

find yourself in deep water."

"Don't threaten me, you . . . you . . . fop!"

"You don't even know what a fop is. And I wouldn't speak. I'm not the one wearing a tuxedo and top hat."

"This is standard for important games, you ignorant . . . . scholar."

"My, what an insult." Roy looked mildly shocked for a moment. He never engaged in sarcasm. Shaking his head ruefully, he walked away with his lips pressed firmly together.

After this incident, the insults were constant from the Nashville team, especially toward Bryon. They called out 'Luke the Mute Fluke' again and again and found increasingly crude ways to tell him what a looser he was. He kept his cool and outwardly appeared calm and unruffled. He let his frustrations come out in his play. In the fifth inning, he hit a triple, bringing in two base runners. The crowd was exultant. It was a thing of beauty to watch the strongly built manager knock the ball so far.

The next striker up was Ethan. He hit a high fly deep to center. The crowd was silent as everyone watched the ball soar. The third base player kept backing up as he watched. He backed right into the umpire's chair and fell backwards over the unfortunate official. This ploy, practiced in advance, allowed the center field player to take off his cap as he ran, and stretching out, he caught the ball in his cap. Once again the crowd reacted and Mr. Bishop returned to the umpire to lodge a complaint.

"Sir, it is against the rules to catch the ball in the cap. Even I know that."

"I didn't see any cap used."

"All you saw was dirt. It was used. Listen to the crowd."

"Occasionally we umpires do ask for help but I try not to use a biased crowd."

"Biased? These are the Athletics fans!"

"Apparently they pity your students. I will ask the players." Turning to the field he yelled, "Did any of you players see an illegal use of the cap?"

"Loud 'no's' issued from the Athletics and only one 'yes' was forthcoming from the Deaf and Dumb School's team. Ethan started marching toward the umpire shouting yes, over and over but Bryon pulled him back reminding him that only the manager could approach the umpire.

The sixth inning began with a surprise. The original ball had disappeared and now the hurler had a ball that was unusually rubbery. During that era, the balls differed, at times being too rubbery and bouncing wildly into the field and sometimes being too mushy and making the striker's job difficult. Now the ball was a great advantage to the Athletics as they scored eleven points in that inning moving ahead of the school, forty-two to thirty-seven.

"Don't worry, boys. Now it's our turn to play with the bouncing ball," Bryon assured his players. Only it didn't turn out that way. Ira was first up to plate and got a good, solid swing on the first pitch. The ball made a thwunking sound, indicating a mushy ball, and dribbled toward Pitcher. Ira was easily thrown out at first.

Hurrying over to Mr. Bishop, Bryon explained the situation. Bishop approached the umpire who rolled his eyes at the tenacious manager. "What now, Mr. Bishop?"

"The ball was changed. Where is the one that was used in the first half of the inning?"

The umpire bent over a black bag, rummaged a moment and pulled out a ball. "Look at this. It must have hit a rock out there and split. Can't be helped, I had to use a new ball."

"It looks as though it was split deliberately with a knife."

"My, aren't we paranoid. I was assured it was a rock."

"Where is the ball that was used before that one?"

"I have no idea what you are talking about. This is the only ball we've used."

Short of calling in the law, Roy had no idea what to do. "You certainly are working hard for your club."

"My club? I have no club, Mr. Bishop."

"You, sir, are a liar and I have no doubt you will find a

229

way to exchange this ball when your club comes up to bat."

The nasty little smirk on the umpire's face confirmed his suspicion and Roy did something he never, ever did. He stomped away in a huff.

Play resumed and a second out followed the first bringing Bryon up to bat. He looked at his boss standing rigidly on the sidelines and winked. He smiled at the insults the catcher was tossing out and channeled all his anger and determination into his shoulders and arms. Pitcher threw the ball and Bryon swinging with all his might connected solidly and the ball exploded into a cloud of sawdust. No more mushy balls. The umpire called him out although he could not back it up with a ruling.

"Since there is nothing in the books to cover this, I will rule against such destruction. Resume play."

Nashville scored two runs in the seventh inning before Bryon scooped up a hard grounder and threw it to the hurler who caught the runner at first for the third out. Now it was the school's turn with a decent ball. When Ethan came up to bat, the bases were loaded and the catcher was talking.

"Since you can't hear, I can say anything I want." The catcher smirked and continued. "I heard your mama was so ugly your daddy asked to be sold."

The ball was a blur to Ethan as he swung.

"Strike."

That insult hit home painfully to Ethan and he gritted his teeth and took a deep breath. *Shake it off, don't let this pasty face get to you, Ethan*, he told himself.

"We can all see why you are with them idiots since no one else would have you."

"Strike two." Ethan wasn't even aware he had swung.

"Yeah, I heard they were all your illegitimate brothers and sisters that got hung last night from jail."

This time Ethan was well aware of what he was doing when he swung. He intentionally missed the ball, swinging so hard the momentum carried him clear around. The heavy bat struck the catcher on the shoulder. Ethan felt avenged. He fell into the catcher where he further avenged poor Chris when his knee accidently made firm contact with the other man's crotch. Apologizing, he tried to get up from the tangle they were in on the ground but he used his elbow as leverage against the man's sternum, finally avenging Slim. The catcher screamed in pain and let out a string of curses. Ethan finally scrambled to his feet and began walking away.

The catcher caught his breath then leaped to his feet and ran after Ethan, jumping onto his back and locking his forearm around his throat.

Both benches emptied in what became the first brawl in Base-Ball history.

Pitcher ran up to Bryon who was the only player not engaged in combat and grabbed his shirt. "You get control of your filthy players now or we'll do some real damage."

Nodding his assent, Bryon headed into the throng. He reached right and left, wading through writhing bodies, pulling (or appearing to pull) his men back from fist fights. It was close work and he was unable to avoid inadvertently giving a number of sharp elbows to Nashville players. He shook his head at his own clumsiness as he repeatedly stamped down on insteps, and once or twice, his knee came up a little too high. He kept his eye on the umpire and when he would catch his eye, Bryon would shrug in dismay and continue pretending to end the fight.

When the majority of the Athletics were wounded, limping and groaning, both teams made their way back to their benches.

Slapping a hand on Ethan's shoulder, Bryon shook his head in disgust. "Way to keep a cool head!" he signed.

"I'll make it up to you, I promise."

"Okay, I'll hold you to it."

The umpire wanted to throw Ethan out of the game but since the catcher had actually started the conflict, he could not go that far.

During the eighth inning, the score was, Nashville 43, the school 37. Nashville had two men on base. Pitcher was up to plate and got a long hit to left field. Ira fielded the ball on the first bounce and instead of relaying it in, he planted his foot firmly and threw the ball toward home. The ball didn't have to go first to the hurler if thrown to home plate. Tom stretched out his big hands and stepped as far as he could toward the ball. The throw beat the runner by two steps. Tom grinned, swept off his cap and bowed to the cheering audience.

"He's safe!"

The umpire had to dodge a few orange peels and hard-boiled eggs as the crowd erupted in shouts of displeasure.

Bryon had all he could take. Now the gloves came off. He motioned to Edwin, his hurler and they came together for a conference. A smile broke over Edwin's face as he nodded and went to third base. Bryon stripped off his black belt and put it on like a headband.

Questioning murmurs came from the spectators and players and grew until loud laughter was breaking out. Everyone was well aware of the rule in Base-Ball that the hurler's arm could not come up higher than his belt. There were occasions when creative hurler's would fasten their belts under their arm pits to allow more motion for a faster pitch. No one had ever seen the stunt Bryon was pulling. Only Ethan knew what was about to happen and he was holding his sides from laughter.

Bryon pitched a new kind of game, one that was only played for fun in the sand lots of New York. When the first striker came up to the plate, the suddenly hushed crowd watched on the edge of their seats as the new hurler wound up, took a big step forward and pitched overhand while being careful not to raise the ball above the belt level. The ball shot forward and flew past the surprised striker who stood a moment as if still waiting for the pitch. The crowd waited expectantly to see what the umpire would call. He didn't call anything.

Tom threw the ball back to Bryon. Again, he wound up and let go with a fast ball. Again there was no call and this was repeated twice more until the striker decided to make a try for it. On the fifth pitch, the Nashville striker swung at the ball but was way too late. The crowd laughed. A second and then a third time, the confused man swung at the pitches. All eyes swung toward the umpire to see what he would do.

Striding forward angrily, Pitcher accused Bryon of

cheating and demanded that the umpire remove him from the game. Roy came up and patiently listened to the other manager's diatribe.

The umpire turned to him and said, "Okay, Bishop, what do you have to say for yourself?"

"Allow me to bring Mr. Hancock and Mr. Brown over for a conference. I understand only I can speak to you according to the rules but I need to consult with them."

"Very well."

The discussion was fast and furious, the finer points of the rules discussed back and forth until finally, the umpire ignored the protocol of only speaking to managers and began speaking directly to the ball players. While this was going on, Bishop slipped away.

The umpire continued to complain. "It may not specifically be against the rules, but it definitely isn't the gentlemanly thing to do."

Ethan sneered, "Oh yes, and you are keeping this game so polite."

Bryon glanced over with irritation when he saw that Roy had deserted them to talk to some man in the crowd.

When Roy finished chatting with an old friend from New York, he returned to the conference, ignoring the exasperated look from Bryon. He got there in time to hear the umpire threatening to ban the school's team from ever playing another club in Tennessee if they did not throw the game.

"The dignity of this noble sport would suffer if your team were to somehow beat the state champions. Of course that seems highly unlikely with you down 44 to 37 in the eighth, but anything is possible."

Ethan snorted. "We're not noble enough for the game, huh?"

"I've heard about your smart mouth, Mr. Brown and I will not tolerate it."

Roy ignored Bryon's glare and told the umpire he understood his predicament and perhaps something could be worked out. Bryon took a step forward and took hold of his dignified boss's lapels but backed off when he saw the small wink.

Trying to appear pleasant and non-confrontational, Mr. Bishop spoke softly. "Gentlemen, I am afraid we may be overheard out here and that could be an embarrassment for all of us. There is more privacy over by the team room, if you would follow me." The administrator led the way to the corner of the team's dressing room. "This is better. Now, sir," he addressed the umpire, "if you would repeat yourself. I'm afraid I missed part of your words."

Clearing his throat, the umpire straightened his shoulders, feeling the importance of his position to save the reputation of the game he loved. "Certainly, Mr. Bishop. As I was trying to explain to your players here, unsuccessfully I might add, the game could be damaged irreparably in this state if students from an obscure and . . . uh, unusual school beat the greatest team Tennessee has ever seen. Therefore, I am forced to let you know that if you win here today by some fluke (Pitcher smirked at the referral to Bryon's nickname), I will make sure your school will never play another official game in this state."

"I see. So we have no option but to throw the game?"

The umpire gave him a patronizing smile, "That's one way to put it," relieved the professor understood. His relief died with the austere manager's next words.

"Carl, how would you put it?"

Roy Bishop's friend from New York appeared around the corner of the building. It was just his luck that everyone was frozen in shock. "Ah, posed perfectly for my picture." A bright flash blinded their eyes as his heavy camera recorded the event. "Personally, I'd call it a threat. I wonder what my readers will call it when it hits the papers. Perhaps extortion?"

Bryon took hold of Pitcher's neck and jerked him back when he went for the reporter's camera. The umpire shrieked and chaos ruled for a moment.

The official, whose face was reddening, stuttered, "M . . . Mr. Bishop, you c-can't do this. I'll be ruined!"

"You don't care if my students are ruined just as long as you and this team come out smelling like a rose. That's right isn't it, sir?"

The man was practically sobbing. "Please, my family .
. . they'll be shamed. Don't do this, I'll call the game fairly, you
have my word!"

"What do you think, Carl? Should we let him off the
hook?"

"Don't know, Roy. Guess it depends on how he calls
the rest of the game, right?"

Before play resumed, a small figure maneuvered her
way through the players and sidled up to Bryon.

"Jenny, what do you need, honey?" he signed.

She handed him her ball. "Teacher, will you use my
ball to pitch? Remember, this ball has the power to throw away
the bad things so it will help you beat the bad guys."

He took the precious ball from her small hand. "If you
kiss it then it will have more magic." He fondly watched the
beautiful little girl bend forward and kiss her ball reverently
then run off the field. He had Mr. Bishop okay its use with the
umpire. With fear still hanging over him like a cloud, the man
agreed.

A few of the Athletics were catching on to the timing
necessary to hit that fast ball by the last inning. That is when
Bryon released his curve ball. When the first striker swung at
the ball that had faded away in the last second, he threw his bat
down and walked away in disgust. Now, they had to be
prepared for either pitch and not one man was up to the
challenge. Three up, three down brought the school up to bat.
The score was 44 to 43. This was the moment it all came down
to.

Ira started the dance hitting a solid single over the first
base player's head. Ethan followed with his well-executed
fair/foul bunt toward first and Ira advanced to second while he
secured first. Horace went down on a fly ball and was quickly
followed by Snap who was thrown out at first on another bunt.
With runners at second and third and two outs, Bryon came up
to the plate. Pitcher began the chant, "Luke the mute fluke."

Bryon looked around remembering how he blew this
situation to lose the big game in Cincinnati. He heard the team

and the few fans still rooting for them yelling that he would choke. The catcher assured him he would miss as always in a clutch situation.

"Everyone will know you for the failure you are in a moment, Hancock."

Smiling, Bryon thought that since he hadn't just been dumped by the girl he loves, he'd do just fine.

The first pitch was high and outside and he relaxed and stood back.

"Strike!"

Turning around, he just stared at the umpire. The man straightened his top hat and sat back in his chair insolently. Since it was unusual for an umpire to call balls or strikes unless forced to, Bryon was surprised he had called it at all, especially since it was so obviously a ball. *Why am I surprised, he's been doing it the whole game against us.*

The second pitch was not as bad so Bryon decided to step into it and let go. The exhilaration of the athletic conflict poured through him and with a light in his eye, he swung his bat and felt deep satisfaction at the loud crack of the ball. The runners all took off as the crowd watched the ball sail higher and farther than anything anyone in Tennessee had ever witnessed. The left fielder was running but it was clear he would never even get close. The collective groan of the crowd started small but got louder and louder as the unthinkable happened. The ball was so high that the wind caught it and was blowing it toward the foul line. Everyone held their breath and even the last two runners, Ethan and Bryon, stopped in their tracks and tensely waited for the ball to come down. Which it finally did; two feet past the line.

"Foul ball!" the umpire shouted in triumph.

Pitcher sang out in a mocking voice, "Hey, Hancock, looks like you are the foul character I always thought you were. You and that little girl freak of yours better get used to being losers cause that's all you'll ever be."

Setting down his bat, Bryon stared daggers at Pitcher then a cunning grin slowly grew on his face that gave Pitcher a sudden chill. Bryon changed his mind at that last instant and instead of attempting to hit a long fly, he decided he shouldn't tempt the wind. It would be irresponsible.

The pitch came harder than normal which played into his hands perfectly. He swung and the ball came off the bat like it was shot from a cannon. It slammed into the startled hurler, cracking a rib and knocking him head over heels. Pitcher lay there screaming and holding his side. The shortstop had to run over and get the ball.

It was a good thing Ira was fast because Ethan was hot on his tail. He rounded third and was barreling home when Ira's tying run crossed the plate. The shortstop threw it to home, attempting to stop Ethan from scoring. The whistle of the ball was audible in the silence and the smack of contact with skin was heard a second after Ethan's foot pounded on the home plate.

Once again, all heads in the park turned to the umpire. He was staring at home plate and breathing rapidly. Finally he opened his mouth to speak, stopped and looked out at the crowd. Thousands of angry and threatening faces glared at him. He saw a dozen cameras focused on him from the press, including Carl. He gulped, wiped his forehead and spoke through a dry throat. "He's safe!"

The fans went crazy. The throng poured onto the field and lifted Bryon and Ethan onto their shoulders and marched them around in celebration. During the celebration, Ethan shouted over to Bryon asking him why he did a fool thing hitting Pitcher and almost losing the game.

Signing back, Bryon grinned boyishly. "I knew you were greased lightning and I knew you hated these Tennesseans enough to fly to beat them. But most of all, I knew you'd keep your promise. I held you to it."

Bryon saw Jenny hopping up and down on the edge of the crowd. As soon as they let him down, he threaded his way through the chaos, bracing himself for all the pats on the back, and reached his little girl. He picked her up and swung her round and round, then gave her a smacking kiss on the cheek. She hugged him tight and squealed. Out of the corner of his eye he saw Roy Bishop waiting to congratulate him. After shaking the man's hand, Bryon asked to borrow the pen he knew the administrator always kept in his pocket. He took Jenny's ball out of her hand and wrote on it. When he finished he saw she was waiting to sign to him. "I knew you could do it, Teacher. You beat the bad guys."

With a huge grin splitting his face, he held up her ball for her to read. She laughed when she read the words written on the ball. "We beat the bad guys."

At length the tumult calmed and everyone cleared the field, waiting for that all important bet to be honored. Photographers lined up to get shots of the losers licking clean the shoes of the winners. The school team lined up in the middle of the diamond and waited for the Athletics to come forward. Bryon motioned to Pitcher with a crook of his finger.

Ethan helped out. "Bryon wants you to go first, Pitcher, since you made the bet. You know, to set an example for your teammates."

"That wasn't part of the deal," he complained bitterly.

His team immediately began to grumble. "You got us into this, you do it first."

Ignoring the snickers of the crowd, Pitcher slowly walked up to Bryon, gave him a hate filled glare and knelt down in front of him. He groaned and kept a hand pressed against his cracked rib. Bending low, he licked the dusty top of Bryon's shoe.

Bryon's teammates tried to hide their laughter as the other players approached. The Athletics would not look at the students but with set faces they were determined to honor their debt as Pitcher was doing.

Wiping off his tongue after the first lick, Pitcher bent to continue.

"That's enough," Ethan said. "Bryon wants you to get up now, he has something to say to everyone."

Surprised hope leaped into Pitcher's eyes and he carefully eased himself to his feet and stepped back.

Ethan watched the message being signed to him, cleared his throat and spoke with serious conviction. "Bryon says that no man has the right to make another person grovel or bow

238

down before him either physically or symbolically. Anyone who shames or belittles another, especially in public, has no honor. He refuses to take advantage of you because of a weakness you can't help. You did your best. He releases you and your team from the wager."

"So why didn't you stop me before I started?" Pitcher yelled. "How dare you make me bow down to an inferior animal like you!"

Ethan carefully watched his friend's hands. "He dared because he wanted you to have just a small taste of what it is like for the people you just played almost every time they go into a public place. Now you understand the humiliation you suffer when a fellow human being treats you like a dog."

Bryon reached down and swung Jenny up on his big shoulder then turned back in surprise when he heard his friend continue.

"And Bryon also wants all of you to know that this crowd taught him that folks can change. When you saw clear injustice here today your eyes were opened. You stopped thinking of our Base-Ball players as handicapped animals and you began to see them as people." Ethan watched heads swinging back and forth between him and Bryon as they tried to understand how the message was being sent. Bryon's hands weren't moving, he was holding a cute little girl on his shoulder. Some in the crowd began thinking of the killings of the Negroes that had just happened and began listening to Ethan with a different attitude; some in growing anger, and some in growing shame.

The tall black man spoke with more dignity than most of the spectators thought possible for a colored person. "This doesn't have to be just a game, it can be more. For these kids from the Deaf School, it can give them hope as they watch your fairness, feel your support; it can hold out the promise given a hundred years ago, the promise that this nation believes that all men, *all men*, are created equal and are endowed by their creator with certain unalienable rights. Can these kids claim a right to life? To liberty? Can they be allowed to pursue happiness or will that be withheld because they are different through no choice of their own?" Dead silence met these words. "And finally, Bryon wants to thank you for your humanity this day. He wants to thank you for not just pretending to be a good Christian society, but by actually living those ancient principles of mercy and kindness, especially toward the less fortunate. Looking at each of you here, our team can see what is truly in your hearts." Ethan watched faces softening, others hardening.

Turning to Pitcher, Ethan said, "I want to especially thank this fine man for making this all happen. Pitcher, without you, we wouldn't have learned how a man loses with grace. And even though you don't play ball as well as Bryon, he promises to never treat you as an inferior man. As far as he's concerned, you're equal. You did your best and that's all a man can do." Ethan reached out his hand for a shake he knew would not come.

Pitcher's face burned with shame. Turning, he began to run, but stumbled to the ground and groaned at the stabbing pain from his injured rib. Picking himself up he ignored the agony and hurried off the field, the laughter of the crowd chasing him like a specter.

The silent crowd held their collective breath as Bryon set the little girl down and signed something to the black man. Waiting for something profound and moving, they listened to Ethan turn back and speak to them.

Last of all, Bryon says . . . Let's eat!"

The National media went nuts with the story of The Big Dog Fight. Photos and details of the win were news for a week. The story even made papers in Europe. One man in England who was especially interested in the events lowered his newspaper, sat back and stared out the window making plans.

The End

240

Joy (Castleberry) Bischoff lives with her husband Roy in Orem, Utah. They are the parents of six children and the grandparents of 7 and counting. Joy has a degree in Ancient Near Eastern Studies from BYU and she enjoys researching and lecturing on ancient topics, especially Egyptology and ancient rabbinical writings.